PRAISE FO[R]

"A bloody, wonderfully creepy sca[...]

"Even careful readers will be caught off guard by twists and unexpected but divine surprises. This first-rate thriller delivers everything a thriller should, and adds more."

—*VOYA Magazine, VOYA Perfect Ten*

"Balog fills every inch with classic horror references, red herrings, and uncertain motivations. This is fantastically creepy psychological horror."

—*Booklist*

PRAISE FOR *THAT NIGHT*

"Downright chilling… A twisted, engrossing tale of relationships intermingling to disaster."

—*Kirkus Reviews*

"The book gives full weight to the complexities and consequences of teenage sex and obsessive relationships, giving readers much food for thought."

—*Bulletin for the Center for Children's Books*

PRAISE FOR *UNNATURAL DEEDS*

"A compelling, dark confessional with pages that will keep you guessing and an ending that will blow you sideways."

—Natalie D. Richards, *New York Times* bestselling author of *Five Total Strangers* and *Seven Dirty Secrets*

"Like a PG-13 version of *Gone Girl*. A page-turner that will keep readers riveted."

—*Kirkus Reviews*

"An unpredictable, shocking ending that most readers will not see coming. This thriller will stay with readers long after the last page."

—*School Library Journal*

YOU WON'T BELIEVE ME

ALSO BY CYN BALOG

Alone

That Night

Unnatural Deeds

YOU WON'T BELIEVE ME

CYN BALOG

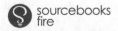

sourcebooks
fire

Published by Sourcebooks Fire, an imprint of Sourcebooks
P.O. Box 4410, Naperville, Illinois 60567–4410
(630) 961-3900
sourcebooks.com

Cataloging-in-Publication Data is on file with the Library of Congress.

Printed and bound in the United States of America.
VP 10 9 8 7 6 5 4 3 2

To Sara and Gabrielle

PART ONE

THE WAY IT BEGINS

PROLOGUE

It begins with the note I received.

DO EVERYONE A FAVOR AND KILL YOURSELF NOW.

Or maybe it doesn't begin there. Maybe it begins with the drive to Miami. In a story like this, it's hard to tell.

It won't make sense to you anyway. Not at first. It didn't to me, the first time I heard it. I can only share what I remember, and that may or may not be in order. Because, well…you'll see. When you circle a net through a pond, you don't catch everything that's in the water. But every single word of my story is absolutely true, or at least it's my truth, pieced together from what I've collected in my net.

Now that I think of it, the start was likely months before we left Pensacola. My father would have a better idea. But I doubt even he would know for sure, because he was under a lot of stress at work. Stress to perform. Stress to save the world. Sometimes he'd disappear into the lab for weeks at a time, then appear in the kitchen one morning, making pancakes as if he'd never left.

That was always his life, but it got worse in those later days. Or those earlier days? I don't know what to call them. His supervisors weren't happy. Whenever he spoke with them, he got this worried crinkle between his eyebrows and murmured all kinds of curses under his breath.

Dad said it would be good for us to get away for the weekend. To escape the bubble we'd been stuck in for months. Little did I know that Dad *needed* to leave, because of the death threats.

From *him*.

But I'm jumping ahead of myself.

I remember my dad loading Mom, JT, and me into the car and telling me that I would be okay. Whatever happened, *I* would be okay. He's my dad, so of course I believed him. His exact words: *You'll be okay, Willow. You'll make it out of this just fine.*

You. Not *We.* He repeated those words, over and over, as if trying to convince himself.

He wasn't wrong about much. You know, MD, PhD, brilliant mind and all. But he was wrong about that. Very wrong.

I wasn't okay. Far from it.

So I'll start there. It's what I remember best.

But looking back, I wish I'd followed the directions on that note. If I had, maybe none of this would be happening now.

ONE

A: You there?

W: Maybe...who is this?

A: August.

A: From history?

W: oh hi

A: What are you up to?

W: I just woke up. What are you doing?

A: Truth? I was thinking about you.

I think about August's eyes. I have all the time in the world now to think, and those eyes are endless and clear as a sky in summer.

You can see it, right? Everyone knows that color. It pulls the corners of your lips into a smile and makes you take giddy breaths until you're dizzy.

August has incredible eyes. That's one of the few things I know.

Mostly, I think. But thinking is not knowing. Thinking

and wondering are useless. You never get answers. Only more questions.

Before, I didn't have to do that. Any question I had, I'd consult my phone for the answer.

Oh, what a charmed life I led.

That was then.

Now all I can do is ponder the many, many things I don't know. It's a great, big, gaping hole that grows wider and deeper the more time I spend here, immobile and staring at the water-stained ceiling.

I don't know when I lost my phone.

I don't know how I got here or who is keeping me here.

I don't know what day it is or what time it is or what came before this. There are so many questions I can't answer. The past is a fuzzy cloud of nothingness inside my head. It's toxic; sometimes, I worry it'll spread like a cancer and contaminate the rest of me.

But I do know some things. That's what I focus on, running those thoughts through my mind, over and over and over again, hoping I don't lose them too.

Those eyes, for one. That smile.

August. His name comes into my head, then pieces of him, like a jigsaw puzzle begging to be put together. When I fit the pieces into place, I sigh wistfully and imagine him, sitting at his computer, smiling at the screen over something I said.

I also know that there are sixty-four tiles on the ceiling.

Most of them are cracked, and the one in the left corner has a brown water stain that kind of looks like an old-time silhouette of someone. Maybe George Washington, with a slim braid tied in a ribbon. He has an odd Cro-Magnon forehead, though.

The bed is too small, a toddler bed, but it's lifted rather high above the dusty, wood-planked floor, and the blanket over me is too scratchy and has a fraying patch that says "Woolrich." My feet hang off the edge, pale and shriveled hooks with chipped neon-blue nail polish.

I can't remember when I painted them. Or did I go to the salon? *Another trip is in order...*

The room is green, and there is a picture of three rabid-looking bears lapping at bowls of bloodred soup. Also, an angry cow with oddly L-shaped limbs jumping over a moon with wide, terror-filled eyes that look like they've seen death.

I think this room used to be a nursery. A nursery for demons.

The walls here always hum. They vibrate. It calms me, if one could call this calm.

There's a table on the other side of the room with one of those old-fashioned telephones with a rotary dial. It has never rung before, but I know it can ring because the bell sometimes goes off, just once, whenever the door accidentally slams too hard, which isn't often. There is also a comb and a hairbrush and one of those handheld mirrors. Sometimes light from the window will hit it and paint a tiny rainbow on the ceiling, creating, for a minute or two, the one pretty thing in the room.

I have never looked in that mirror. But I know I won't like what I find. And comb my hair? I think I still have hair, but I can't be sure. My scalp used to itch, but I've gotten used to it. I can feel oil slipping down my temples. The restraints have prevented me from investigating.

Not sure I want to anymore.

The old lady who keeps me here wants me to believe she is my granny. I don't think she is my real grandmother.

She has told me two things: I can't leave, and I must not ever make a sound, because *he* can't take it.

Granny has green eyes with hardly visible pupils. They are not like sparkling emeralds. They are like sickness. Like pea soup vomit in the gaping holes of a skull. She has black witch hair, all scraggly against her pale skin. She came close enough for me to touch it once, and the strands broke in my frail fingers.

Granny opens the door twice a day: once in the morning, and once at night. The rest of the time, it stays closed.

Other things I know?

No one is looking for me. Scratch that off the list because I've been here too long. I'm not sure how long, but long enough that my legs feel like jelly, my feet look like tumors attached to my ankles, and my body is withering. I think I used to have a shape but now I'm all angles, like that cow on the wall.

At least he can jump. I can only lie here.

The medicine makes my mind fuzzy. Two pills every morning. I drift in and out during the days, but I am more awake during the nights. I listen to the humming of the walls and the mice scurrying about. Sometimes I will hear the old one-eyed cat skulking about, pouncing. He—or she?—has plenty to eat around here.

Granny—the old lady who is not my grandmother—comes in with the sun, which glows behind a yellowing roll-up shade. The shade is always down. All I see beyond that thin shade is the silhouetted skeleton of a bare tree. Sometimes its branches scrape the pane in conspiring whispers.

When Granny arrives, it's soft like a breath. The door creaks open, then she has a slow, steady, rhythmic sweep to the table by my bed. It takes her an eternity to make the trip across the room; I don't stay awake for all of it.

The next thing I know, a bedpan's shoved under my butt. Then, while I do my business, she starts shoveling lumpy white food with the consistency and taste of paste between my lips. For this, I stay awake. If I nod off, I will choke to death. She looks fragile but the way she pries my lips open with the spoon is anything but. It is a wonder I haven't broken a tooth or two. Granny is on a mission when it comes to the feed. The metal spoon, which tastes like silver polish, will make its way between my lips if it's the last thing Granny does. She is slow and methodical when she walks, but during the feed, she shovels food quickly and haphazardly, like trying to stuff an overflowing garbage can. The slime dribbles onto my chin, and she shovels it back in. Not a drop to waste. No matter how much I fight. How badly I choke. It only stops when the bowl is empty.

The bowl is a baby's bowl. It has a faded clown face on the bottom and says ALL DONE.

Then she lifts a red straw to my mouth, and I suck down bitter, tepid water. Out comes the bedpan. And just like the clown says, I'm all done.

This morning, I suck down the horse pills and start to dream that I am a horse. A horse in a field, running. I do not know if I've ever run before. Even in my dreams, my legs don't seem to know the movement.

Sweep, sweep, sweep, and it's dinnertime.

Let the shoveling commence.

I only gag once or twice. All in all, a successful day.

Oh. One other thing I know?

I'm going to die here. She's never letting me out.

TWO

A: How was your day?

W: Dull. Yours?

A: Same. How'd you do on the history test?

W: 💣

A: lol same. Low, you're a trip

W: Low? No one calls me that

A: Can I be the first?

Sleep, wake. Sleep, wake. Wash, rinse, repeat.

I stare at the door. It has a nail in the center where the faint outline of a crucifix can be seen. I have all the time in the world to wonder where the crucifix went. If Granny lost her faith the way I've lost hope.

The most interesting time of day is when the door is open. When the door is open, it almost tastes like freedom.

Almost. Not quite.

At least I have more to look at.

Beyond the doorway feels like an entirely new world. Unexplored—by me anyway. The walls of the house are wood paneled, which makes everything shadowy and dark. In the hallway, there's a painting on the wall that looks like blotches; it's too far away to make out. Another old telephone the color of wheat is tethered to the wall, a long, curly cord hanging down and coiling on the floor like a copperhead lying in wait.

If I tilt my head, there is yellowing wallpaper with brown baskets of red flowers and a cracked, butter-colored Formica counter. Probably part of a kitchen where Granny prepares my delicious paste.

Besides that, almost directly across from my room, is another door.

It's painted black, with another nail in the center. Something must've hung from that nail too once. Not a crucifix. A calendar, I think, because there's a little paper scrap still attached to the nail.

Someone, or something, sometimes pounds on that door. Not in a quick, desperate way. More like the strike of a gong. Slow, deliberate, rhythmic.

I've heard that thumping sound as Granny feeds me, so I know it is not Granny making that noise.

Granny is not alone.

I think Granny has captured other people.

Yes, that is what I am. What I must be. Granny's captive.

One day, if I manage to get some hope back, I will get myself free. I will open that door. I will tell whoever else is hostage here that we will get out. Together. Together, we will be safe.

But right now, all I want to do is sleep.

No. Can't sleep. Granny is here. And she's brought food.

She fits her substantial backside onto a stool. Puts the tray on the night table.

I open my mouth. She shovels it in. Faster than ever.

Are the walls humming more slowly, or is it just me? It's probably me. There are a lot of things wrong with me, in case you hadn't guessed.

Bang, bang, bang goes the door across the hall. She ignores it.

Something is wrong. I can't keep up with my feeding. She's on edge. Or maybe I am. Maybe it has to do with the humming in the walls. A fly lands on her nose. She doesn't flick it off. She just keeps shoveling. The fly turns on the bulb of her nose, posing. One of her green, pupilless eyes twitches. Once. Twice.

I swallow, but not fast enough. Suddenly I'm choking, gasping for air.

"Quiet!" Her whisper is phlegmy.

I cough and spray paste. Some dribbles off my chin as I nearly die.

"Quiet!"

She's always scolding me. Her voice sounds like old pipes. The creaking stuff of nightmares. She catches the goop with the spoon before it can fall onto my chest.

Something is definitely wrong.

It's not any one thing. Just little differences. The slower hum. The louder banging. Granny shoveling faster, her forehead damp with sweat, eye twitching.

Then, something big happens. Or doesn't happen.

Granny doesn't give me my pills.

I wait for them. But she never gives them to me. Or does she? I don't think she does. I'm so tired, I might have fallen asleep, and now I'm numb to the pain in my throat from the swallow of those massive pills.

My eyes close, heavy. I blink, and she's standing there, black blood leaking from one nostril. She wipes it away.

I blink, and she's gone. I fall into merciful sleep.

I wake a second or a lifetime later.

Someone is screaming. It's not Granny. The voice is male. *He'll come back!*

It's not coming from the other side of my door. It sounds like the words are coming through the walls.

Wondering why Granny hasn't told him to be quiet—he's a hell of a lot louder than I've ever been—I fall asleep again.

When I wake, it's dark and the house is silent except for the scurrying mice and the cat, slowly and stealthily creeping along the baseboards.

This time, I can't fall back to sleep. I think it's because I didn't get my pills.

I spend the entire night staring at the back of my door, hardly blinking at all.

THREE

A: Willlllllllow

W: Auggggggggust

A: Are you blowing in the breeze? Are you weeping,
Willow?

W: Like I haven't heard that about a billion times in my
life

A: but never from someone so charming

A: Right?

A: 🙂

W: Riiiiiight

A: What are you up to?

W: Just back from walking the dog

A: Ooooh. You got outside.

W: I'm adventurous like that.

A: Thank god for Ventex, right? What kind of dog do you
have?

W: Akita. She's named JT.

A: Interesting name.

W: Not really. Was a big Justin Timberlake fan.

A: I think there's a lot of interesting stuff about you.

W: Nope. That's it.

My name is Willow Lafayette.

I am sixteen.

I am a junior at Pensacola High School.

By the time the door opens in the morning, I've remembered new details. Each time, I give myself a pat on the back. A hypothetical pat on the back because I'm still bound by these freaking restraints.

But my mind is much clearer now.

I think it's the pills. Or lack thereof.

I'm an only child. My parents are Doctors Beatrice and Vince Lafayette, research scientists at Latrobe Scientific, one of the only employers in the panhandle that pays really well. We live on the gulf in a sprawling, two-story modern home that's all white angles and picture windows and palm trees. I have a fluffy Akita named JT and a blue Mustang convertible I got for my birthday last year, which is April 12. August said I look hot driving it.

I do not have a granny. All my grandparents are dead.

January 21 is the last day I remember. I remember it because it was my father's birthday. My mother bought him an expensive cake from the only bakery in town that was still open, and she had to order *months* in advance. But the bottom of the box busted when she took it out of the fridge and the cake practically detonated, sending frosting and strawberry filling everywhere—the walls, the appliances, even the ceiling. My mother cried. JT had a field day.

Look at all the memories I have! I can catalog them, pull them up at will. It's a small miracle. I almost feel human again. *Sorry for ever having doubted you, brain.*

The only thing I can't seem to remember? How I got to this godforsaken place with Fake Granny to begin with.

I'm able to do other things too. I can lift my head off the pillow, though there's a considerable pain slicing through my skull. At least my vision doesn't swim. I've kicked off that scratchy wool blanket and can see legs that don't look like mine. They're white and bruised and skeletally sticklike, a nice complement to my ugly, hooklike feet.

I used to have strong legs. Nice legs. Cheerleader legs—though I am not a cheerleader, but *I could be one.* I'm too shy. August said that was even better. All the hot without the attitude.

August was all about hot. That was his running joke: *And I know hot because I'm August in Florida.*

Ha ha.

My sort-of boyfriend, August L. Rule. Son of Mayor Tom Rule and Pensacola High's best-looking junior.

This? This isn't my bright white mansion on the gulf shore. This isn't August's house either. I haven't been inside his house yet, but he lives six doors down from me, and his home is almost a mirror image of mine.

This...*place*...wouldn't even qualify as a shed on either of our properties.

But I got here somehow. Was I driving? When my parents gave me the Mustang, I wasn't happy. I know, I sound spoiled, but it's not for the reason you'd expect. My parents said they were sick of driving me places, so it was on *their* list, not mine. I didn't ask them, not once, for a car. Besides, I didn't think I needed one, because by the time I turned sixteen, the pandemic was in full swing and no one was going anywhere. But truthfully, I didn't want to drive because I was afraid of getting into an accident.

Did I? Did I drive off the road and this psychotic pseudo Granny took me in?

I gnash my teeth, trying to remember.

Nothing comes.

Why did Granny give me these pills? To make me her prisoner? To make me docile?

That must be it.

Or...

No, wait. The pills. *Ventex.* We have to take them. They keep us alive! I remember that. For the past year and a half, everyone has had to take those giant pills. If not, they might catch the virus since it's airborne. It's called the bunyavirus, but most people call it the screw. Because if you got it, that's basically what you were: screwed. You got sick, hemorrhaged, and died.

Thousands of people—hundreds of thousands of people, actually—died before the pharmaceutical companies came out with that lifesaving pill. Everyone took them, every man, woman, and child.

Ah, the screw. Good times.

Oh, hell. Why didn't I have any pills today?

Slowly, as dawn breaks, I notice new details of my surroundings. Like that paddle hairbrush? It has long bits of hair and large flakes of dandruff clinging to it, too much to be normal. The numbers 9 and 1 on the rotary phone are all but faded away. The bears on the wall look at me with warning eyes, as if to say, *Get out.*

Yeah, can't exactly do that, friends. For obvious reasons. I tug on the restraints to prove the point. *I need those pills.*

The smell in this room, in this house, is wrong. It's sickly sweet, foul. I heard on the television once that that's what death smells like: *sickly sweet.* But I guess you never really know until you smell it yourself. Is this death? It makes my empty stomach churn.

As the sun comes up and I take in my room with my newly clear brain, I am struck with a new fear.

I'm going to die if I don't do something.

Because when I lift my chin to my chest, straining my stiff neck muscles, I see it huddled in the corner.

A pile of mangled white fur covered in blood.

FOUR

A: What is it like to be the prettiest girl in school?

W: Give me a break.

A: Truth. I cannot tell a lie.

W: Okay, George Washington.

A: You're hot—and I'm August in Florida. I know hot.

W: Ha

A: You stab me. Right in the heart.

W: Zzzzzzz...

A: Hey. Your dad works for Latrobe right?

W: Yeah why?

A: That's what I want to do when I graduate. If we ever graduate from this nightmare.

W: You do?

A: Why are you surprised?

W: Because you're you. And Latrobe is Zzzzzz

A: You think what your dad does is boring?

W: YES

A: And what excites you?

W: Very little.

A: Name something.

W: Can't think of anything right now.

W: What is it like to live in the mayor's mansion and have everyone in school wanting to be your friend?

A: Only one person I want to be friends with, Low. And she's cold as ice.

W: Whatever!

A: Another stab. I'm bleeding. For you.

W: Can you hear the tiny violins over there?

The walls have been humming slower and slower. Now I am sure of it.

I have been looking at the dead cat. Despite being inside, flies have been accumulating on it, buzzing around. They buzz on me too. It's gotten so hot in here that I've kicked my blanket to the end of the bed. I'm wearing plaid boxers I don't think are mine and a man's threadbare undershirt that I *know* is not. Where did I get these clothes? And why does it feel like I've been wearing them so long they've become a part of me?

That afternoon, Granny comes in with my meal. She sets the tray down, and when she sees the cat, she doesn't say a word. She simply sweeps, sweeps, sweeps out the door. A moment later, she sweeps back in holding a dustpan and broom.

She stoops over it, her knees making cracking sounds like

brittle branches in a windstorm. Sweep, sweep, sweep. And the mess is gone. The flies linger, then find another target—my sweaty skin. They tickle. I know I am not the cleanest, but at least I am not the cat.

Yet.

Granny returns to the tray a moment later. The banging on the door outside has risen to a fever pitch. She shoos the flies away with her hand, and they begin to congregate on my paste breakfast. They seem to like it a lot more than I do.

I shouldn't talk. But I have so many questions, I can't seem to hold them back. August always said I was too curious for my own good. I wonder if curiosity killed the white cat. Will it do the same to me?

When she sits, I notice it among the whiskers on her wrinkled upper lip. Dried blood.

Part of a news report I heard back home comes to mind: *Early symptoms include fever, aches, and pains, such as severe headache and muscle and joint pain, weakness and fatigue, sore throat, and loss of appetite. Gastrointestinal symptoms include abdominal pain, diarrhea, and vomiting. Unexplained hemorrhaging, bleeding, or bruising...*

She stirs the bowl and the flies scatter.

Before she starts shoveling the food, I open my mouth and whisper, "What happened to her?"

Granny settles her body on the shaky stool, shifting her weight so it rocks a little. No answer.

"Or…him? The cat?"

She reaches for the spoon. The flies have returned. One lands on her wrist. She is not going to answer.

This is where August would crack a joke, like, "Hello? Anyone out there?"

August is such a pisser.

Go to the emergency room immediately if you experience any of the following symptoms: bleeding under the skin or from the mouth, eyes, nose, or ears…

To that, he'd say, *Uh-oh. Code Red.*

"You didn't give me my pills," I remind her gently, in case she's forgotten. "In case—"

Before I can say more, she shoves that spoon home, so hard the rim of it scrapes against the roof of my mouth and rattles my teeth. The paste is different. It's clumpier, warmer, with a strange, almost sour taste. My stomach is empty, but I'd rather give this to the flies. Is it spoiled? Is it going to make me sick?

She's feeding me faster, making me think of something my father used to say as if I were three. *Eat every last bite, so you grow up big and strong.* My sweet father. As busy as he was, he would always make pancakes.

The memory's gone with the next choking spoonful. I can barely breathe between swallows. The paste sticks to the insides of my mouth, clogging my esophagus. I imagine it closing. My stomach churns from the smell. Not only does it taste foul, the paste smells rancid too.

I nearly cry with joy when that ALL DONE clown appears. It happens sooner than I expected. Was there less paste today? Fine by me.

When she raises the straw to my lips, I'm so thirsty I could suck the whole thing down. I only get an inadequate gulp.

She puts everything onto the tray and sweeps out of the room. But she stops in the doorway and looks at me when she says two distinct words: "No more."

No more. Before she turns away, I see desperation in her eyes that wasn't there before.

Then she closes the door, and I am alone.

There is a red smear on the floor where the cat once was. Flies buzz noisily around it. I listen for a while, thinking.

No more. Does she mean that I am not allowed any more pills? Or that there *are* no more pills?

Or does she mean she can take no more of this?

I get the feeling it is all three.

FIVE

Lavani: Whoa girl why did you sign on late to 1st period

W: I was up late

L: Lemme guess...A?

W: Yes.

L: He is totally playing you.

W: Why do you say that?

L: Bc he plays everyone. He's not sincere AT ALL.
   Everyone says it girl.

W: You are so wrong. He's not who you and everyone
   else thinks he is.

L: Ok so...who do YOU think he is?

W: Forget it. Gtg

I am fully awake now.

Horrifically awake.

It is nighttime, and the walls have stopped humming.

Now that it's gone, I hear everything. Every last sound. The flies buzzing. The crickets. The wind. My heart, beating like a drum in my chest.

And…far away, someone's snoring. It must be Granny.

It's hot. Too damn hot. Hotter than a freaking oven. That humming must've been a generator for an air conditioner. There isn't one in this room, which is why it was usually warm, but there must've been one somewhere. The sweat is pouring off me, and the flies are having a field day with my damp skin. I feel them in the darkness, landing and taking off, like the planes at Pensacola International. With the cat out of the way, the mice are playing, scurrying under the bed and across the baseboards—I imagine them having wild celebrations in the darkness.

At least someone here's happy.

This is the longest night. I barely blink. I'm so awake.

At least I haven't vomited. The food may have been spoiled, but I kept it down. That's good. If I'd vomited, I would've had to lie here in it all night, and the flies probably would've devoured me.

Slowly, daylight filters into the room, seeping over everything like maple syrup.

God, I miss pancakes. My dad, Vince Lafayette, is a world-renowned scientist but also the world's best pancake maker. *Eat every last bite so you grow up big and strong.* It was hard not to. The secret, he'd say in a whisper, was applesauce. Always put a spoonful in the batter. Funny, he always said it was a secret, but then he'd tell everyone who complimented his breakfast. My dad's like that. Above all, he wants to help.

I hope he's okay. Because if he were here, if he knew where I was…he'd be the first to help me.

The first thing I see is the dark red blotch where the cat bled out. I wonder for the thousandth time why it did and if I'm next.

The bunyavirus will infect men, women, and children. It will infect your pets. Be sure to have an adequate supply of lifesaving Ventex on hand at all times.

That's right. Some people got caught in a snowstorm and couldn't get to their supply. They got screwed. A lot of people, back when the virus was new, simply forgot. They got screwed too. Some people believed wild conspiracy theories that the screw was government mind control. Others said they couldn't deal with the medication's common side effect, which was nausea. Screwed, screwed, screwed.

Some people survived getting screwed. Very few. It weakened their bodies so much, they died shortly after. The survival rate was 0.0001 percent.

Yep. As that cheery thought drifts through my mind, something comes over me. A momentary burst of energy. I start to pull on the straps. Wildly. I wriggle my wrists in different ways to see if I can slip my hand out. I try to lift my chin toward the headboard, imagining myself biting through my bindings like some animal.

Nope. Nope. Nope. I think I tried this trick before. I got the same result then as I am now. That's the definition of insanity right there.

My escape attempt lasts only until the sun's rays begin their assault, bright beyond the shade of the window. I've got to be in Florida still. Only in Florida is it this ridiculously hot without AC as soon as the sun comes up.

That's when two things happen at once: I decide these restraints are never going to give out on their own, and the sweeping comes.

I lick my lips, readying myself for the morning choke fest. If August were here, he'd tell me to stop being a drama queen. The first time I met him, freshman year in gym class before all the crap hit the proverbial fan, they needed someone to tend goal. I started to make excuses—*I'm totally not athletic, my back hurts, I've never played handball in my life*—but he gave me a look like a mother gives her toy-grabbing toddler at Target and said, in a voice that clearly meant *I don't have time for bullshit*, "Tend goal, Willow." Predictably, I failed miserably, and we lost 6–0 in fifteen minutes, which had to have been some kind of record.

But that's August. His dad was pretty high up in the military before he got into politics, served a bunch of tours overseas, got decorated with medals. August's probably going to West Point when he graduates, like his dad.

Well, that is if we ever get to go anywhere.

The pandemic, which started the summer before my junior year, put a big question mark on all our futures.

Everyone at school knows August's destined for West Point, though, because very little about August is a secret. He's one of those people you want to get to know, and he loves to talk about himself. Loves to talk about how his dad expects him to be just like him. There are a few things only I know, like how he doesn't want to go into the military and would much rather be a boring scientist, like my father.

He could probably do anything he wants. He's at the top of our class every year. But August smiles, unlike his dad.

Sometimes I wonder if life can steal a person's smile. If things can become so bad, it's physically impossible to twist your mouth upward.

I wonder if that will happen to me.

I used to smile a lot. I wasn't popular at school, not by a long shot. I was less interesting than eggshell-colored paint. My freshman year, I was always trying to devise ways to get noticed by that upper echelon. I chipped away at it, and it was working. Even when classes were forced online junior year. My friend Lavani said I couldn't do it, but I *was*. How else could she explain August finally noticing me after years of being in the same classes?

She never liked August, though. Lavani was my closest friend at school, my "best" friend, but we weren't really all that close. I didn't invite her to my house for sleepovers or trade clothes with her or get drunk with her at parties. In fact, though we texted a lot, we never saw each other outside school. That's probably why I don't miss her, not like I miss almost *everything* else about my old life.

The sweeping is slow. I don't know if I'm hungry or she's slower today. It takes her forever to open the door.

When she does, she doesn't come in right away. Her scraggly hair sticks out in all directions, rats fleeing a sinking ship. She stands there, her thick body hovering in the doorway. Her hands shake at her sides. Her sweat-slickened skin and eyes appear to be melting.

I'd say she must've had a worse night than I had, but I'd heard her snoring. At least she got some sleep.

Something's different.

She's not carrying a tray.

There was less food yesterday. Maybe there is no more food, like there were no more pills.

Well, get your lazy butt to the store and get some. I would, but I'm a little tied up. Ha ha.

I don't care about the food. But I do care about my pills. Quite a lot, actually.

She looks at me as if she's staring into a mirror and noticed a blemish. Her eyes fixate on my face and narrow. She takes a step in. Her wrinkled crevasse of a mouth opens, and at first, I think she is going to tell me to hush.

But then she lets out a long, powerful hiss, like air being forced out of a tire.

"He's going to get you one day."

She wobbles on her feet. Her pea-green, pupilless eyes roll back into her skull. She pitches forward, then back.

Then she sort of slumps to the side, falling in a heap at the foot of my bed with a *ba-dum-bump*, like the cymbal crash after a bad joke.

I blink, still, listening. There is a clock somewhere, ticking away. I've never heard it before. Flies buzz louder in glee. *New target acquired!*

That didn't really happen, did it?

I count to three. Then ten. Then a hundred.

Nothing changes.

I imagine what August would say right now. *Well, that's a great way to start our morning.*

I lift my head and scuttle against the headboard as far as I can go, then inch my body to the edge of the bed as far as the restraints will allow so I can see her.

Granny's lying on her side on the worn rug, facing me. Those vomit-like eyes stare under the bed. She's still.

So very still.

Her chest isn't moving.

Nothing is moving.

Except the flies. They're loving their new feast.

But there's something else. It's like someone turned on a faucet in her skull, because before my eyes, the lower one starts to fill, turning black as coffee. When it reaches the top, it begins to leak out her tear duct, a long, dark trickle onto the floor.

Blood.

The bindings on my wrists suddenly feel tighter. Because I know exactly what August would say. *You, Willow, are royally screwed.*

SIX

A: Low. You there?

W: maybe...who is this?

A: lol very funny

A: You really don't know who this is?

W: jk what you up to?

A: Thinking about you

W: I hope I'm clothed in those thoughts of yours

A: Barely ☺

W: You're sick.

A: You love it.

A: Hey, you looked good today. Yellow's your color.

W: Thanks. I don't post very much, but I was feeling cute.

A: You're always cute.

This is not a problem.

Really, it isn't.

Without the old shush-happy woman here, I can make a little noise. Someone, maybe another captive or a neighbor, will hear me. Maybe we can free ourselves and run for the hills.

This is good actually.

The door to the bedroom's open. There are noises coming from beyond, a nonrhythmic scraping from deeper inside the house. Someone else is here.

I'm going to get out of here. I can feel it.

Taking all the air I can into my lungs, I shout, "Hello!"

My voice doesn't sound like me. It's gravelly. Quiet. And it cracks halfway through.

I clear my throat and shout again. "Hello! Can anyone hear me?"

I lift my head as far as it'll go. That irregular scraping sound continues. Nothing else.

All right. Third time's a charm.

"Help me! I'm tied up and there's an old lady here! I think she's dead!"

A fly lands on my shoulder. I shrug it off. It lands a second later about an inch away.

The first thing I'll do when my hands are free is smash that fly.

"Help me!" I shout louder, taking another deep breath. "HELP ME!"

Nothing. Maybe nobody is here. Maybe the screaming I heard before was a television. Maybe I'm isolated and there are no neighbors. Maybe I am completely alone now that Granny is dead.

Okay. This *could* be a problem.

Just then, across the hall, I hear it. Thumping. And in a sliver of light under that door, shadows sway.

Someone is there.

"Help! Do you hear me? If you're there, say something!"

Thump, thump, thump.

Enough knocking. If they can move, why won't they open the door? Scary Old Lady is gone. Why won't they answer me?

A horrible thought scrapes into my brain. Maybe it's *something*. Something not human. Maybe it's behind closed doors, trapped, for a reason.

Yeah. Right. Too many horror movies as a kid, I think.

Except Granny kept me trapped. And I can't think of a good reason why. I'm your average high school student, with a sometimes-overbearing boyfriend, SAT fears, the occasional zit, and a weakness for Big Macs. None of those faults qualify me for being kidnapped and tied to a bed for weeks on end. Do they?

My throat is already aching. On cue, my stomach growls. Maybe it knows there's a good chance that, unless I get out of here, I'm never eating again.

No. I have to get out of here.

If I don't, who knows when I'll be found? Maybe years from now, someone will come by this house and find me, tied up like this, nothing but bones.

At least I'd be able to slide out of these restraints. Ha!

I peer over the side of the bed one more time. It's worse than

I thought. Like the cat, Granny's bleeding more, this time from both eyes. Thin rivulets of blood trickle down the side of her doughy face, giving her a slightly clownish appearance. Great. I'm trapped in here with a Pennywise wannabe, only scarier.

The flies love her.

I do not.

Granny is right. It's going to get me one day.

Or wait. She said *he's* going to get me one day. He who? I'm alone. Completely alone, with no hope. No he, she, anyone to be found. The least Granny could've done before she passed was untie me, give me a fighting chance.

But I'm apparently not that lucky. And it doesn't matter what she meant. It, he, she, they… I'm going to be gotten, one day soon. Gotten good. That's inevitable.

Thanks to you, Granny. I'm going to die and become a putrefying mass of goo. Your goo will be right beside mine. Maybe we'll drip together and become one, a unified body of putrescence. Your heirs will have to burn this place down to get rid of the smell.

My stomach rumbles again, this time from disgust rather than hunger.

Those days, in high school, I thought I had problems. Getting into college was one of them. Bullying? Yeah, I was a little goofy and had my share of that too. Whether August was going to quit messing around with too-gorgeous-for-real-life Jana and finally notice me, that was another.

Those aren't problems. This? This is a problem. A big one. I sort through my nonexistent options, and I realize that nothing in my life has equipped me to deal with it.

All those days, chatting incessantly about nothing with August and trying to get him to ask me out, thinking it was the most important thing on Earth, I never thought I'd wind up like this. Dead at sixteen.

Why had I passed up survival YouTube videos for tutorial offerings like, "How to make out like a pro!" and "Ways to do your eyeliner so your eyes pop!" I should've paid closer attention to the ones by the girl who'd successfully broken her way out of zip ties using nothing but her shoelace. Not that I have a shoelace to my name, but…

No one is going to care what my eyeliner looks like when I'm a pile of goo.

I start to laugh at my joke, which becomes maniacal chortling before turning into another scream. It's a loud wail, no words at first. Then I finish with a prayer, even though I've never been religious in my life. "Please. Please, God. If you're up there…help."

Sweat trickles down my forehead, tickling me. I tilt my head to the side to wipe it on my upper arm. I had this cute yellow dress that August liked. I remember feeling good about myself, really good, snapping a photo for my Instagram. God, it's been so long since I've felt good about myself. Look at me! I have no reason to.

Suddenly, the thumping stops, and the irregular scraping resumes.

That's someone. It's got to be.

"Help me!" I scream again.

Somewhere in the house, out of my line of vision, a door creaks open, and along with that, the floorboards creak under someone's substantial weight.

Yes, yes. It's definitely someone. It's working!

Shadows darken the hallway. A human shape. Yes! It's a person. A knight in shining armor to save me. Today is the day that I get out.

And then he appears. Nothing about him is shining. He's a dark, oily nightmare, covered in grime, filling most of the doorway.

For a split second, all I wish is that I'd kept my mouth shut.

The rusty tool in his hands—a wrench, I think—clatters from his grip, and he winces before lunging at me. He throws all his weight onto the bed, onto *me*, covering my mouth with a rough paw that smells of earth and motor oil.

I choke on the breath he's caught in my throat.

Beyond the black mop falling in his face, there are pinpoint yellow eyes, fixed on me. He whispers one word, a word that I've heard time and time again.

"Hush."

SEVEN

W: I can't talk.

A: What's wrong? You looked worried in history today.

W: Yeah. I don't want to talk about it.

A: Willllllllooooooooow...

A: Tell me.

W: My dad had a bad day at work. A REALLY bad day.

W: I'll tell you later.

I let out a muffled growl under his hand, which is pressing against my jaw so tightly I think he might crush my teeth into my mouth. Forget using the self-defense skills I learned at that assembly freshman year. His hand is so tight, I couldn't open my mouth to bite it. And I can't kick him off me. He's too big.

He's going to get you one day.

Right. Gotten.

Eyes wild with terror, I stare at this boy—no, he's a man, I think. His face is lean and boyish, but he has a man's chin strap field of stubble. His lower lip is pierced, right in the center, and he has the dark points of a tattoo snaking up from the collar of his shirt.

I don't like tattoos. Or piercings. My parents raised me to like the clean-cut, all-American, unblemished type. Like August.

I wonder if he's the *he* Granny was referring to.

Maybe there are worse things than being tied up alone in a house.

Mercifully, when I quiet, he loosens his grip and backs up. Then he puts his hands in the air, like he's surrendering to me. He's so tall, his head nearly brushes the transom. Despite the heat, he's dressed in faded jeans that hang from his skinny frame, probably many days or even weeks unwashed. He also wears a buffalo-plaid flannel, open to reveal a black T-shirt underneath. The sleeves are rolled up to the elbows at least. The skin that's visible is partially tanned, partially dirty. Mostly dirty.

I pull on the leather straps, not like they'll let me go anywhere. "Who are you?" I ask.

He doesn't say anything. Instead, he grits his teeth and puts a grimy finger to his mouth.

Hush.

Granny's lying on the floor, but it can't be *his* Granny either, because he steps over her like she's a crack in the wood. He's more interested in the window. Lifting his shaggy, oil-slick hair and scratching at the back of his neck, he walks toward it on tiptoes. Strange for a guy that big to be walking like a ballerina.

Is it because he wants to be quiet? Why? Ding, dong. The witch is dead.

He's barefoot. His feet are even dirtier than the rest of him. His toenails are outlined in black. At least I'm not the only one who's in dire need of a shower.

He makes a motion as if he's going to push aside the shade and look out, but he must think better of it, because he stops. With his hand lifted, I notice a red, raw scar encircling his wrist.

He was a prisoner here. Somehow, he's gotten out.

I pull on the straps. "Can *you* let me out?"

He whips his head toward me. Brings his finger to his lips. Jabs his finger there a few times in exasperation.

Right.

Seconds pass, and I get the feeling he's contemplating whether to help me.

Then he goes to the foot of the bed. He crouches and a second later straightens with Granny bent over his shoulder, his arm wrapped around her knees. He lifts her like a sack of potatoes.

When he turns to face me, I let out a cry. Blood seeping from every one of her orifices—eye sockets, nose, ears, mouth— splatters my legs. It's warm and sticky and *everywhere*.

His eyes widen in warning.

Yeah, I get it. *Hush.*

Then he stoops slightly to pass under the transom, reaches behind him, and closes my bedroom door.

Great. Nice meeting you, jerk.

Well, Willow, your situation has not improved.

Although not having a dead body on my floor is a slight step up.

And not being completely alone in the world is another.

Possibly.

But there is also a very real possibility that my new Mr. Shush-Happy is a demented serial killer.

Of course, he could've killed me already if he wanted to.

I listen for sounds from beyond the door, wondering if he was the one who'd been shouting all those days (weeks?) ago. If so, someone's definitely put him in his place.

There is the sound of metal clinking and a key being turned. Then a door opening.

Is he opening the door across the way? The door with the thumping?

Wait…he's putting dead Granny there? Doesn't he want to…I don't know, *call the freaking police?*

Thump-thump. Was that Granny's body falling to the ground? I hear a click, a door closing again. Then silence.

My eyes trail to my bare legs, now covered in droplets of Granny's blood.

And I thought I couldn't feel any dirtier.

In the hallway, more footsteps sound, and a second later, my door opens.

The guy doesn't look at me. He stands in the doorway, rubbing his face as if trying to decide what to do. He has one of those little divots in his chin, right above the hair and below his silver piercing.

"I need pills," I whisper. "The Ventex. The ones that are supposed to keep me alive? Know where I can find any?"

He glares at me.

Okay, so I'll take that as a no.

Then he goes to the side of the bed and sits beside me. Instead of untying me, he pulls on the glass knob of the night table and slides the drawer open.

How many days have I wondered what was inside that drawer? Now, I get to see. It's a disappointing lead-in because it isn't much. A little plastic case filled with beads. No, a rosary. And a little golden statue of a man in a loincloth, sprawled...no, wait. That's Jesus, probably part of the crucifix that used to hang on the wall. So *that's* where it went. I'm guessing someone had a little crisis of faith. Why else would someone smash Jesus and shove him in a drawer?

My shush-happy friend pulls out a small pad and a pen, as if he knew they were there all along. How, if I've never seen him, if he's a prisoner here like me, does he know what is in that drawer?

The question simmers in my head as he flips the cover on the spiral pad and writes, scratching out the words in an angry way. He holds it up:

Did he shoot you?

I stare at the paper. Shoot me?

He points to his inner arm, streaked with blue veins, and mimes an injection.

There are only more questions in that question. I don't even know where to start. "What about me makes you think I'm a drug addict?"

He winces, then writes more, underlining like his life depends on it. Then he holds it up to me.

DO NOT MAKE NOISE!!!

He jabs at the paper a few times with the pen to really drive his point home.

Fine. I'd like to write my own questions on the pad, but there isn't enough paper there to hold them all. Not that he'd let me. I'm still tied up, and it doesn't appear that's going to change.

I don't get it. Granny's dead. What else do we have to be afraid of? Is it some monster with freakish hearing? I saw a movie like that once. Can't remember the name.

He turns to the window and sucks in a deep breath. Then he lets it out, his chest stuttering under his black T-shirt.

This man, this huge man, is afraid of something.

EIGHT

A: Tell me something about you that no one else knows.

W: Like what?

A: Anything. You're so quiet in history.

W: I'm not good at history, and I hate talking in groups. Even online. It feels weird.

A: If I called you, we could talk one-on-one?

W: Of course.

A: So what are you really good at?

W: Nothing.

A: Stop being mysterious. Everyone's good at something. I, for example, am good at looking good.

W: Shut up. You're good at everything.

A: Come on. Tell me.

W: Okay. Fine. I'm a pretty good singer.

A: ???

A: Why have you never auditioned for the spring musical?

W: I was too shy. But I have a YouTube channel

A: !!!!! No! Link?

W: Here.

A: Holy shit!!! You're...WOW. Now I'm the one who can't talk.

I wonder if I still have the voice to sing.

I had a few hobbies, but nothing I was really good at. Nothing I was confident about. Except singing, and I wasn't really confident about that either.

But I was a *damn* good singer. My parents were constantly telling me to quiet down, because I was always singing. Well, at first. Then, when they realized how good I was, they wanted me to sing all the time. Just for them, though. Then I started a YouTube channel and got all these followers. The funny thing was no one in my school knew about it. Especially with the pandemic going on, I could remain sort of anonymous.

And then...

Then...

Hell if I can remember what happened after that.

My gaze travels to my arms, restrained to the headboard. His intense eyes follow it.

He stares for a moment, two. Takes a deep breath. When he lets it out, his breath smells like cigarettes.

Smoking. Gross.

I flinch as he grabs the nearest strap and starts working.

Oh my God. He's letting me go free.

I look at his face, this time in a new light. He's not as evil as I thought. No, he's just afraid. Yes, that's it. He's not fully a man yet. Seventeen maybe? Or…maybe he's a little older. I'm a bad judge of these things. The tattoo and piercings say older. The fear on his face makes him look younger.

His brow wrinkles in concentration as his big hands pull at the leather tie. Occasionally, he pinches my skin, but it doesn't matter.

Free. I'm about to be free.

When the bindings fall away, I almost sob in relief. It feels so good to move my arm. "Oh, thank you," I say. "I can't even tell you—"

He stiffens.

Sorry, I mouth.

I point to the pad, and he hands it to me. I write: My name is Willow. Were you a prisoner here too?

He looks at me, confusion on his face. I point to the scars on his wrists, which mirror mine. There's a war in his eyes. When he nods, I get the feeling that it's been a long time since he's had any normal human interaction. I feel sorry for him. I wonder how long he's been here.

I scribble more. Your name?

He stares for a moment, then takes the pad and pen from me.

He writes carefully this time, so carefully that his pen shakes and the letters wave:

ELIJAH

I was hoping that when I had a name for him, I'd be satisfied. No such luck. I need to know more.

I take the pad back and write: Why do we have to be quiet?

He stares at the question. I try to hand him back the pad, but he shoves it away.

After a moment, he picks up the pen and starts to write, then shakes his head. He sets the pen down and in a voice I can barely hear, murmurs, "Doesn't it bother you?"

I whisper back. "What? The noise?"

He nods.

I shake my head. Why would it bother me?

He considers this. "It might. Later. Different for everyone. Never bothered…" He shifts on the bed. "Forget it. You can whisper. But not too loud. It hurts me sometimes."

All right. Now I'm getting somewhere. "Why?"

He winces, like even my whisper is too loud. Then he shakes his head solemnly. He doesn't want to say.

All right. It doesn't matter. I know anyway: It's because of who or whatever he's afraid of.

I pick up the pen again: What happened to Granny?

He looks at the question, takes the pen from me, and scratches out her name. Then he writes: VIRUS.

Now it's my turn to wince.

Reading my mind, he writes: YOU'RE SAFE

Right. At first, kids seemed immune to the screw. But during the second wave, everyone got it, and it was vicious.

At first, there were a few empty seats in class. Then more and more. By the end of my sophomore year, school was online to prevent the spread. Then Ventex came out, and things almost returned to normal.

Almost.

He circles the question again, then raises his eyebrows: Did he shoot you?

"He who?"

He frowns and rubs his chin. I guess he was expecting a different answer.

"Pills?" I ask. "Can I have them?"

He bites his lower lip and nods. "In a minute."

"Why didn't Granny…"

"She wanted you to have what is left."

Oh. What is left. That means there's a shortage. I remember the news saying that there might be one. Too much demand, not enough supply. In some areas of the country, people were fighting for Ventex on the streets.

I misjudged Granny. Who knew that woman shoveling paste into my mouth like she wanted to kill me was a martyr?

I squeeze my eyes shut, trying to remember more. The more questions I ask, the more questions I spawn. I'm tired and hungry and want to get the hell out of this bed.

Maybe then I can get some answers.

I point to the edge of the bed, silently asking permission. He gets up and nods.

Glaring at my feet, I issue a silent challenge: *You better not fail me now.*

For the first time in I don't know how long, I slide my skinny legs over the side of the bed. My toes hit the ground. It's colder than I thought it'd be, considering how warm and stuffy the air is.

When I try to put weight on them, pain shoots up my legs. I stifle a cry that makes him wince.

I think of my dad, my ever-patient dad, when he tried to teach me how to ride a bike. A billion hours, running after me and my Dora bike on the sidewalk outside our house. *These things take time.*

I curl my toes to stretch them. Try again. Slowly, slowly, a little more pressure, then pain unlike anything I've ever felt. Pain that makes my stomach squeeze and want to expel everything inside it.

Sweat beads on my temples, slips down the sides of my face. I can feel the veins popping out on my neck.

Maybe today *won't* be the day we escape.

I've been here too long. Although every single pore of my body wants to leave this room, my legs are not getting with the program.

He watches me carefully. Then he reaches down and grabs my legs. I'd fight, but I don't have the energy. He moves them back on the bed, so I'm at square one again. "No, I need to—"

He clamps a hand over my mouth.

Right. No talking.

I lie there, silent, unmoving, until he lets go. When he does, I don't think I can go anywhere. I might as well still have the tethers around my wrists.

He runs his tongue over his top teeth. Then he wraps a big hand around my bare ankle.

My every hair stands on end. My mouth shapes to say a W, like, "What are you doing?" but then he lifts my leg, bends it at the knee, and moves it up toward my chest.

He takes the other one too and moves it, gently. Then he gives me a look, brow creased. *Do you understand?*

I do. My father volunteered at the VA hospital, and I went with him from time to time. The nurses would do that with the injured soldiers to help them start using limbs they might not have exercised for a while. I nod and start to bicycle my legs.

It hurts like a mother.

I keep working. Getting sweatier and sweatier. There was a time when I could run the mile without breaking a sweat. Now the tiniest movement sends pain shooting up my spine. My legs are still splattered with Granny's blood. In the back of my mind, I'd thought that once I got up, I'd wash up, because who knows when I last did that?

A shower. Oh, God, do I want a shower.

But dammit. That's probably not happening today.

Especially since it doesn't look like my friend here has had one in quite some time. Maybe this place doesn't have indoor plumbing.

The horror.

Finally, my limbs fall like cinder blocks on the yellow sheets. I shake my head. *No more.*

Crouching, he picks up the wrench and starts to leave.

I wave my hands frantically.

He stops and looks at me.

I take the pad and pen and write: Is there any food?

He nods. He plods out the door and returns a few moments later with my pills, a half-full glass of water, and a bowl. I expect white paste, but I find six mostly green cherry tomatoes.

Eureka. I swallow my pills, then start shoveling the tomatoes into my mouth, pressing my tongue against them until their bitter goodness pops against my taste buds. They taste delicious, sweet and fresh, a little like earth too, so I have to wonder if they've been washed properly. Not that it matters. In seconds, they're gone.

When I look up, so is he. As big and imposing as he is, he managed to escape without making a single sound.

And here I am, no more restraints, yet stuck. Again.

NINE

A: Can you sing to me?

W: NO

A: Please. Send me a video or something.

W: Fine.

<video attachment>

A: Wow. Beautiful.

W: Thank you.

A: The singing was good too.

I lie on the bed for the rest of the afternoon, moving my limbs, massaging feeling into them, thinking of August, and trying to be silent.

For what, I don't know.

I imagine August, swooping in here like the hero everyone always thought he was at school and saving me. He'd scoop me up in his arms, and when I thanked him, he'd say, "Of course, Low. I couldn't let you be here like this. I couldn't let them do this to you."

But he's not a miracle worker. He doesn't know where I am. No one does.

I feel my head. My hair is thick and knotted with oil but no bugs, I think. I feel my face. My skin is covered in pimples. *Your normal hygiene routine has certainly suffered, girl. You really think August is going to ask you to prom now?*

Prom. Oh God. That was the fantasy, wasn't it? I used to dream of August asking me to prom. Not that we thought we'd *have* prom, but all of us were hopeful life would be back to normal by then. I didn't want a social-media-worthy promposal. I just wanted him, quietly and earnestly, to ask me to be his date.

My heart flutters at the thought of what could've been.

Because he never asked me. I think I'd remember that. He never even officially broke up with Jana, did he? Even though he promised, time and time again.

Who knows? Maybe prom has already happened. Maybe August gave up on finding me and went with Jana. Maybe they're a thriving couple again, now that I'm out of the picture.

I wonder how long he worried about me. *If* he worried about me. Or if he cried on Jana's shoulder until they got back together. Not that he could—social distancing and all. Maybe he didn't even cry. Maybe all those little love notes he sent me were games, like Lavani said.

Maybe I'll never find out.

Elijah doesn't come back. It gets hotter in the room. I get the feeling the AC broke and he's outside, trying to fix it. I mean, it's Florida. Even old shacks have AC in Florida. Otherwise, it's suicide. Would've been nice if he cracked a window.

Maybe he is afraid of diseased bunyavirus air getting in.

But it's already in here, isn't it? Granny…

I can't think about her.

Still, as I lie there, staring up at the water-stained ceiling, I imagine it slipping into the cracks in this old house, slowly trying to infect me.

My father is an epidemiologist, so disease has always been a big part of my life, even before the screw. Dad's always been big on the ways infection spreads. His favorite movie is *28 Days Later*. I must be my father's daughter, because my mind hitches on that.

We'd left Pensacola. Had we been running away from something, my family and me? If so, I'll be damned if I can remember what we were running from.

Did he shoot you?

What does that mean?

An image of August pops into my head. I always imagine him the same—in nothing but gym shorts, his blond mess of hair in his eyes, one bare foot pulled up under him in his chair, face lit by his computer screen. That last time I messaged with him, before we left. *I think I have an idea.*

I didn't get a chance to tell him I was going anywhere, much less give him a proper goodbye before we left Pensacola. My father peeled us out of the driveway in my Mustang so fast that my head spun.

Don't give me that face, he'd said, peering at me through the rearview mirror. *We've got to get on the road, Willow.*

Little did he know...

I remember some of our luggage falling off the rooftop rack, but he didn't stop. I'd looked out the back window at August's house, wishing he'd come out, wave to me. Wondering if he'd meant what he'd promised.

What had August promised?

I can't remember.

The thought of the unease on my father's usually placid face makes my stomach churn. He didn't do worry. But he'd torn out of Pensacola like the devil was chasing him. Something *big* had to have been up. I think it had to do with his job. He was on the news. Something about his work. About...escape.

I can't recall a damn thing.

I get so annoyed by the Swiss cheese holes in my memory, by my inability to do anything, that I decide to give walking another try.

When I throw my feet over the side of the bed, the pins and needles are back, but they don't shoot quite as high up to my spine as before. Now, it only hurts like hell up to my knees. I put a hand down on the mattress and lift myself to standing.

I'm upright! Huzzah.

I peer around. The room looks different at my full five feet, eight inches. When you can look down on things, you always feel a certain power over them.

I'm just getting comfortable with the view when my hand slips off the table and down I go, caving in on myself like a pile of broken furniture. The resulting smash as my knees and hips hit the floor is so loud, I expect Elijah to come running.

I breathe in, out. In. Out. Waiting.

He doesn't come.

It's actually not so bad, crawling. I can scoot my backside across the dust-covered floor. Ignoring the pain in my bones, I stretch my heels, touch the ground, dig in, and slip my butt close to them, again and again, like an inchworm.

I get to that table that was across the room. The one with the telephone, comb, brush, and handheld mirror. From here, I can see the old, heavy cord of the telephone, heading toward but not quite making it to the outlet on the wall. When I pull it toward me, it gives easily. The line has been cut. It's frayed, maybe even gnawed by the cat or the mice. Guess no one has been calling 911 recently.

Reaching up, I pat the surface of the table, feeling around. Bristles, no. Teeth of the comb, no. Smooth and cool handle.

Aha. Got it.

Grasping the mirror, I lower it and peer at the surface, bracing myself for the horrors.

But I see none. Just some dusty, shiny metal.

It's missing most of the glass. There's only a small shard, like a crocodile tooth, still fixed to the frame.

Great. So why is this here? What good is a hand mirror without the mirror?

I place it back on the table. Scoot, scoot, scoot.

There's a closet on the same wall as the entry door. I move to it, reach for the knob. It's locked.

Boo.

More scooting.

At the window, I hook my fingers on the sill. Limbs shaking with the strain, I try to lift myself again.

Suddenly, the shade snaps up, a sound so loud it pops in my eardrums. Punishing white light brands my eyeballs.

I fall back on my ass and shield my eyes as the sun invades the room.

I wait for Elijah to come running again, to scold me for making too much noise. I listen for the sound of the screen door, the creak of footsteps.

Nothing.

Blinking the starbursts from my vision, I peer through my fingers. The branches of the tree I always glimpsed through the shade are now visible, burned black, another victim of the relentless sun. That dirty shade is fully coiled on the spool at the top of the window, and the sun is so menacing, I imagine it creating tiny fires on my skin as it passes through the pane. I'm burning. I may be a Florida girl, but right now, the sun is an enemy.

But I don't care. I need to see what's out there, what's beyond this room.

I try again, my fingernails scraping the top of the sill as I lift myself, feeling like I'm presenting myself to the firing squad. Or a zombie hoard. Or a plague of bumblebees. Whatever.

When I'm eye level with the bottom pane, it's nothing like the chaos I was expecting.

The dead tree is the only once-living thing near the house. Tufts of yellow saw grass struggle hopelessly from the dirt.

But beyond that, in the hazy distance, there is a line of trees, thick, scraggly trees, covered in Spanish moss. A swampy forest—a dark, thick one, so thick I imagine that being inside it must feel like nighttime all the time.

Cool, quiet, wet, *alive*. The vegetation in the distance is so lush, it drags a sigh of relief out of me.

At least something in this world is capable of living.

And I know where I am.

My family took me here once, after we did a cruise to the Caribbean out of Fort Lauderdale.

I'm in the Everglades. Well, somewhere in the Everglades at least. They're huge. Like, lower-half-of-Florida huge.

And desolate. And remote.

We'd gone on a tour of the national park when I was a kid. On one of those big airboats with the giant fans in the back.

I remember thinking, when I was out on that boat, surrounded by all that dark, swampy water, how someone could come here and get lost.

Disappear.

Forever.

People have, you know.

My father loved the water, which was why his office was on the third floor of our house, directly overlooking the gulf. He'd always go out on the balcony for hours at a time and stare at nothing in particular. I'd ask him what he saw out there, where the deep blue of the water met the cornflower blue of the sky, and he'd say, "The end of the world."

Now I stare into that thick line of trees, and I wonder if the end of the world is *here*.

Had we gotten turned around on our trip? My father was awful with that. He could lose his sense of direction in our own neighborhood. Even with GPS guiding him.

Did he get us lost *here*?

I'm about to stand to grab the edge of the shade so I won't be roasted here like a half-mad fly on a windowsill when I see him.

Walking away from the house, staring out toward the line of trees, he shields his eyes from the sun. He's wearing a white, loose shirt, a stark contrast to his deep tan.

He turns to me suddenly, and his laugh lines wrinkle as he smiles. *The end of the world*, he mouths.

All feeling that was gradually returning to my limbs drains right out again. I push my nose against the scalding glass, ignoring the burn.

It's him.

It's my father.

TEN

A: Willllow.

A: Willlllllllllllow

A: Where are you?

A: Are you ignoring me?

W: Yes.

A: What did I do?

W: What do you think?

A: No clue.

W: Come on. You're never going to break up with J, are you?

A: It's complicated.

W: Not really. Lavani said you were playing me. And
   she's right.

A: Willow.

W: Just leave me alone.

Sweat slips into my eyes, making them sting. I blink. Again and again, I blink, eager to see what my father is doing out there. Like I said, above all, my dad wanted to help.

So why isn't he helping me? Why is he smiling?

But when my eyes adjust, he's gone.

In his place is a little girl. A girl in braids and a pink dress. She's also barefoot, walking along a dirt path with a long blade of saw grass in her hand, weaving it into a chain. She's so placid. So sweet.

She doesn't see me.

But I want her to. I wave. As I do, I notice the once pale-blue sky being crowded with black clouds. Lightning slits the sky.

I gasp. She needs to get in from the storm. The sense of foreboding nearly suffocates me. Something terrible is going to happen.

I shake the glass. It rattles so hard, I'm surprised it doesn't break. I start to shout, looking for a way to lift the window. It's locked or doesn't open, because there are no pulls. Still shouting, I throw my weight against it, pounding with both fists.

The girl ignores me and ignores the coming storm, even as the rain begins to pelt her face.

Suddenly a hand clamps over my shoulder, yanking me back. I topple to the ground.

Breathless, I lie on my back, staring up at Elijah. He stands over me, his hair wet, matted against the sharp lines of his face. He pulls down the shade. Then he crouches in front of me, dripping rainwater off the edge of his pointed nose onto my face.

Don't, he mouths. *Ever again.*

"But there was a little girl out there," I say, my voice not more than a whisper. The rain's pelting the window louder than my voice.

He stares at me, eyes wide. He doesn't believe me. He didn't see. He mouths, *What did you see?*

"A girl. And my father. I saw…" I start to point.

He reaches down, shoves a hand under my armpit, and drags me upright, then drops me on the bed like I'm nothing. I struggle to get up. If my dad is out there, I need to—

He throws his forearm over my chest and forces me to stare into his eyes. He shakes his head. Then he grabs my arm and looks at the inside of my elbow joint. There's nothing there. He shrugs and mouths, *You don't need the pills.*

What is he saying? Does he think I'm a drug addict?

I stop struggling. Maybe I am. "Where is my father?"

He loosens his grip and shrugs both shoulders, not meeting my eyes.

He's lying.

I don't know what makes me think that. Actually, everything he *hasn't* said so far, everything he's done, could be a lie. I don't know him. I don't know anything. And damned if I can remember what brought me here.

Suddenly, lightning flickers through the sky again, and the house shakes as a gigantic boom follows. He boxes his ears with his hands as if he's in physical pain.

I stare at him. *Dramatic much?*

He pulls his hands to his lap and whispers, "Sounds really don't bother you?"

I don't understand. Now I really want to scream.

The rain falls harder, pinging against the roof and metal gutters. The dead tree branch outside scrapes against the window, and it moans as if in pain too.

"Wait. They will. And you might see things that aren't there. It's normal."

"Normal? For who?"

He opens his mouth, then shakes his head. "If you know what's good for you, you'll stay away from the doors and windows." For the first time, I hear his regular voice, not a whisper. It's lower than I expected, with a bit of a southern twang. "Just stay put."

"Why?" I scuttle back against the headboard and pull my knees to my chest.

"I can't let you out there. Not with…"

"With who?"

He shakes his head. "No one."

"Tell me."

"There are *monsters*."

My blood turns to ice. *The end of the world.* "What monsters?"

Thrum, thrum, thrum goes the rain. *Screeeeech* goes the branch on the window. He sits down, carefully choosing his words. If the only time he'll talk to me in a normal voice is when it rains, I need him to hurry. I have so many questions.

"It started a year ago. The screw. It killed a lot of people, but then there were the pills to prevent it. You remember?"

I do and I don't. It sounds unreal as he tells it, made up, like a bedtime story someone read to me years ago. "Ventex."

"Right. But it had side effects. Made people tired. And when you stopped taking it, you lost your protection. There were shortages. Scientists were trying to come up with something more permanent. But that takes time. People were getting desperate… scientists were under a lot of pressure…and then…"

Déjà vu creeps over me, and it's like someone opened a window to the past. This sounds familiar.

BST-14D.

A miracle.

That was what my father called it.

BST was my father's baby. He spent most of his life working on a drug with a broader application than the antiviral medications on the market, ramping up his work during the pandemic, only to have to scrap it. He'd been destroyed over that.

"They haven't found a cure yet," I murmur, remembering. My father's work had made the news. My mother had turned off the television, but I'd caught the press conference on my phone. For whatever reason, the Federal Drug Administration had not cleared BST-14D to go into clinical trials. But there were accusations that my father had moved forward anyway, without Latrobe's knowledge. He and his team had been disgraced. There was talk of governmental investigations and him losing his job.

Did he? Was he fired?

I can't remember. I *do* remember him looking haggard as the press stuck their microphones under his nose. *It's perfectly safe, and I stand by it…*

Elijah shakes his head. "Developing a vaccine is a long, slow process, then there is laboratory testing, clinical testing, FDA approvals, production… There are protocols that must be followed to keep people safe. But someone didn't follow that process, and their experimental drug made people monsters."

Monsters. Each time he says it, I feel like someone's playing a trick on me. "How do you—"

He rakes both hands through his hair. "Because I saw it happen. It started small, like the pandemic. With the pandemic, it was a couple people overseas who died. Nothing to worry about, they told us. You remember? But it got worse, fast…much worse. The second plague."

I don't understand. "When did this happen?"

"Last month. It went fast."

"But how do you—"

"I *know*. I saw it with my own eyes. You haven't seen them," he snaps, shooting a wounded look at the window. His body shudders, and there are goose bumps on his forearms. "You don't *want* to see them."

"I don't—what's wrong with them?"

"They kill. They like the sight of blood. The taste of it too."

I wait for the punchline. The "just kidding." It doesn't come. He's serious. He's talking, straight-faced, about zombies.

"Does it spread like the screw?"

"It's worse than that. A million times worse. Unless I, *we*—"

He puts a finger to his lips, and I hear the rain is slowing. He mouths, *There's no stopping it.*

"How do you know all thi—"

Shhhhh! he mouths.

But there's so much I want to talk about. How could this happen? My father developed a lot of different drugs, including the one he thought was a miracle. It was supposed to stop humans from contracting *all* viruses. And he was never more excited about proving it right than when the screw came along. He was so confident. Like I said, my father always wants to *help*.

It killed him that his life's research was scrapped when people needed it most. He would've sooner died than see people suffer. But even though he was working for the common good, he got his share of hate mail. People asking why he couldn't work faster. And he hated that. I had a *bodyguard* once, for two tense weeks when some stalker had threatened my father. My parents shielded me from the particulars, but it wasn't a good situation.

Then my mind hitches on what Elijah asked me. *Did he shoot you?*

Why would he ask me that, unless…

Dread settles over me. I open my mouth, but Elijah's staring death into me. I grab the pad out of the drawer and quickly scribble: Where did this drug come from?

He reads and points at me.

My stomach roils. I mouth, *My father?*

He nods.

That's impossible. There were accusations, but BST-14D never made it to testing. Latrobe scrapped his project. Didn't they? I don't know. It was all confidential. I was close to my dad, and I don't know.

So how does this random stranger in the middle of the marsh know more than I do?

I mouth, *How do you know?*

He writes: You won't believe me.

He's right. I don't believe any of this. How does he even know who *I* am? I grab the pen and write: Yeah, and I don't believe in MONSTERS.

He shakes his head, snatches the pen from me, and writes over the word MONSTERS, making it darker.

He underlines it a few times to make his point. I almost laugh aloud.

"I don't…this is insane," I whisper. "You expect me to believe that something my father developed turned humans into, what, psychopathic killers? That he started some kind of zombie plague?"

How stupid. What is this, *The Walking Dead?*

But he nods. Entirely serious.

"Prove it."

Scowling at me, he shoves the notebook into the drawer, closes it softly, then goes to the door. He closes it behind him, and once again, the silence is a killer. The only sound is the water trickling through the downspouts outside.

I wait for him to come back. One minute. Two. He doesn't. So either he doesn't have proof, or he doesn't care if I believe him.

And I don't believe him. I really don't.

But it's clear he believes something bad is out there. So I keep running it through my head. Either he's mad, or...

Or...

Or...there are monsters. Real ones. And I am here because of it.

Where is my father? And who was that little girl?

It starts small...

Does it start with people seeing things?

Am I going crazy?

Did he shoot you?

No. Absolutely not.

I never took anything experimental. I'm sure of it. Whatever my father was working on was killed before it went to trials.

I squeeze my eyes closed and try to focus. But only one thought comes to mind.

I don't want to live in a world with monsters. Especially if I am one of them.

ELEVEN

W: Thanks.

A: ???

W: Shut up, I know the flowers were from you.

A: I'm sorry.

W: Fine. I accept your apology.

A: How are you?

W: Scared. So many people are dying...that's all I hear
on the news.

A: Yeah. I know. But your dad will fix it.

W: I don't know. I feel like it's about to steamroll over him.

W: My mom's suspicious about who's sending me flowers.
She thinks it's some internet creep.

A: Sorry. I'll be more careful next time.

W: No. Just be more honest. All the time.

I'm thinking about flowers when I finally get out of the bedroom.

August left flowers on my front stoop at night. Twice. With
a card that said, HI, LOW.

In all the darkness of those days, that tiny gesture gave me hope. God, my mother was so freaked out. She thought it was the stalkers who wanted to kill my father over the press he was receiving because of his miracle cure. But Dad's stalkers left death threats, not flowers, and I'd told August that white roses were my favorite. An Alice in Wonderland thing.

Anyway, a second or a lifetime after I've let the full weight of Elijah's words settle over me, I stumble to the door and try the glass knob, hoping to find something there to give me the same hope as August's flowers. I need something right now, and God knows I'll never find anything in this room.

Surprisingly, the knob twists. It's not locked.

The door doesn't creak open. Someone has greased the hinges with some runny amber stuff. I hadn't noticed it from the bed, but I can see it now, dripping down the white paint, coagulating in the rusty crevices of this old door's fixtures. *Hush, we must be quiet.*

The floorboard creaks under my weight.

I wince.

Nothing happens.

No one appears. No monsters attack.

The cigarette smell is strong out here. Choking. The air is slightly hazy with smoke.

In front of me is that door. The banging door.

Whatever lies behind it is being good for now. It's quiet.

I reach out to jiggle the glass knob, identical to the one on my bedroom door. It's locked, as I expected.

I lean forward, cock my head to the left.

There is the kitchen in all its wheat-colored glory. I imagine that sixty years ago, this might have been fashionable. Now, it barely looks functional. The space is neat, though the cabinets are chipped and cracked and the dead-flower wallpaper is peeling. The ceiling is brownish, burned over the stove, maybe from a kitchen accident. There is a massive fruitwood spoon and fork attached to the wall. And a smell mingling with the cigarette stench—not a good one. Something's rotting. Flies buzz over the sink.

I inch over to it, ever so slowly. There is a dead rat there, curled in a fetal position. It's been there awhile. There are maggots in the smile-like gash in its side.

A lifetime ago, I'd be disgusted. Now, I just stare.

Mr. Rat, are you a monster? Or a victim of one?

I lift the lever to run the water and scatter the flies, but when I do, nothing happens. Nothing except a hellish groaning noise emanating from under the sink. It grows louder.

I quickly push the lever down.

No water. Instantly, my throat goes dry.

Then I turn toward a dark living area beyond a small pass-through with dark fruitwood prison bars. I peer inside, past an ashtray with a large pile of cigarette butts, each one smoked efficiently to the filter.

There's a large sofa, one that looks like it's been beaten into submission by the weight of too many too-hefty backsides over the years. Draped over it, a handmade afghan of two colors that go terribly together—brown and stoplight red. There's an old AC in the one window. The blocked window and the faux-wood paneled walls make the room tomb-dark.

Beyond that sits a relic of a television set with antennae poking up at an almost right angle, like the arms of a traffic cop. Another ashtray, filled with even more thoroughly smoked cigarette butts, one still smoking slightly, rests on a table. And in the corner…is that what I think it is? I've seen something like it before on television. It's one of those two-way ham radios.

Hope ignites in me for a split second, until I remember that it probably runs on electricity. And we clearly have none.

I scan a wall of pictures. The one in the middle is a photograph; the others are painted scenes of some cobbled street somewhere. Maybe they're supposed to look pretty and quaint, but they're not particularly good, and to me they just seem lonely, washed out.

I step out of the kitchen and inch down the hall toward the pictures. As I do, I see two more doors. The one farthest away is a half door under the staircase, a Harry Potter cupboard-under-the-stairs kind of place.

The bigger door, the one closest to me, is open. I peer inside. There's another bed there, with a lumpy, misshapen mattress. My eyes are drawn to the old leather straps wound to the rusted metal rails of the headboard. Just like mine.

Is that where Granny kept Elijah?

The bed is neatly made, with almost military precision. I move a little closer and notice dark, reddish-brown splotches on the sheets, close to the headboard. I imagine someone like me, screaming and writhing and wringing his wrists raw enough to bleed as he tries to get free, and my heart speeds up.

Then I notice a bookshelf filled with what looks like textbooks: biology, mathematics, and U.S. history. Old, worn ones without slick covers, only gold-embossed titles. An old wooden desk with a lamp. A poster of a solar system. And a drum set.

A drum set. I certainly wasn't expecting that in the quietest house in the world.

But really, except for those straps and the bloody sheets, it looks like an ordinary bedroom. I wonder if that's what it was once. A normal teenager's room. I wonder if the monsters changed that.

I back out of the doorway and turn toward the living room. On the opposite wall is a framed cross-stitch with Snoopy and Woodstock. It says BLESS THIS MESS. I have to wonder who stitched it. It seems so…benign and monster-free.

I look past it, into the living room. I creep over, reach out, and touch the radio. Tap the mouthpiece. *Hello, August? Can you hear me?*

Of course not.

I take in the wall of pictures. From here, I can make out a happy family—Mom, Dad, gangly kid, apple-cheeked, pigtailed girl. Just what I needed to see. Something nice. Something cheerful.

I get halfway to the wrought-iron scrollwork railing of the

stairs when I see him. Well, only his dirty bare feet and the hems of his jeans, which are coated in dirt and frayed.

I bristle.

He shoots down the steps in a flash. I glimpse something in his hand, long and black and sleek, but I barely have a chance to recognize it when he lunges forward, and this time, he grabs me by my hair. He pulls me back toward the bedroom, lifting me up so my feet scrape the ground. I yelp. He clamps a hand over my mouth.

No. I can't go back in there. Not yet. Not when I just got out.

I pull open my lips and bite down as hard as I can. So hard that I taste motor oil and dirt, and blood and saliva run down my lips.

His face twists in agony. But he doesn't let go, and he doesn't cry out. If anything, he grips me harder, pushing his sweaty body against mine as he hoists me onto the bed.

"They're here," he whispers in my ear.

TWELVE

A: I miss you, Low.

A: Low.

A: Speak to me.

W: I'm here.

W: I miss you too. I wish I didn't. But I do.

Monsters.

That's all I can think as he shoves me on the bed.

When I was in school, we studied a television show called *The Twilight Zone*, and our English teacher made us watch an episode called "The Monsters Are Due on Maple Street." People on an ordinary suburban street became so convinced that their neighbors were part of an alien invasion that they all wound up turning on each other, causing chaos, proving that *they* themselves were the true monsters.

The monsters are here.

I can't help thinking that I might be one of them.

My elbows and knees hit the mattress, and before I can look up, he's grabbing the straps and tying me up again.

"Oh no! Please," I beg as he holds tight to my wrists. If monsters are coming, I can't be tied up. I need a fighting chance. He doesn't listen until I say, "I'll scream."

He pauses and whispers, "If I don't tie you, will you stay here and be quiet?"

I nod feverishly. "What are you going to do?"

"Get rid of them."

He can't be a monster, because he has a heart. He lets me go, then stalks to the window. As he does, I see the bow, along with a quiver of arrows, strapped to his back. What is he going to do with those?

Lifting up the roller shade, he finds a catch on the window I didn't notice and releases it. He shoves it up with the heel of his hands. He looks back at me and presses a finger against his lips.

Then he peeks his head out, wiggles the rest of his body through the opening, then hoists himself up.

I jump to my feet and rush to the window, peering after him in time to see his shadow disappearing beyond the rooftop eave.

Leaning out, I try to glimpse him, to figure out exactly what he's trying to do, but the sun bears down upon me, making me squeeze my eyes shut. When I open them again, lights float in my vision. I blink the bursts away, trying to spot the monsters in the distance. A zombie horde, shambling its way to us.

Nothing. Only trees, faraway branches bending in a sauna-hot breeze.

Maybe the danger is on the other side of the house. I listen for far-off eerie moans of the dead. Instead, I hear his footsteps on the roof. I press my sweat-soaked palms against the window-sill, spotted with dead gnats. That's when I see something moving out in the tall saw grass, near the marsh. A dark shape, winding between the sun-dried brown grasses, swaying in the wind. A thick haze, like the kind that settles over a street in the summer, crowds over the horizon.

I tilt my head. Even as I blink, it doesn't get any clearer.

An animal? Or…

My father?

Then, there's a quick *thwack!* and something sails over my head, straight for the mysterious reed-dwelling thing.

It occurs to me what it is when the dark shape drops from sight.

Now, I'm leaning so far out the window, it's a wonder I don't fall out.

Someone—a man—starts to scream. First, it's a distant buzzing, and then it gets louder and louder, reaching a crescendo before dissolving into sobs and wails of pain. "Help! Helllllp!"

My father.

No, not my father. Granted I have never heard my father scream for help, but the voice is all wrong. It's gravelly. Older. Less confident.

And Elijah has just shot him with an arrow.

I don't think. I throw one leg over the windowsill, then the other, landing among a bunch of wooden posts and old seashell edging that must've once been a garden but is now scraggly weeds. My hair catches in the branches of the dead tree and rips from my scalp as I race toward the reeds.

It only occurs to me that Elijah is behind me...with a bow and arrow...that he used to shoot a man...when I break free of the shadow of the house. Amid the man's tortured wails, I hear the slow stretching of the bow's string.

I turn, raise my hands to the sky in surrender.

Because Elijah is standing on the sloped rooftop, the sun a halo behind him, I can't make out the expression on his face.

But I can see he is aiming the arrow right at my heart.

The man in the tall grass behind me is screaming, again and again, clearly in agony.

I raise my hands higher and let out a shaky breath. For a moment that feels like an eternity, I wait for Elijah to make the next move.

Without a sound, without so much as a breath, he raises his aim, and then, *thwack!*

The arrow sails narrowly over my head.

And the world goes silent once again.

THIRTEEN

W: Another kid from class died today. He didn't take the pills.

A: I know. You all right?

W: Been better.

A: Low, I've played that video of you about a million times. You're so beautiful. I was wrong. I'm sorry.

W: Stop. I'm talking about death and you're back on that? I already told you. We're fine.

A: I don't think so. I can tell you're different. Why?

W: You know why. J

A: I'll do whatever you want me to do. I'm ready.

W: Do what YOU want. But just know that right now, you're not being great to either of us. And it's not a good look.

I sink to the ground, covering my mouth with my hand.

Somehow Elijah slides from the roof and jumps from the

gutter to the ground. His footsteps are silent as he approaches, like a hunter inspecting his latest kill. A kill lying not twenty feet away from me. A man who was crying out for help.

"You killed him. You killed a man," I sputter. "An innocent man who wanted our help!"

"He'll be back," he murmurs, staring at the sky.

Is that what he thinks? Is he mad? The man is lying dead. Does he think that normal humans are monsters? That this man, who was crying for help, is a zombie? That he needs to shoot him in the head to end him for good?

I stare past the saw grass at the lifeless body, almost waiting for it to sputter to life again. But that's crazy.

It's *not* coming back.

He's crazy. Is his brain diseased from being Granny's captive?

And if the monsters are on the ground, why is he always staring up at the sky?

I shake my head. "No. You don't know that. He was a man. He looked normal."

Facing away from me, he whispers, "Go back to the house."

I crouch there, the saw grass tickling my legs and arms. Flies buzz around my damp skin, which is still covered in Granny's blood and my own thick sweat. "No."

He puts a hand solidly on my shoulder and shoves. Hard. I fall on my side, sloshing into the muddy ground.

"*Yes.*"

When I look up again, he's holding the bow in front of him.

He's not aiming it this time, but his face says, *Don't make me use this on you.*

I don't scream. Somehow, I scrabble to my feet and start to run.

It's a feeble attempt, because I have no idea where to run, and my legs are still rubbery and borderline useless. I fall, get up, fall again, squinting in a sun so bright it scalds my eyes. It's like I'm running into a vast white heaven.

Before I know it, he's grabbed the back of my T-shirt. He pulls back, and I lunge forward at the same time. There's a *pop-pop-pop* as the stitching gives way, and then a tear. He wins the tug-of-war, getting me in a choke hold and dragging me back. Kicking is useless. He's too strong. He yanks me toward the house. The screen door opens and slams.

Another door creaks open. I expect he'll tie me to the bed.

I'm wrong.

Instead, he drags me past the bedroom. I hear him working the latch on another door.

Then, huffing, he sets me down, and with a shove that knocks the breath out of me, he sends me reeling into blackness. Into a rabbit hole. My head bangs against something hard, and something jabs into a shoulder blade. Still in shock, I crawl toward the only light, toward him and that small doorway. He's shoved me under the stairs.

He snarls, "I *could* kill you right now. I *should've* already. Then I wouldn't have to—"

I don't hear any more as he slams the door. It clicks closed with a resounding finality that echoes in my eardrums.

The smell is like garbage, garbage that has sat in the sun for way too long. My eyes water. I don't want to breathe in the rancid air.

And it's darker than my worst nightmare.

I scream.

Of course I scream.

I scream until I can't anymore. Every name I can think of. I call him every curse word in the book. Then I beg for him to save me, pleading to his humanity, if he has any left. I scream because I know he doesn't like the sound and because I don't want him to forget me in this small space.

He doesn't come.

I sit there for what seems like hours.

After a while, I explore with my hands. I reach for the door first. Of course it's locked. I shove against it, and it doesn't budge, doesn't even rattle.

Then I run my hands across the ground. It's grooved. Wood planks, I think. Covered in a soft powder. Dust bunnies. I feel several small, hard objects with my fingertips. Dead insects? Wisps of cobwebs tickle my nose. I hold back a sneeze.

The place is so small that I cannot fully stretch myself across the width of it, but I can stretch my arms out on either side of me and not touch a wall. It's much longer than it is wide.

And here I thought there wasn't anything worse than being strapped to that bed.

I reach my hands up and feel the underside of the staircase, the Ls and angles. Following it as it descends, I crawl until my head bumps it.

On the ground, I find something soft.

It feels like a lumpy pillow. Beside it is a rough woolen blanket, like the one that had been in my room, then disappeared.

Did someone once...sleep here?

Is this a prison?

Another place for one of Granny's captives?

I pat around on the floor, stirring up the dust, until I find something else. A pile of rags, mixed with something hard but yielding in places. I slide my fingers around it, picking out something long and thin, but also...slick and greasy. Sticky. Just when it comes into my head how very wrong this is, my fingers catch on matted, scraggly strands of something much thicker than cobwebs.

Hair.

This misshapen lump was once a human body.

I skirt away, as far away as I can, kicking out my feet.

And I scream.

Louder this time, as loud as my body will let me.

And this time, I do not stop, even when every bit of air has left my lungs.

I fall into a place where the sun is warm on my skin, where my belly is bloated from the hamburger I just ate, where my SAT scores, chipping nail polish, and whether August's ever going to give Jana the brush-off are pretty much the only worries on my mind.

I'm on the balcony of my house, enjoying the last rays of the sun. I'm supposed to be working on an English paper on *Wuthering Heights*, but instead, I'm looking over my messages from August. You looked so pretty today.

Ah, the flutters.

He always knows what to say to make me feel better. Today was a bad-hair day, so I'd worn a ponytail, and I'd had a zit coming out over my eyebrow. I'd held the camera far away and dimmed the lights in my room.

I type in: Are you blind?

But August isn't blind. He may strut about school like he's hot stuff, but he has this whole other side, a side he only shows me. He's sweet. Sensitive. Kind. Perceptive.

He sees everything.

Except that he's way too good for Jana.

Jana, who spent most of freshman year twirling her white-blond hair around her pencil and giving pissed-off looks to anyone who came into her orbit without first bowing down in adoration. Jana, who made us yearbook geeks change the super-lative "Most Likely to Succeed" to "Most Successful" because she *already* has 1.2 million social media disciples following her makeup tutorials and has cosmetics sponsorships that would make the Kardashians take notice. Jana, who always looks like she's practicing her Instagram angles, even while standing in front of her locker, trying to fish out her algebra textbook.

Jana. *Groan.*

Not that I'm better than her. Far from it.

But August and I have so many favorites in common. Like caramel M&Ms. The Beatles. Going barefoot. Happy Meals. Tie-dye everything.

His response makes my whole body warm, from my hair to my toenails. You blow Jana away.

So what if it isn't remotely true? It's *his* truth.

"Hey."

I blink. The sun setting on the Creamsicle horizon disappears, as do the white wicker balcony chair at my Pensacola house and the computer in my lap. I'm left with darkness. Dust.

"*Hey.*"

Something nudges my foot. Hard.

My eyes snap open. Elijah's standing in front of the door, a dull gray light filtering in behind him. The day is ending or beginning, or a storm is coming in.

I've somehow pushed myself so hard against a wall that it feels like my spine might crack. When I start to relax, I remember.

I open my mouth to scream, but my throat is bone dry and useless. Instead, I manage to point. "There's a dead girl over there. In that corner."

One of his thick black eyebrows arches. He follows my finger, then steps in with a lantern, crouching when the ceiling gets too low. He kicks with his foot. "Just some old rags."

Is he insane? I squint, trying to see what I'd felt. The stringy hair, matted together, that I'd ripped through my fingers. The bones. The stickiness. I press forward on my knees, not wanting and yet wanting to prove him wrong. But he's right. It's a bunch of old, yellow-green flowered, dirty rags.

I sniff. Even the smell is gone. "But that…that's not…"

Elijah looks as confused as I feel.

Sucking in a breath, I close my eyes. Maybe if I wish hard enough, I'll be back on that balcony, overlooking the gulf. My belly full, smile on my face, typing messages and procrastinating work on *Wuthering Heights*, flirting with a boy.

Nothing makes sense.

He slides a tray over to me. More cherry tomatoes.

Well. That's something. It's the first time he's done anything for me that I didn't have to beg for.

He peers at me. Shadows obscure the wayward whiskers on his chin, his tattoos. He looks less intimidating. Smaller. Almost boyish. Handsome. No, I've been here too long.

"You gonna shut up now? If you do, I'll let you out."

I blink at him, confused. "What is this place here for?"

His eyes go up to the ceiling. "For when we were bad."

"Granny…?"

He nods, then leans against the wall, sliding down it. He sets the lantern by the rags and…yes, they really are just rags.

Whoever Granny was, however she came to have us, it's clear there's history here. "Who was she? How did you get here?"

He shakes his head, then points to the tomatoes with his dirty toe. "You waitin' for an invitation? Eat."

I do. Even faster than the last time. I'm so hungry I hardly take breaths between shoveling the fruit in my mouth. They barely burst on my tongue before sliding down my throat. When I'm done, I lick my fingers and realize he's watching me. Half like he hates me, half like he wants to...I don't know. Figure me out?

Since when has a boy ever wanted to do *that*? Well, August is the only one. Still, I have zero experience in this matter. It's not like I'm very good at reading guys.

Especially this one. He's a murderer. He killed that man, out in the field, without hesitation. Then he turned his aim toward me. I think he's killed before. Maybe more than once. I have to wonder if he would've killed me too.

"What did you do with that...that man? The one you killed."

He draws his long legs up to his torso and crosses his arms over his knees. "Don't give me that. That's not what I did."

"I saw you."

His eyes burn. "You don't get it. Whatever your dad shot into his trial subjects was contaminated. It made people go crazy. Made them strong. They bite people. The contamination spread. Nobody could contain it. The world went under martial law, fighting against it. And they're losing. Or they lost. Everything's gone. Everything was lost."

Everything's gone. "That man didn't look crazy."

He squeezes his eyes closed. "He will be."

"What? How do you—"

"I *know.*"

Well, what a wise Nostradamus he is. If I am to believe him... I swallow, thinking of my parents. August. Everyone I left behind. I didn't have many friends in school, but that doesn't mean I want them to suffer. "I need to get home."

He lets out the closest thing to a laugh I've heard in ages. "You'll never make it to Pensacola."

I blink. "How did you know I was from Pensacola?"

He doesn't answer.

I draw my chapped lip between my teeth, gnawing on it until I taste blood. "That man didn't come back."

"He will."

"What?"

He shakes his head. "Forget it. That's the thing. They don't look like monsters. Till they get close to you and they snap. They talk all crazy. See things that ain't there."

They see things that ain't there.

I let out a shaky breath. "How do they get like that? From being bitten?"

"Or scratched. Or somethin'. It don't happen right away. Takes a while to mess with a person's brain. Two weeks, two months... It's different with everyone. That's why Granny tied you down. Tied me down too. She was trying to see if you were infected. When your hearing starts to get supersensitive, that's when you know you're in deep shit."

"Hearing? But you—"

"I've been like this for six months. I didn't get the full course of your dad's medication, though. I don't think I got enough of it in me. I don't think you did either."

"I *told* you, I didn't get shot. So does that mean I'm going to be like Granny?"

He presses his lips together. "Different for everyone. Don't think it's gonna happen like that to you. At least not now."

Like that. But something happens.

Of course, Willow. It's clear something *is happening to you. Something's wrong. Maybe your brain is turning to mush already.*

But why?

Did he shoot you?

No.

I straighten. "I can't stay here. I need to get to my family. My parents. We were probably trying to run from this. And somehow—"

"Your parents are already dead."

I freeze. "What?" When he doesn't answer, I press on. "Did you see them? How do you—"

"Trust me," he adds.

It's a guess. He's not being straight. There's something he's not telling me. I don't trust him.

Not. At. All.

I sit there, silently running these words through my head. *They see things that ain't there.* And *It don't happen right away.*

My eyes trail to the rags.

Is my brain turning? Am I going to become a monster?

One thing I know for sure: if I start losing my mind, I'm not telling him.

I know what he does to monsters.

FOURTEEN

A: Hey

W: Hey.

A: Missed you the past few weeks. Sorry. Was sick.

W: Not with the virus, I hope.

A: No. Thank God.

W: Things have been a little weird.

A: Why? Are YOU sick?

W: No...it's worse than that. With all those people dying, and...

A: You want to talk about it?

W: You know my dad works for Latrobe, right?

A: Yeah. You said. Did he get fired?

W: No...but I think he's losing his mind.

A: What do you mean?

W: I'm a little scared of him.

"Come on," he says after a few moments, after I've finished all the tomatoes in the bowl and my stomach is rumbling for more. "If you'll be quiet."

"Where are we going?"

"To get rid of him."

"I thought you said he'll come back."

"He will. But I still got to bury him."

I blink. "Is that what you do?"

He stops with his hand on the door. "What did you think I did?"

"I thought…" I don't know what I thought. "What is in that room? The one across from mine?"

He averts his eyes. "You thought I put bodies in there? Why would I—"

"I don't know."

He starts to push open the crawl space half door. "Quiet now."

I do as he says. I follow him out the little door. I can finally stand up straight. He's already down the hall at the front door. He holds it open for me.

I tiptoe to reach him, trying to make as little noise on the creaking floorboards as possible. But it's not easy. He's so good at creeping around, almost as if he's had all his life to figure out which boards make the noise.

At the door, he grabs a shovel that had been leaning against the wall.

I guess we're going to be digging a grave.

The humidity, combined with the sun, is enough to steal my breath. I'm not sure how good of a digger I'm going to be, considering I'm so weak, my head's swimming.

Plus, it's a grave. Never did I think I'd have to dig a grave.

He goes to the edge of the grass, and that's when I see them. Heaps of dirt, six large, two small.

Eight bodies.

There are eight dead people buried outside this house.

This place is a graveyard.

"Who are—"

I stop when he presses a finger to his lips. Right. Another question I'll have to let simmer in my brain until I go mad.

If I'm not already there yet.

I follow Elijah through the tall grass. He doesn't stop to look back at me. As we walk, the earth gets spongier and wetter until it makes a squishing noise under my bare feet, mud oozing between my toes. Then I'm in brown, stagnant water up to my ankles. The long saw grass slaps against my thighs, my elbows, and insects buzz around the sweat on my skin. I can't tell if that thick stench is me or the swampland.

My feet turn leaden when I see the man.

He's lying on his stomach, half-submerged in the swamp, so I can't see his face. Thank goodness, I can't see his face. But he's large and shaped like a doughboy, wearing a chambray shirt and jeans rolled up at the cuffs, and old white Reeboks covered in mud. He has snow-white hair but is bald on top, the crown of his head horribly sunburned and dotted with yellow blisters and liver spots.

He looks like someone's grandfather.

Except, of course, for the arrow, sticking out from between his shoulder blades. The other one is lodged in his lower back.

Something tickles in the back of my mind. It's like he saw Elijah aiming at him and tried to run away. How many blood-thirsty zombies do that?

It's not much blood, just a small circle, more black than red. A cloud of flies swarms above him.

News flash: He hasn't come back.

Elijah waves the shovel in front of him to shoo the insects and stands at the dead man's head. He motions to his feet.

Oh God. He wants me to help lift him.

I take in a deep breath. I can do this. I can lift a dead body. This is the second dead body I've seen, after Granny. I won't have to touch him. Not his skin, just his sneakers, maybe the ankles of his jeans.

I have to wonder when dead bodies will stop being terrifying. Like a fly carcass on a windowsill, easily flicked away.

It's not now, that's for sure.

Splashing a little in the warm water, I shuffle into position. When Elijah crouches at the head, I crouch too, mimicking his moves. He wraps his hands under the man's beefy shoulders, hooking them under his armpits.

He's buried those other bodies. To him, this is nothing but a dead fly that needs to be flicked.

I reach down into the water, which feels oddly oily, and grab ahold of the man's cuffs, readying myself to lift.

The man lets out a guttural noise, something awful from

deep within his throat. Before I know it, his arms are flailing, grasping. His stubby, dirt-encrusted fingers take ahold of the first thing they can find.

Elijah's neck.

His legs animate, thrashing and splashing. I stupidly lose my grip. Legs now free, the old man scrabbles forward and launches himself atop Elijah, scratching at him. No more *help me*. This man is a rabid animal.

A monster.

I half expect him to growl, but when he opens his mouth, he speaks actual words, unlike any Hollywood zombie I'd ever seen. "You..." he seethes as a wet, white booklet falls from the front pocket of his shirt, landing with a plop in the water between them. "You..."

For the first time, Elijah's making noise. It might be words, but I can't make them out because they're strangled. He's kicking, fighting back but not getting anywhere as the man pounds him into the water.

This monster is trying to drown him.

For a moment, I can do nothing but watch in horror.

Then I remember the shovel.

Grabbing it by the handle, I hold it like a baseball bat, and the funniest thing comes to mind. *Just keep your eye on the ball.* My dad said that when he coached me in softball every damn spring for six years, even though I was the worst player on the team.

I draw the shovel back.

And I swing.

The flat end of the shovel makes such perfect contact with the back of the man's head that a certain excitement surges through my veins. It's the same rare feeling I used to get when I knew I'd gotten off a good hit.

Home run.

Except the difference? The man's head gives way under the force of the shovel, sending bits of blood and scalp flying through the air.

He falls forward onto Elijah.

I hold the shovel at the ready, breathing hard, ready to get in another hit.

When the monster's body judders a little, I think I might need to.

Instead, Elijah sits up, pushing the motionless creature off his lap and into the water as he gasps for air.

I stare at the body lying facedown in the water, the back of its skull smashed in.

I killed a man.

Or maybe he was already dead? Maybe he wasn't a man but a zombie?

Elijah was right. *He came back.*

My fingers tremble around the shovel's splintery handle. All my strength leaves my body, and I drop it to the ground like a lead weight. When I do, I see what fell out of the man's pocket, half-submerged in the water. They're brochures. I see a cross and the words, You can find God's love again!

I think the zombie was a Jehovah's Witness.

Elijah's wet hair hangs over his eyes. He sweeps it back and stands up, grimy water dripping down his chin strap, making his T-shirt cling to his slim, lanky frame. Then he reaches over, grabs the shovel, and stalks toward the house.

He murmurs something under his breath as he sweeps past me. Not a thank you. It's something like, *Just leave him there and let the animals eat him.*

All right. That's fine.

Because I'm not touching that body again.

FIFTEEN

W: Everything's awful.

A: Except you. You're beautiful.

W: I'm serious

A: What's going on?

W: Don't tell me you missed 7ft tall Bubba the Bodyguard standing in my front yard.

A: What's that all about?

W: My dad's gotten death threats. People are crazy.

A: Seriously?

W: I don't know. You saw the news. All those fights. The Ventex shortages. People are dying. And the scientists are the scapegoats, I guess.

A: How long do you have that bodyguard?

W: Just for a few days.

A: Is your father acting any better?

W: No. Worse. I can't say much but...I have no idea what he's going to do.

Night falls fast, and in moments, the sun is beyond the horizon, and strange shadows creep across the walls like uninvited guests.

I sit on the bed in "my" room while Elijah works outside. A while ago, I heard him digging outside. I guess he finally decided he had to bury that body rather than leave it to stink in the marsh. Now, he's trying to fix the generator, which powers the window AC in the living room as well as all the electricity. I saw the thing outside. It's a big, gray hulking mass in the weeds next to the small house. It looks a hundred years old. No wonder it's broken.

When the light is just about gone, a thin line of pink against the trees in the distance, he comes in. He comes in because the light is gone, not because his work is done. The walls aren't humming. The generator's still broken.

"Why can't you fix it?" I whisper.

He puts a finger to his lips, then mouths, *It's old. Missing parts.*

There have never been lights in this house since I've been here. When the sun goes down, the light is gone. I suppose because unnatural light draws the monsters, but I don't know that for sure. Even so, a fat full moon floods abundant light into the room, spilling over the bed, so I get the feeling he can see me just fine.

Then he disappears for a moment, and when he returns, he has more tomatoes.

God, I'd kill for a Pop-Tart. A s'mores one. Heck, even one of the berry kinds. I am going to get sick of tomatoes. I think, when this is over, I will simply look at one and want to cry. I can already taste the tang and the texture of those gooey green seeds, and it makes me gag a little, like the paste once had.

Mmm, paste.

Oh God. I've fallen so far. I shake my head.

He gives me a confused look.

I grab the pen and pad from the drawer and write: I NEED TO PEE AND I'M THIRSTY!

Then I shove it into the moonlight.

He reads it, something like horror growing on his face, and then he shakes his head, like, *Sorry, that ain't gonna happen.*

One of them is going to happen, whether he wants it to or not.

I give him a look like, *Well?* Really, does he want me to pee on the mattress? Granny at least had that bedpan for me. I don't know where it went, but it doesn't matter. I sure as hell am not using a bedpan now. Granny's death feels like a lifetime ago, and all the time before? I must've been drugged because I can barely remember it.

Finally, he pushes off the bed and motions me to follow.

I do. In the darkness, with the crickets and insects outside making so much noise, the creak of the floorboards barely sounds like anything. He stops at the door and points through the dirty screen.

At first, all I see is a massive, leggy mosquito, about the size of my hand, bumping up against the other side of the screen.

Then my eyes focus on a small white structure, about a stone's throw away from the front door, near a garage with a caved-in roof and the rusting carcass of an old-time lawn mower. I didn't notice it before, because it's drowning in weeds and looks abandoned, like the rest of the junk on the lawn.

A freaking outhouse?

I take a step back. I'm about to ask him about the bathroom, but then I remember the dead rat in the sink. "Don't you have running water?" I whisper.

In the darkness, I can't see his face, but I already know the answer.

An outhouse.

That bedpan is sounding better and better.

The more I stare across the expanse of yard to the small outbuilding, the farther away it seems. It's on the edge of the clearing, beyond the graves.

I'm not sure what will be worse—the walk through the tall grass to get there or what I'll find beyond that peeled-paint door.

I wonder, for a split second, if I can hold it until morning.

My bladder isn't wondering at all. It knows that's a fool's hope.

I make a promise to my heart, which is beating much too fast, that from now on, if I survive this journey, I will only pee during daylight hours.

But I'm being silly. It's been a long time since I've been afraid of the dark. I learned long ago that what's there in the day is the same as what's there in the night. No difference.

I push open the door. Elijah holds it for me so it doesn't

slam. Humidity hugs me like a coat, drawing the sweat out of my body, making my skin cold. I slip down the steps, and I run and run and run. A fly buzzes up my nose. I snort it out and keep exhaling. Then I'm dizzy and out of breath, the outhouse no closer than it was before. It's like one of those dreams where the more you run, the farther away a door gets.

But I eventually get there. I wrap my hand around the metal latch and take a deep breath before I pull, imagining a monster, ready to jump out at me.

Of course, that doesn't happen. But the smell hits me like an even worse force. It's sweet yet putrid. Refusing to inhale again, I go in, spotting the dreaded hole. The hole of darkness and death. Who knows what's down there? I should look, but I can't. Not like I could see anything down there anyway.

My bare feet catch about a thousand splinters on the rotting wood platform floor. As I lower the boxer shorts and my panties and move into squatting position, I imagine a creature reaching up to grab me, pulling me down to the most horrible death I could imagine.

Nothing comes. No pee. My bladder's scared.

Don't! Hurry! Don't! Hurry! I scold myself, trying to think of waterfalls and oceans to make this easier.

Eventually, it comes, and when it does, it's a veritable torrent. I hear it splashing not so far below. Relieved, I accidentally take a breath and nearly gag.

Then the wind shakes the walls, whistling through the slats in the rotting wood, and I hear it.

A moan.

A low, long, otherworldly sound, like someone in pain.

Not outside, though.

Below me, echoing in the unknown.

Gripping my shorts, still in mid pee, I pitch forward, toward the door, letting out a scream. I don't know if I open the door or pull up my pants first, but my legs are wet with pee and I don't even care. I run and run and I don't stop until I run headfirst into the wall of Elijah's body.

He skirts backward, his hands up in a *get away* posture, like I'm one of the infected. Like I'm a monster too.

He knows. He can probably smell the pee and feel my wet skin and he must think I'm disgusting.

But I'm not one of them. Not yet at least.

And I can't help it. I keep coming at him. Because I can't do this. Not anymore. Eventually, he drops his hands and lets me in.

Heaving great big sobs into his T-shirt, I can't stop shaking.

And Elijah does the first human thing he's ever done.

He wraps his arms around me and holds me.

SIXTEEN

A: What's up?

W: I think my father wants to leave.

A: And go where?

W: I don't know. I heard him whispering. Making plans.
Somewhere south of here.

A: Why?

W: He says that it'll be better for us. That the world is
going to end, and he wants to save us.

W: August. I'm scared.

A: I have an idea. What if I met you down there?

It comes to me in that split second, as I'm pressing my face into
the damp cotton of Elijah's T-shirt. The lines of his firm, lean,
not-quite-boy-but-not-yet-man frame mold to my body. His
heart beats against my forehead, and the muscles of his biceps
thrum around me.

August.

I can't even count how many times I dreamed of being close to August. Of being held like that, so all my worries and cares drained away.

When he'd said he'd meet me, take me away from all this, I was on cloud nine.

Now I remember. He was going to meet me there.

And then…

Then…

Nothing. I can't remember. Was he there with me? Did he hold me? I can't remember.

Elijah doesn't hold me for long.

A moment later, he pushes me away, like I'm one of the infected, and the memory disintegrates in my head.

Anyway, he can probably smell me. He smells too, pungent but not terrible. Kind of like the outdoors, like earth and rain and fresh air, but a little like old sweat and unwashed body.

He motions for me to follow him across the rickety front porch to the side of the house. He points to a giant barrel, half buried in weeds. There is a downspout from the gutters at the top of the house dripping into it. He lifts off the cover, which looks like it's been half-eaten by termites, and shows me the water. It looks black from here, and the surface isn't smooth, like there are things floating in it. "If you need water," he says softly, grabbing a glass that's sitting nearby and filling it with a ladle that's hooked on the side. "Just get it here."

I guess that's the water I'm going to be drinking. I read once that people can die from dehydration in a matter of days. So I will drink enough to make sure that doesn't happen. I need something to moisten my prickly throat.

Without a word, he turns inside the house again. He sets the glass on the kitchen counter. Even in the moonlight, I can tell it's not clear. It's brown.

I lift it to my nose, inhale, and smell gasoline. Meanwhile, he goes to the sink and twists the handles, showing me that the plumbing isn't working, like I didn't already know that.

The generator? I mouth as I stare into the glass, and he nods. He shrugs and the hair falls in his eyes, like he's shielding his shame from me.

Shame because he doesn't know how to fix it or shame because we shared that weird, almost-tender moment outside?

He must be thankful for the darkness…and I am too. I don't think I want to know what else is in that water. I bring my lips to the rim and suck it down.

I'm almost done with it by the time I notice its chalky texture, its bitter taste. The tepid, funny-tasting water Granny fed me was like heaven compared to this. And there are chunks in it.

I don't want to know what those are. When I finish swallowing, my tongue swells and burns. It tastes like what I imagine gasoline tastes like.

I once knew a kid from school, Bobby Barnes, who lived in a house next to a gas station. He was in sixth grade when doctors discovered his body was riddled with thousands of little tumors.

Especially his brain. His parents sued the gas station, because their underground tanks had leaked into their well, but he died before his twelfth birthday. The tumors practically ate him up from the inside.

I can almost feel the tumors inside me, worming their way through my already diseased brain. The thirst and bitter taste are still there, taunting me.

I set the glass down and look around. *What now?*

It is probably only nine in the evening, if that. At home, I'd be winding down in my bedroom, preparing for another long chat with August. He and I got into the longest and weirdest conversations, about everything from the best Beatles song to the flavor of M&Ms we'd like to have if stuck on a desert island. I didn't go to bed until well after midnight most nights. Sometimes, I wouldn't go to bed at all. I'd get lost chatting and suddenly look up and the sun would be spilling through the blinds.

I think I loved him.

Well, the closest to love I've ever gotten.

Funny, because I never even touched him. I don't think.

Love in the time of screw.

Now I want to go to bed. Close my eyes and wake up from this nightmare.

Elijah looks around too. I can tell he's not used to having company from the way he fidgets his bare feet. Usually, he moves like a ninja, but in his nervousness, he makes the floorboards creak.

I point to the bedroom and shrug. I guess I'll lie in there. Lie down and think of happier times. Which really is any time before I landed my ass here.

Before I can get away, though, he reaches out and grabs my wrist.

I look up at him, confused. I mouth, *What?*

He has something to tell me. I can almost see it, dancing at the tip of his tongue. But then he closes his mouth, shakes his head, and lets me go.

I go to the bedroom. Close the door and climb into the bed. I roll onto my side, thinking about what my boyfriend would do.

Wherever my parents took me, did August try to meet me? Did I meet him? Or did something happen with the monsters before that, like Elijah said? Are my parents dead?

I can't believe that. I *won't* believe that until I see it with my own eyes.

August. I can't stay here. Right?

Right, Low. You've got to go. Even if the world is ending out there.

I take deep breaths and then flop over on my back. It's still unbearably hot, even at night since the windows are all closed. Flies buzz around my ears. I rub under my nose and feel something hard come out on my fingers. It's the fly I inhaled on the way to the outhouse, a dead black ball, drowned in my snot. The mice scurry around the baseboard.

I'm back to where I was before, when Granny was alive.

It's go time.

I have to go. Somehow. I'll gather whatever I have, even if I have to go alone, and head out, tomorrow morning, with the sunlight. I'll head away from the sun. West. Toward home.

And I'll hope I won't see any monsters.

It feels like progress to have made that decision. Even if I'm still lying on this smelly, old, stained mattress.

I close my eyes and try to sleep.

That lasts about two breaths. Two breaths, and I feel something tickling my feet. The cat. The one that always used to climb on the mattress and step on me, sit on my chest and try to steal my breath.

As I'm about to take a third breath, something occurs to me.

That cat...died.

Didn't it?

My eyes fly open. At first, I think I'm bound to the bed, but then I remember I'm free now. I sit up in bed.

No cat. Just my feet.

I suck in another breath and reach for the pillow, ready to hug it and roll over onto my side again. Yes, side sleeping is my most comfy way of sleeping, and now, finally, I can do it. My situation *has* improved, if only slightly. I should take advantage, get a good night's sleep, so I can start out early tomorrow morning.

But as I'm grabbing hold of the pillow, my fingers tangle in hair.

Not my own. Something is resting on the pillow beside me.

Someone.

I know that hair. That scraggly seaweed, falling apart in my hands. With a sinking sensation, I peer over at the thick silhouette of a woman, her face caved in, eyes puckered like they're sewn shut, skin wrinkled like a prune.

Granny.

I don't have the voice to scream. I let out a strangled cry and throw myself off the bed, so ungracefully I land on my hands and knees on the hard wood floor. Scrabbling away, I make it to the door and turn around, hoping that what I saw was just a nightmare.

But she's still there, stretched out across my bed.

In a single, sweeping movement, she sits up and turns to me. Arms stretch out to me.

"Oh God!" I moan, throwing open the door and racing into the hall.

I slam the door behind me, and then I hear it. *Bang, bang, bang*…coming from the door across from me.

I cover my ears and turn to leave. I rush to the front door and stand with my hand on the doorknob, thinking of that thing inside the outhouse. Of all those graves. In my mind, I see hands reaching out from the dirt, the dead, coming after me. Granny's dead, and yet she's in my room.

There is something very wrong here.

Here, in a place where the dead don't stay that way.

Bang, bang, bang goes the door across from my room.

And then I watch as the doorknob to my room…the door I just slammed…slowly starts to turn.

Oh God.

I have nowhere to go.

There is a straight shot down the hallway to the kitchen, then the living room. And then there's that room under the stairs. I can lock myself in there. Be safe. Maybe.

I dash down the hall through to the kitchen as the door to my bedroom flies open. Shrieking in fright, I pick up the pace. I'm making a racket, and I'm sure if Elijah were here, he'd tell me to shush. But I can't.

I'm going to die. Those monsters are going to get me. They are right on my tail.

I reach for that half door, but I can't seem to pry it open. There's no knob, it's flush against the frame, and my fingernails are nothing but stubs so I can't seem to get it up. I fall to the ground, curling up in a ball, as the form of Granny bears down on me.

"Hey."

A male voice. Gentle and soothing. Not Granny.

Still trembling, I look across the living room.

Elijah is sitting on the couch, legs spread, hair all over the place, looking like he might've been napping until I came in.

I peer around the darkness, confused.

No Granny.

Elijah meets my gaze in the darkness. He's looking at me like I'm insane.

And maybe I am.

"What?" he whispers.

I cover my face in my hands and finally bring myself to say what I've been thinking all day. "I think I am turning into one of them."

SEVENTEEN

W: That's crazy. I'd be in so much trouble.

A: Me too. But only if we got caught.

About five minutes later, we're lying in the room under the stairs, face-to-face, on our sides, our heads propped up by our elbows. I'm using that pile of rags I thought was a dead body as a mattress. It doesn't bother me in the slightest now.

I have far greater things to worry about than a dead body that stays dead.

Granny's sure didn't.

He's lit a lantern, which I so desperately need, because I can't stand the darkness. The shadows. I can't stand the thought that any time I turn around, I might see Granny's hands—or something worse—reaching for me.

He doesn't really say anything.

Frankly, after what I told him, I'm surprised he hasn't shot an arrow into my heart, the way he shot that man outside.

Maybe that comes next. Maybe he's biding his time. He certainly seems to regard me very carefully. His eyes haven't left me since I made that surprise appearance in the living room while he was trying to sleep.

A long silence passes before he says, "What did you see?"

I shake my head. "When?" I laugh miserably. "Everywhere I look, I see something terrifying. These rags, I thought they were a dead body. When I was in the outhouse, I could've sworn there was someone in there with me. And lying on my bed…Granny. She woke up. She came after me. And her face was all…dead. Shriveled like a walnut and her eyes were sewn shut."

He grits his teeth but says nothing.

"What keeps banging on that door over there?"

His eyes narrow. "That? Wind, probably. I keep the window open. It's the bathroom. Plumbing's all fouled up."

I let out a laugh. "I thought you kept dead bodies in there, and they were coming back to life."

He stares at me.

"Are people coming back to life?"

He shakes his head a little, his fingernail tracing a ridge in the wood floor.

Then he says, "Guess you're sick."

I nod, glad he's finally agreeing with me. I wait for him to say more, but he doesn't. "You said people come back."

"I know. Not like that, though."

"Like *how*, then?"

He opens his mouth, and I think he might tell me, but he closes it. "Doesn't matter."

I squeeze my eyes closed, trying to understand. "What does it mean? I'm going crazy, right? Is that what happens?"

He considers this for a long time before nodding.

Well, that's that, then.

I want him to say something like, *It'll all be all right.* Isn't that obligatory? When someone gets bad news, you're supposed to say stuff like that. *God only gives you what you can handle. After the rain comes the sunshine.*

Instead, he says, "Too bad. Kind of liked you."

What does that mean? He says it like I'm a favorite shirt that got too small and now he must donate it. And *did* he like me? Could've fooled me. I got the feeling I was more of an intruder he constantly had to shush. A pest he wanted to be rid of.

But I guess being here alone would kind of suck. Even if I am a pain in the ass, at least I'm company.

I take a deep breath. I'm sixteen. I thought I'd graduate, go to college, marry, have a career. I never thought I'd be asking the question that leaves my mouth: "Does that mean I'm going to die?"

He lies there, still running his thumbnail across the ridges in the wood floor. He doesn't look at me. "We all die."

I click my tongue. "I mean soon."

He considers this so long that I think my heart stops and starts about a thousand times in the interim. "Yeah. But by then you'll be so out of it, it won't matter."

Oh God. Way to soften the blow, dude. August, if he were here, would be kind. He knew how to reassure me. He was the king of the joke to lighten the mood, but he knew how to phrase things so that he never hurt anyone's feelings. For this, he would be diplomatic. He'd tell me that it would be all right, that this would blow over, and everything would be okay.

But there's no August.

I'm alone.

"What happened to you?"

His answer is immediate. "What do you mean?"

"Your hearing."

He sucks in a breath. "Cash was tight, so we all signed up for a trial." He lets out a bitter snort. "Us and six other people. Your father's. Turns out it did just what it was supposed to do. It's protection from all disease. Only…the side effects are pretty bad."

Yeah, I'd say thirsting for blood is a negative side effect. But as far as I know, he's not there yet. "And me?"

He shrugs. "Don't know. You say you haven't gotten a shot. I think you're full of crap. Because seeing things is a symptom. It's different for everyone, but it's a definite symptom."

"You see things?"

He nods. "Sometimes."

I swallow. "I *know* I haven't gotten the shot. My father would never do that to me. I don't know why I'm seeing things, but it's not because of that."

"Really? Because I think your dad saw that it was working

on us, protecting us from the screw, then gave you the first course during the Ventex shortages because he wanted to make sure you were protected. But that was before we had symptoms."

"Okay, so I'm getting worse. I'm becoming a monster. Does that mean you're going to kill me?"

He presses his back against the door and winces when it creaks.

The answer I'm looking for doesn't come. I rest my head on my upper arm and watch him. He's not an angry dick like earlier. He doesn't look worried or anxious or anything that I'm feeling. I guess, most of all, he just seems sad.

I can't blame him.

But I guess I trust him. Because as my eyes grow heavy, I don't worry that he's going to take that shovel to my head.

Maybe an hour later (but who can tell), my eyes blink open to the candle in the lantern, nothing more than a black wick drowning in a waxy puddle. Elijah is asleep.

Well, huzzah. He didn't kill me while I slept.

Maybe he does like me.

I scuttle on my hands and knees over to the door, but he's in front of it. I nudge him.

He rolls over and is fully awake almost immediately. Something tells me he doesn't ever sleep soundly. He sits up, rubbing his eye. "What?"

"Is it morning?"

He shrugs, then cracks the door. Brilliant light pours in even with the shades drawn.

"Guess so."

He scoots out, picks up the old blanket, and folds it neatly, draping it over the back of the sofa, which is such an odd thing. The world is going to hell, and he's tidying up.

I slide out behind him as he goes to the mantle, opens a small silver box on it, and pulls out a gun.

I take a step back. I have never been this close to a gun before. Is he going to shoot me now? He was waiting for me to be awake?

He twirls it on his finger like a gunslinger, grasps the barrel, and hands it to me, butt out.

I stare at it.

It's loaded, he mouths.

I shrug, really big, like, *What do you expect me to do with that information?*

He thrusts it toward me and whispers, "You might get better, or you might get worse. Or you might stay the same. I don't know. But I'm sick of killing. If you want to die, do it yourself. But do it in the little room, so it doesn't make noise. I'll clean it up later. Or maybe I won't."

It's like an invitation to dinner. One he doesn't care whether I accept.

My jaw drops. He's not serious. I shake my head and back away. "I can't. I can't kill myself. Are you...crazy?"

No. But I am.

He stares at the gun for a while, shrugs, and puts it back in the silver case, dropping the lid. It taunts me there, so easily accessible, the silver surface shining and winking in the bright sunlight. *I'm here if you need me.*

He's probably opened that case and stared at the gun a million times. Contemplated. Imagined. I have to wonder if that's what that gun is for. For the moment he gets up the courage.

I turn from the box and my gaze lands on the family portrait. In the bright light, I notice something.

The lanky boy in the picture is Elijah. Why did I not notice that before? Oh, he's a few years younger in the picture, maybe thirteen, and well groomed, clean-cut. No tattoos or whiskers or long shocks of hair flying in his face. He looks like the kind of honor roll kid you'd trust to watch your pets while you were on vacation.

Not like the kid who'd hand you a gun and casually invite you to off yourself.

I don't realize I've gotten close to the frame until my nose nearly bumps against it. I point at it. *This is your house?*

He looks away.

I tap him on the shoulder. *I thought Granny kidnapped you?* I mouth. *She was really your grandmother?*

He nods.

Wow. Didn't see that one coming. He'd picked her up and tossed her away like a sack of potatoes. Like she didn't matter. Had sadness even touched his face after he saw her lying on the floor?

No. Not at all.

Which means either he's a monster too…or…he's been through a lot of death.

Of course he has. That's why there are all those graves outside. That's why he killed that man without a second thought.

Or maybe he thinks Granny is like that other guy. *She'll be back.*

And in a way, she was. In my head. She was lying right freaking next to me.

That guy hasn't tried to come back again; he's still lying in the yard, liquifying into the marsh. Fortunately, he's half-covered by saw grass. The abundant swarm of flies and the stench when the wind shifts are good indications that he's gone for good.

I peer at the picture. The mother is a bit overweight, wearing glasses, an unfortunate perm, but she has his eyes. And the father has about everything else of his. She looks like a coupon clipper. He looks like a guy who works with his hands, who has grease under his fingernails and watches NASCAR. They're the average, everyday middle-class family…

But it's the little girl who gets to me. Probably about six or seven, she has two pigtails, and even though they're sprouting out of the top of her head, they nearly reach her waist. She has so much hair and hardly any body. She's stick-skinny, with glasses that magnify her eyes, freckles, and a gap where her two front teeth should be. Strawberry Shortcake T-shirt. Scabby knees.

All at once, it hits me.

His family is not here.

And there are plenty of graves outside.

He's in shock.

And his family...

They are all out there in the yard. He buried them. Maybe one by one. Maybe he *is* a bit mad, though not mad enough to see living Grannies.

Or maybe he has. Maybe he's just better at hiding it.

My breath hitches in my throat before I can think of something to say. When I do, I turn. He's not there.

He comes inside a few moments later, with a bowl of tomatoes and a bucket of water. He must've slipped away while I was hypnotized by his family photo.

He doesn't meet my eyes as he sets out the tomatoes. He takes one and pops it in his mouth, then pours two glasses of very murky, almost brown-green water.

Delicious. I take a tomato, wondering whether humans can subsist on tomato alone. Who thought planting a garden with only tomatoes was a good idea? Can't we have, maybe, a cucumber to shake things up?

Then I pop a tomato in my mouth. I gag a little.

Doesn't matter. I'm getting out of here.

Today.

Elijah eats a few tomatoes but leaves the bulk for me, then stalks outside, maybe to work on the generator. As I finish the bowl, I peer in the refrigerator. It's dark and warm in there, and while there is food, it's all jars and condiments. Pickles, relish, ketchup. A buffet of absolutely zero nutritional value.

I close it and look in the freezer. Empty and wet, with a moldy smell that turns the tomatoes in my stomach.

I start opening cabinet doors, finding the same boring stuff a person finds in every kitchen. Plates. Glasses. The drawers have some silverware and odds and ends—pens, buttons, quarters, a few AA batteries and spare parts, hexagonal items that look like they belong on a piece of lawn equipment.

As I'm about to give up, I open a cabinet and find dozens of amber bottles. I lift one but the label's peeled off.

I shake it. One pill. I push down on the childproof cap and pry the lid open. A single Ventex greets me.

All at once, I find myself heaving. I throw myself over the sink and vomit a little, right on the dead rat, which is a little mushier than before. The maggots are gone; they must've matured and flown away. So nice that even when the human race dies, the insects of the world will continue to thrive.

I spend five minutes gagging over the sink, thinking about those pills.

We don't have enough to last even another day.

EIGHTEEN

A: Just think about it.

W: Are you kidding me? It's ALL I've been thinking about.

A: When do you think you're going?

W: I don't know. He's being very secretive.

A: Then I'll be ready.

I go outside, stomping as I do. Screw the noise.

Elijah is at the side of the house, working as quietly as a person can with a wrench. Every so often, there's a *clunk*, but it's dull. My stomping on the porch's wood planks is loud. He hears me before I round the corner and greets me with a scowl.

Before he can tell me to hush, I hold up the medicine bottle.

I don't think Elijah does emotions anymore. I should probably stop expecting him to. He has no reaction. He goes back to the knobs on the rusty old generator.

I shove it in his face again. "There's only one left," I whisper hoarsely.

He shrugs.

I grab ahold of his bony shoulder, meaning to make him look at me, but the second I do, he throws up his hands and shoves me away.

"So?" he mutters, still not looking at me.

"How can you say that when—"

"We're safe."

"I don't understand."

He glares at me. "Because you were shot."

"For the last time, I was not—"

"That's what you think. But you had to have been. When you said you were seeing things, I knew. You don't need the pills. I was shot too. We won't get sick."

I stare at him, thinking of that room beside mine with the leather straps. Thinking how it looked like a boy's room. It was his room. He'd liked school and the planets and playing the drums. He'd been normal. And now…

"How do you—"

"Because we ran out of Ventex weeks ago."

I stare at him, uncomprehending. Then I hold up the bottle. "But—"

He grabs the bottle. Opens it and plucks out the pill, then holds it up so I can see it. "See that? That's not Ventex. That's regular ol' acetaminophen. You were too out of it to notice."

He's right. Now it seems silly that I couldn't tell the difference. "But I was so loopy. Ventex makes you—"

"You were loopy because of the accident."

"Accident?"

"Yeah. When I found you, you kept babbling about some accident."

"You found me...where?"

"You stumbled up to our front door. I found you there, half-dead." He's looking away from me, up at the sky again. "We brought you in, started giving you what we had in Ventex. Until we ran out."

I shake my head. This doesn't make any sense. "Didn't she need it? Why'd she waste it on me if she needed it?"

He looks away, refusing to answer. But I don't need him to answer. He said it before. The martyr.

I could understand Granny doing that for Elijah, her own grandson. Wanting him to survive, she'd give him the last of the pills. But me? Why would she care about me?

Either she'd refused them, like he said, or...he's lying. *He's insane.*

"So this shot my father developed...it works."

He laughs. "I told you. It stops you from getting screwed, yeah, and any other disease for that matter, as far as I can tell. That's the only good thing it does."

"Why didn't your parents get the shot too?"

He shrugs. "They did. And Suzy."

I swallow. "Who is Suzy?"

He doesn't answer. Doesn't have to.

"Did she snap?"

He draws in his lower lip, lets out a breath, his long, dark hair a veil between us. "Yeah. She's smaller. The drug affected her different. Worse. By the end, she was one of them. That's how I knew—"

"What did she do?"

"At one point, all she ever wanted was to play on that ol' swing set of hers. Death trap, we told her. She didn't care. She'd swing on that thing for hours." He motions to the rotting carcass of an old metal swing set with the metal slide, U-bar, and plastic swing. Except the swing's gone, and the thing is practically consumed by grass.

He seems reluctant to say more, so I gently prod him along. "What happened?"

"She pulled the swing down and tried to strangle Granny with the chains."

My mouth opens. I cover it with my hand to keep in the gasp.

"She killed my parents. With that gun."

I think of that girl. That little scabby-kneed girl. "How? She didn't take—"

"She did. Like I said, we were the first test subjects. Me and Suzy and my parents. Few other people. You too a little while later, I guess, even if you didn't know it."

"I never heard anything about trials."

"It was weird. Now that I look back, there were a lot of red flags, but a lot of trials were being done, and my parents needed the money and saw the Latrobe name, and they trusted it. Turned out, Latrobe—the FDA—knew nothing about it. I think when they found out, they fired your father, and there was an investigation." He fixes me with a stare that makes me wither. "But by then, the damage was done."

My world tilts slowly. I think about something I overheard my father saying to my mother at the kitchen table, back when he found out that his funding was being cut off. *I can prove it to them. I will prove it. Even if they won't give me a chance. They'll see.*

My mom had been livid. *You can't just play with people's lives like that, Vince.*

He'd pounded the table. *I'm SAVING lives!*

I blink away the memory. "I'm telling you. You're insane. My father never used me as a lab rat, giving me shots—"

"How do you know? Didn't have to be a shot. Could've been mashed it up in your food."

"My dad would never—"

"He would if he thought it'd help. And things were getting desperate."

Well, sure. My dad was all about helping people. Me especially. But this?

I shake my head. He can't be saying what I think he's saying. Yet my mind hitches on pancakes.

Those delicious pancakes.

Eat it all up, Willow. Every last bite. We want you to grow up big and strong.

Oh God.

You'll be okay, Willow. You'll make it out of this just fine.

"How did the truth get out, then?" I ask.

Elijah shakes his head. Either he doesn't know or doesn't want to tell me. Instead, he gets up, drops the wrench, and stalks toward the graves. He points at the first one. "My momma." He points to the next. "My dad." The third is smaller. "Suzy." The next few—and there are four more of them beside the one he just buried—he shrugs. "No idea who they are. Wandered on the property."

It's funny. The first one, the one belonging to his mother, is neat. There is an ornately carved cross at the head. The next one has two sticks tied together. The third has nothing at all. "You were very religious."

"They were. Me? No."

That explains why the cross was broken, along with the rosary, in the bedside drawer. Why I've never seen him praying. He's given up his faith. Guess I can't blame him. People have had their faith shaken for far less.

"You said they're coming back."

"Not them. It's too late for them." He scrubs a hand down his face. "Granny will. She was after."

I don't understand what that means. I stare at the others, a second small one. Another child maybe. "Who is that?"

He shrugs again. "Either that one or that one's granny. Don't know anymore. They'll come back. They died after, I think. Does it matter?"

I shake my head.

It doesn't matter.

But it means one thing.

Whatever is in our veins has made us immune to the screw. There is absolutely no reason for us to stay.

"We need to go. To get out of here."

He shoves his hands into the pockets of his baggy jeans and makes no reply.

I try again. "I'm going. You can come with me."

He swings his head toward me. "What for?"

"We can find someplace safe. Like the CDC. In Atlanta?"

"There's nothing for you out there."

"How do you—"

He points toward the corner of the house, the driveway, raising his voice as loud as he dares, which is still only a whisper. "I listened to the radio. Again and again. It was spreading. It was everywhere. Even the CDC was overrun. It's over. Everyone is dead. Don't you see? This is the safest place. You don't want to live in a world like that."

I stare at him. "I can't believe everyone is dead. That's impossible. How could that happen?"

"Dunno. But it happened."

"But—"

"You think I'm lying? Okay, maybe I'm lying. About some things. But it's for your own good. You want to die to find out the truth? You want to be the one killing people after your own sheer stupidity?"

I shake my head.

Either I can't believe it, or something inside me won't let me. "But there's nothing for us here. Nothing to eat. We're essentially waiting to die. Isn't it better to fight to live?"

I'm really hoping he'll say yes. Because I'm not sure I can make it alone. Oh, maybe I'll make it off the property, to a road with some indication of where I am in the vast state of Florida. But I don't know what comes after that. I've never traveled anywhere without my family, and there was usually a nice hotel to stay at. How far can I get on foot without help? What if I meet a monster?

He shakes his head. "You'll die."

"Likely. But I'll die here too."

He tilts his head back to the sky. It's blue and perfect, and the sun is climbing into it as if nothing is wrong. Funny how the weather can be so glorious when everything is falling apart. Didn't it get the memo?

He squints, then pushes his hair off his forehead and shrugs, like, *Your funeral.*

"Could I...maybe borrow that gun?"

It's so stupid. Borrow. Like I'm going to come back next week and return it. By next week, heck, probably by the end of the day, if I get on the road soon enough, I'm going to be dead.

He nods.

The second I have his permission to head out on my own, it's like I've fallen into a tub of cement. I can't move. Terror grips me. Where will I go? Do I even know west from east? There are other wild things out here that can claim me, even if the monsters don't. I've never camped out before. I prefer being indoors. I'm not one of those people who likes adventures.

Why did I think this was a good idea?

"Um...do you have a backpack I can carry?" I look down at my dirty bare feet. I love being barefoot at home, on the beach, but for this, the unknown, I'll need shoes. "Did your mom have shoes I could use? Clothes?"

He nods.

Okay, so there's really nothing stopping me. I'm doing this.

And yet I'm not sure I can. Not alone anyway.

He can sense it. He studies me like he's daring me to take the first step.

After a few moments, he retreats into the house, probably to pack what I need. I stand there, rooted to the spot, sucking in breaths of humid morning air. My lungs feel heavy. Achy. I can't imagine how much they'll protest when I actually start to exert myself, trekking to God knows where.

Then I walk down the drive, a winding path so choked with vegetation that branches feel like arms, reaching out to hold me back. I've never been to the front of the house before. It's like a new world, even though it's steps away.

What will traveling from here be like?

When I break through the brambles, I look back at the house. The front is melting into the tall brown weeds. The rusted air conditioner hangs from the window's jaws like a cigarette from a rebellious kid's mouth. The front door is solid, black, and unwelcoming, lording over a crumbling concrete front step.

There is a mailbox where the driveway meets the road. Someone painted the name on it in a purely functional, unartistic way—ROWAN.

Elijah Rowan. I mouth the name as I reach over, unthinking, and grasp the latch. The metal scalds my finger, and in the split second before it opens, something pokes out of the opening I've afforded it.

It's a wasp. I slam the thing closed, but it bounces open, unleashing a fist-sized cloud of them. The inside is one massive wasp's nest. No, the Rowans have not accepted mail in that thing in some time.

I stare as the wasps buzz around me, then head off, directionless, into the air. ROWAN. The name is in commanding all capitals, as if the painter meant that there would always be Rowans in this place. It makes me think of a poem I read last year in English class by Percy Shelley. "Ozymandias." *Look on my Works, ye Mighty, and despair!*

I spin in a circle, taking it all in. *Nothing beside remains.*

It occurs to me then that it doesn't matter how much we try to isolate ourselves. The world—good, bad, and everything in between—always trickles in eventually.

I don't care what Elijah says. He is holding on to the last threads of something that is all but gone. The world changes, it grows and contracts and infects, and we have to change with it.

I spin again, trying to determine where to go. Using the sun's position, I find a westerly direction. I step out onto a dirt path—it's sparsely rutted with a couple automobile and bicycle tire marks, but it's not wide enough to call a road—stretching out in both directions before disappearing around a bend.

A bird flies low, dodging in and out of the tree limbs overhead before heading down the path. It's remarkable how unaffected it seems, considering the human race is in shambles. The bird's proof that, contrary to what we believed, the world will go on without us. In fact, it might even be better off.

That makes me hopeful. I decide, when I set out, I will follow the bird. Maybe it's good luck.

I go back inside to gather supplies. I hear floorboards shifting above. It strikes me then that I've never been upstairs. I've seen the stairs, known there was a second floor. I even climbed past a boarded window when I'd gone up to the roof. But I have no idea what is up there. I suppose in the back of my mind, there was some half-baked notion that the space belonged to his parents and had been set aside as a shrine to them, one he wanted to keep to himself. The nursery—the room I was in—was Suzy's, the room with the drum set and textbooks was Elijah's, so it only makes sense.

I go to the stairs, avoiding the portrait of Elijah's family. I imagine it like the picture of Dorian Gray, times four—all eyes, following me across the living room. My eyes catch on the silver box on the mantle. The lid gapes open like a mouth. *Here if you need me.*

When I reach the foot of the stairs, I peer up the narrow staircase. It goes straight up, ten or twelve dusty cherrywood steps with worn treads nailed into the surface, ending at a dark-paneled wood door. Grabbing the railing, I take the first step.

As I do, the door opens a crack, and Elijah appears, arms full of clothing. He squeezes through, like there's something in that room he doesn't want me to see, and closes it behind him.

He doesn't meet my eyes as he comes down. I continue to stare at the door. "What's up there?" I whisper.

He brushes past me and places clothing on the sofa. A shirt dress with a strawberry pattern on it. A ribbed tank top. Shorts that two of me could probably fit into. In better times, I'd have laughed, because it's like a fashion show without style. Like those cooking shows that challenge a chef to make something edible using only stinky tofu, sea cucumber, and truffle oil. The way he's laying everything out so carefully makes me think that he's imagining his mom wearing these things.

I'm still standing at the foot of the stairs. "Elijah," I whisper. "What's up there?"

His silence confirms it. It's his parents' room. Maybe the place where his parents died. *Where Suzy killed them.* I gather he doesn't go up there much.

When he finishes arranging the clothes on the old sofa, he hands me an empty backpack. "Get changed." He goes to the door of his own room and turns, hesitating there, dark eyes slowing scanning the place, like he's committing it to memory. Maybe because it's the last time he'll see me in it.

He reaches for the doorknob and starts to close it, and I think that's it. He doesn't want to see me leave. He knows it's certain death, and he wants absolutely no part of it.

But before the door clicks, he whispers, "I'm coming with you."

NINETEEN

W: Another kid died today. From my English class. Did
you know Joe Nolan?

A: Yeah. Not well. But I heard.

W: The Ventex shortages are unreal. I'm so nervous. My
parents say we have enough, but...

A: I have enough too. To last for years. And by then,
there will be a cure. We'll be okay.

W: You promise me you'll be there?

A: Absolutely.

It's probably after noon by the time we set out on the path,
bags filled with clothes and enough tomatoes for a lifetime. I
wonder if it'll be too much to hope we pass a raspberry bush on
the way to wherever we're going. The heat probably wouldn't
let anything like that survive. The sun is so high in the sky, it
doesn't seem possible for it to get any higher or for the air to be
any stiller or thicker.

Sweat clings to my brow. I could probably grab a handful of air and wring it out.

I'm wearing the strawberry dress. It hangs past my knees and looks *ridiculous*. If I was my old self, I'd sooner be caught naked than wear this thing to school. But it's soft and shapeless and doesn't slide off my hips, not like the boxer shorts I was constantly having to yank up. I'll deal.

I'm thinking they must've belonged to his father. I've been wearing stuff that belongs to dead people. I'm not sure how to feel about that. When my grandmother died, my mother had to clear out her house, and I remember all the clothes in her drawers being tossed unceremoniously in garbage bags for donation. The thought of wearing those things, things that smelled like her Jean Naté, with fibers that had probably captured some of her microscopic skin cells that hadn't been removed in the wash, made me feel sick.

His mother also had a pair of iridescent-strapped, knock-off Birks that feel almost as comfortable as the real thing, though she was a size or two bigger. The black imprint of her foot is on the cork sole. I scuff a lot to keep them from sliding off my feet, but I try not to, because I'm worried it'll make too much noise and not only upset Elijah but alert any zombies that might be nearby.

Maybe that's why Elijah's barefoot. He's used to walking that way, so his soles are probably tough. I love going barefoot at the beach, but the dirt here is covered in tiny, sharp flecks of stone. I have to wonder if Elijah has any shoes at all. Maybe he's always lived like a backwoods redneck.

Elijah has a backpack with the gun slung over one shoulder, his bow with all the arrows he could find—five of them—over the other. He looks like a dystopian warrior. Every time he looks at me, I think he sees his mom. Maybe that's why he walks a few steps ahead, so he can't see me. I keep feeling like a tail he's trying to lose.

When we get down the long dirt drive, he turns left at the mailbox.

I'm already glad I brought him because I would've gone right. I just hope he knows what he's doing.

After a few steps, I peer around his form and notice the dusty road continues as far as I can see, toward trees and sky and reeds. I was hoping for another house, for some sign of civilization.

We walk on a few minutes. When I look over my shoulder, his house has disappeared from view. Funny, he doesn't turn back, not once.

It looks like there is nothing behind us and still nothing in front of us. Just haze in the distance and those sad, crooked-limbed trees all around, hanging with Spanish moss.

I'm lagging. I scuff into the Birks a little to catch up with him. When I do, I whisper, "Are you sure this is the way?"

He doesn't break stride. Doesn't answer me either.

I guess I know the answer. Maybe there isn't a way.

More silence. We round a weedy bend, and it's more of the same, but instead of trees, we're surrounded by swampland.

Not a swamp, of course. I learned that much in social studies class every year of my public school education. The Everglades isn't a swamp; it's a massive river.

But it sure looks like a damn swamp. A hot, smelly, dank, putrid swamp. The only place in the whole wide world where alligators and crocodiles live together, *in peace and harmony*.

Or something like that. It's true, though. This is the only place on planet Earth where you can find them both. I learned that in school too.

I'm going insane. We haven't been walking more than a mile, and I'm already losing it.

He's far away. I break into a jog in my happy little strawberry dress to catch up with him and accidentally leave one of my Birks behind.

Just like Cinderella. Those weren't her shoes, any more than these are my Birks.

Rushing back to get the shoe, I realize I'm focused on these inane things to block out much, much worse thoughts.

Like that I'm never going to find my way home.

Like monsters might come after us.

Like somehow, I was my father's lab rat, and now I'm forever disease free, but my brain is full of wormlike tumors, consuming every last bit of my sanity.

Like…

No. Not thinking of that.

Maybe if Elijah talked to me, I wouldn't be going crazy.

So in my demented head, the head that sees things that aren't there, I say, "Tell me about you."

He looks back at me. Mouths, *What?*

"I just want to know."

He allows me to catch up to him and mouths, *Not a good idea.* He touches his lips.

But there's no one around.

"Please," I whisper. "I'll speak quietly."

He starts walking again. I try to keep up. After at least a minute, he murmurs, "You know everything."

"No, I don't. Like…have you lived your whole life in that house? Where did you go to school? Were those drums yours? Did you play? What did you want to be when you grew up?" Once I open my mouth, I can't seem to shut it.

Chin to his chest, he's not going to answer. I've drowned him in questions, overwhelmed him.

But then he says, "Yes. I was homeschooled. Yes. Yes. And I don't know."

I have to smile at that. He's clearly not someone who likes to share, yet he answered every one of my inquiries. "You don't know?"

He shakes his head. "Why? What do you want to be?"

Do. He says it in the present. *What do you want to be?* As if we still have a choice. I like that. I smile wider and answer without hesitation. "A singer."

He doesn't seem surprised. That was always the reaction. Shy wallflower Willow Lafayette, who barely made a peep at school, wants to be a singer? They didn't know that I used to walk around my house crooning whatever songs were popular on the radio. All. The. Time. It was only when I was in public that I clammed up.

"I was a good drummer," he remarks after a long silence. "I mean, I never played for anyone, but I practiced all the time. To music videos."

"You did? Like what kind of music?"

"Rock. Like Steward Copeland. John Bonham."

I'm so thrilled he's talking that I wish I could add something to the conversation. "I...don't know who they are."

"You don't know The Police? Led Zeppelin?"

Well, sure. I've *heard* of those bands. But they were even before my *parents'* time, I think. "That's cool."

I want to say more, but he'd probably laugh if I told him I once waited six hours with my mom for a ticket to a Taylor Swift concert when I was twelve. My mom is the biggest fan of pop music, and the reason our dog is named JT. She was always dancing around the house with me, making me shake it up—*Come on Willow! Shake it!* I shove aside that memory before it can take root, and another thought pops into my head: How funny that we both wish we could make noise for a living. Especially in a world where it's best to be quiet.

Not that either of us would have anyone to perform for. I really doubt anyone is wondering what happened to small-time YouTube star WillowL.sings.

"You were homeschooled…" I start, not sure how I'll ask the next question that's been bouncing around my brain, almost since I first met him. "Have you ever gone to school?"

He shakes his head.

"You never had…like, um, sports you belonged to? Friends? Social stuff?"

"Nope." He glances at me. "I…my parents were strict… Religious, you know. They made sure I stayed away from all that."

"Oh." If he's embarrassed or bitter, he doesn't show it. It's simply a fact of his life. Maybe now that his parents are dead, he refuses to speak ill of anything they did for him. Or maybe he respects it. He's nothing like August, who thrives on his social circle, his sports, his friends…

There I am. Thinking of August, when I promised I wouldn't.

I concentrate on putting my feet in front of me so I can get back there.

"You said there might be more of us, who took that first trial."

"I know there are."

"Where are the others?"

"Don't have to worry about the others."

"How do you know?"

"I just know."

There's that fortune-cookie Elijah Rowan I can't stand. "How? I mean, aren't they the ones who started this?"

He shakes his head.

"Then who?"

He's slow to answer. "I'll tell you sometime. But I don't think you'll believe me."

"Try me."

He looks over, amusement on his face, and I can tell he's thinking about it. Then he shakes his head. "Someday. I might."

Boys. Such contradictions. It reminds me of August, how he'd act a certain way whenever I'd see him in person and a totally different way online with me.

A few steps later, I stop. There is thick black smoke billowing up over the reeds in the distance. When I bring my hand to my forehead to shield out the sun, my forehead burns. I'm getting sunburned.

In another time, another place, my mother would've swept in and insisted I slather myself with sunscreen. Even though I'm older and that's totally embarrassing to have my mom checking up after me, she'd do it anyway, because…moms. But she's not here, and though I tan beautifully after I get a base, this is too much sun. I'm going to be tomato red by nightfall. I bet there'll be blisters and that shivery-sick feeling where my skin feels like it's on fire, but I can't get warm.

I study the smoke in the distance until I'm sure it's real and not something my mind has conjured.

He notices I've stopped and turns, a vaguely annoyed expression on his face. I point and mouth, "What is that?"

He shrugs. "Something's on fire."

Well, aren't you a regular Sherlock.

He reaches into his pocket and pulls something out. When he opens the cover, I recognize it's a compass. He sucks in a breath. "Probably Fort Lauderdale."

I almost laugh. He's saying the whole city of Fort Lauderdale is burning?

Then I realize that's exactly what it might be. I don't find it funny anymore.

We keep walking. My feet are covered in a fine layer of brown dust. I was dirty before, but I was covered in black dirt. Now I've added a brown layer. I'm like gross tiramisu.

Ha ha.

I don't know if I can take much more of this.

We go around a bend, and there's more of the same. Reedy dark waters as far as the eye can see. I stop for a moment. That burning city looks closer. No buildings in sight. Only smoke. It's so far away. It could be anything.

"We can't go that way," I whisper, pointing. "I have to go home. To Pensacola. The other way. Right?"

He shakes his head. "Too far."

He's saying I can't get home to my family. But it we go down toward Miami, I'll be even farther from Pensacola. Maybe I'll never get home.

I plant my feet. "We have to go that way. We have to try. August would—"

"August?"

"My boyfriend." I realize I've never called him that out loud to another person. Because we were still in that iffy, unnamed phase of our relationship. I backpedal. "Sort of."

"Boyfriend." He says the word like its foreign and in a way that makes me certain he's never had a girlfriend. "What's he like?"

I stare at him. I wouldn't expect him to care.

"Amazing," I gush without really thinking. It's nice to talk about August to someone who doesn't know him, since everyone at home does. "He's blond and so hot. He's tall, and he has this dimple...and these freckles... He plays, like, six sports, and he's the best on his team in all of them. Captain, you know. But even though he's really popular, he just got me. We used to have really great conversations, about anything and everything, and—"

I stop talking when it hits me. I sound so dumb. August could be dead, and I'm going on like I have any chance in this world of seeing him again.

"You talk a lot. You know that?"

I drop my chin to my chest. I never used to. I was the quiet one. But I guess having to be quiet has brought out the loud-mouth in me. "Anyway. I want to get back to Pensacola. Which way is that?"

He pauses, and for a second, I think he's actually considering my question.

Then he shrugs and continues on the path. Toward the burning city. A city we can't even see, it's that far away. I hurry to catch up to him again, my stupid dress catching between my legs. It's too much sweaty fabric. "Where are you going?"

He shrugs. "Closest city."

"Are you sure that's the closest? I can't even see a building! That must be hundreds of miles away." Not only that, it's in the totally wrong direction.

He nods.

"If that's east, we should go west. Toward Pensacola."

He scans the area around us. "This is not...not in the plan. Not what we should be doing."

"Plan? Since when have we had a plan?"

He shakes his head and mumbles something like, *I broke it the first time I met you.*

"What?"

"Nothing. I told you this was stupid."

Nevertheless, he keeps moving. I follow him. Because he's right. The closest civilization is on the eastern coast. At least in the nearest town, I can get to a phone, call my parents. Hope they answer and have been as worried about me as I've been about them.

About a mile later, the smoke from the burning city has spread halfway across the sky, but it doesn't look much closer. In fact, now it looks farther away. There is nothing along the horizon but trees and marsh. I'm sure I'm dreaming this, seeing things. The air looks like it should smell like a bonfire, but it doesn't. It smells like swamp stink, coating my nostrils with the stench of death.

I scuff into my Birks, which I've lost for the thousandth time.

I had a blister, but it's popped, and now the sweat is burning and the strap is rubbing. "Wait. Stop," I call to him.

Elijah turns back and whispers, "We're never gonna get there if you keep stalling."

I blink. "I didn't know we were going somewhere."

He looks up at the sky as if he's afraid of something. "I know a safe place to camp. That's what I mean."

Maybe two hours later, when my body's bathed in sweat but my mouth is so dry I can feel every ridge on my tongue, we've gotten somewhere. Instead of reeds as far as the eye can see, there is a big, gnarled cypress tree, its limbs all misshapen like a crooked old man, bent double. The branches spread wide, some bare, some covered with whispery leaves.

He motions to it with his chin.

So that is the safe place to camp? A tree? The only thing it seems to save us from is the sun, and we're not going to have that problem at night.

We haven't seen a single soul yet, but I feel like the biggest threats at night will be on the ground, ready to jump out of the shadows when we least expect it.

He heads toward the trunk, which is easily twice as wide as he is; that's how big the tree is. I whisper, "Maybe we should keep going."

He doesn't turn around. "There's nothing else for miles."

The tree is half-submerged in black marsh water but bending toward dry land, almost like someone tied a lasso around it to pull it in. I follow Elijah to the base of the tree and drop my bag on the dry side. He drops his bow and his bag and stares up at the leaves like they're a blessing, then rakes his hands through his sweat-soaked hair. It's a little cooler in the shade, but not much. I get out my water bottle and suck down half of it, but it does no good. Elijah holds out tomatoes, but the thought makes my stomach turn. Instead I grab a tube of lip balm I found in the side table and slather it on my chapped lips.

Elijah grabs a pair of binoculars I didn't know he had out of his bag.

I motion to them, and he hands them to me as he skirts up the limbs of the crooked tree, using its knots like steps. He swings a leg over one of the branches as I bring the binoculars to my eyes.

First, I look at the burning city. It's too far to see much more than the smoke. The smoke is dissipating. Fort Lauderdale, a ruin. Can that really be?

I turn in an arc, squinting as the sun dapples my vision and sweat pours in my eyes.

I see her, walking down the path, toward us. Pigtails, skinny knees, covered in scabs. An impossibly white dress, considering how dust and dirt cling to everything around here. I know her because she's the girl in that old portrait.

"Suzy," I whisper as she catches sight of me. A smile spreads over her cherubic face.

A warm, content feeling spreads over me, the first one I've felt in a long time. I want to tug on Elijah's foot, tell him, *Look, look, good things exist. It's possible.*

I reach behind me to jostle his foot, but I don't want to lose the sight of her, so I grab air instead. "Elijah." The excitement makes my voice shrill. "Loo—"

Thwack.

Behind me, Elijah lets another arrow fly.

It hits her right between the eyes as she's smiling and waving at me.

Even with the arrow cracking her head apart, the blood coursing down her face, around her eye sockets, running off her chin and staining that pure white dress…she smiles. She waves. She cracks in half before my very eyes.

I stagger back, trying to peel the binoculars from my eyes, but I can't.

She's coming closer, her lips moving, blood on her teeth, saying my name while her body rips apart, almost as if that arrow split her in two, right down the center. "You did this to me," she whispers, her voice not that of a happy child. No, her voice is that of a man, full of spite.

"Suzy," I whisper, again and again and again, getting louder and louder, as my pulse pounds in my ears.

Elijah pulls the strap of the binoculars from me and plants his hands on my shoulders. "What the…*what are you doing?*"

I point to that spot across the way, unable to look for fear of what I'll see. "Suzy," I whisper.

He follows my outstretched finger and then lets me go. He stalks across the road and picks up something, dangling it by its feet. It's bloody and white and…

Not Suzy.

It's a giant bird.

He comes back. "Smoke might attract them. But I really want something other than these shitty tomatoes."

I nod, clutching my heart to calm it, and whisper, "I guess it's worth the risk."

He slouches to meet my eyes. "What did you see?"

"You don't want to know."

We cook the bird—I think it's an ibis—or at least, *he* cooks it. Something tells me he's camped before, cooked birds over an open fire before, because he gets the fire built and plucks the feathers, preparing the animal to roast. I don't look. I don't want to turn and find Suzy on a spit.

"Why aren't you seeing things?" I ask him, still thinking of her, bleeding in front of me.

"I do. I ignore them. Mostly, I hear things."

"Like what?"

"Voices. Telling me to do things. Telling me not to do things. It's been so long, I've learned to block them out. But some sounds are too loud."

"Why do you think Suzy went crazy but we're still here?"

The bird is done. He pulls it out of the fire, rips off a leg, and hands it to me. "She was first. I don't know how the trials work, but I think different people got different doses. I think I'm getting better. My hearing don't bother me so much."

I wish I could say that my visions are going away, but they're not. The thought that my father could've…but now it makes sense. He was gone a lot of the time. Having trouble at work. Little had I known how much trouble. His job was everything to him, after me. No wonder he became unhinged.

"But how did you know that I was—"

"Not now. Like I said, I'll tell you sometime."

Why not now? It's on the tip of my tongue, but it drips away, unasked, because my mouth is watering. The bird smells heavenly. It tastes heavenly too. I never knew any meal could taste that good. We devour the food like animals, to the very bones, licking our fingers clean. He extinguishes the fire. The air is cooler then.

The sun has set to a pink line on the horizon, casting us in utter darkness except for the dim glow of the moon and a few fireflies. We both lean against the tree trunk, which is so massive we don't touch shoulders at all.

He says, "Keep alert. In case something saw us."

Something. A monster.

I stare at every firefly, every leaf that rolls in on the wind, and sure hope that bird was worth it. My belly thinks it is, but as I look around, expecting to see horrible things that aren't there—or even worse, horrible things that *are*—I don't know.

The worst part of all this is that I can't tell the difference.

TWENTY

A: Willow. It's D-Day. Decision Day.

W: I know.

A: And?

W: I don't know. Are you serious?

A: Yeah. 1000%. We can do this.

W: All right. If you're in, I'm in.

A: Low, I promise, everything will be okay. Hold on. Let
me send you something.

Somehow I nod off. In the morning, I wake with my chin against my chest, a crick in my neck, and a thousand red, angry bumps on my legs.

Something wasn't sleeping last night. *Something* was lurking in the darkness, preparing an attack. Many somethings, actually. And they succeeded. I'm vanquished. The mosquitoes spent all night feasting on stupid me, their buffet.

I look around for Elijah, but he's not where I left him. Maybe he's been vanquished too.

All the blisters on my feet have popped; they're raw, burning, crusty, and yellow. Itchy too. I crawl over the dusty earth to the muddy marsh. Pushing away the saw grass and keeping an eye out for alligators, I dip my toes into the water. Salt water's good for all that ails you, which is what my grandmother—my real granny—used to tell me when she'd take me down to the beach before she died. I'd have a cut, and she'd tell me to get down to the gulf and get my medicine. And she was right—whenever I'd come out, the wound always looked better.

This water isn't ocean water, but maybe it has good in it. As I sit there, wriggling my toes, I see a tadpole, trying to become a frog. I twirl my finger in the water near its round green face, and it swims away.

Then I hear a branch break. I look up. Elijah's sitting on the branch above me. He holds up a tomato, a question on his face, pretends to toss one down to me.

The taste of that bird is still on my tongue. It's probably too much to ask for another one. But my stomach is still full, and for the moment, I am not hungry. I think I'll savor that rare moment.

I shake my head, stand, and straighten my strawberry dress as I scuff my wet feet into the Birks. He climbs down, jumping most of the way. The sky is pale blue—no smoke at all, not even a wisp. "We should go."

He doesn't argue. He might have been reluctant before, but I hope he sees how important this is. How staying still is waiting to die. Our stomachs are full, and we haven't been attacked by monsters—this is a definite step up.

He may be alone in the world, but I have family, friends, a life waiting for me. At least I did. I'm not giving up until I know the life I once knew is over. I won't. I can't.

I'm glad Elijah finally understands that and is willing to help me.

We're in good spirits as we gather our things and head down the road. At least I am, and I think he is too, because though he's silent, there's a spring to his step that wasn't there before. A purpose. The glare of the white-hot sun nearly blinds me, and my sunburn only worsens, but this is good. Taking action. Making things happen instead of waiting for them to.

After hours, when my stomach is growling and I'm starting to think those tomatoes sound good, something changes.

When I shield my eyes to view the road ahead, there's black on the hazy horizon.

I break into a jog, thrilled by the prospect of different.

I get only a few steps when I see it's a traffic barrier, set up across the road. BRIDGE OUT, it says.

I run up to it. Maybe it's one of those construction signs to keep people away because whoever set it out doesn't want trespassers. But sure enough, there's a big, hundred-foot gap where a road is supposed to be and lot of murky water in between, covered in duckweed and a thick miasma of morning fog.

I scan up and down the bank. "There's another way around, isn't there?"

He rubs the whiskers on his chin. "No."

"What do you mean?" I almost cry. My spirits had been so high, and now they're plummeting. "You live on an island in the middle of the Everglades?"

He nods.

That would've been good to know before we set out. "Didn't you know this bridge was out?"

He gives me an annoyed look. "You think I would've taken you here if I did?"

I suck in a breath, let it out, pace back and forth. "Can we swim it?"

"Not unless you want to lose a few limbs."

"What?"

"Alligators."

And crocodiles. Don't forget the crocodiles. Living together in peace and harmony. I peer into the dark, stagnant water. It looks so innocent, but in the last few days, I've learned that seemingly innocent things can be anything but.

I throw up my hands. "Well, this is great!" He puts his finger to his mouth to quiet me, but what difference does it make? There isn't anyone over here. We're on a damn island. I don't even know how that guy—the one Elijah shot with the arrow—got here. Did he walk on water? Swim with the alligators? "This was all a waste of time!"

He squints at me, hitches a shoulder, mouths, *Sorry.*

Part of me thinks he's unconcerned, but a larger part of me

thinks that when you get enough bad news, it doesn't faze you anymore. He's had so much of it piled on his shoulders, what's one more disappointment?

He didn't know. He never left his home. *I'm* the jackass who forced him out here. "Is there another bridge?"

He doesn't answer, almost like he's afraid of disappointing me again. He doesn't meet my gaze either. He stares at his feet. Because of course the answer is no.

Tears pull at the corners of my eyes. I'm going to lose it if I don't get some good news for a change. *Any* good news. How is it that the dead bird was the best thing that's happened to us all trip?

Then I remember. "Hey. That boat, behind the generator. Can we use that?"

It wasn't much of a boat, a rusty two-person job on a couple of buckets under a holey tarp. Maybe it had holes in it too. But we could fix those. We don't need fancy. We just need *out*.

Or at least I do.

He shrugs. "You want to go back?"

Scuffing the gravel from the smashed cement bridge with the toes of my Birks, I go to the edge and lean out over the cement piling. Up there, it's a little cooler. I scan the area, looking for another solution, but nothing presents itself.

I nod. We might have to travel back a day, but who cares. I needed a plan. A reason to hope. Now I have one. Years from now, when I look back at this moment, I will consider it a minor setback. "I guess we have to, right? Let's go."

Before I push off the barrier, something catches my eye about fifty feet downstream.

Half-submerged, there's a piece of metal covered by brackish water, glinting in the sun.

I lean forward, pointing to it. "Do you see that? What is that?"

I inch my way to the edge of the bank to get a better look. As I'm doing so, Elijah says, "A car?"

I squint, trying to focus. Is that what it is? Yes, he's right. I can make out the metal bumper, which means it's probably an older model. A classic, maybe. No, a sportscar. I can tell by the graceful lines. Tilting my head, the duckweed drifts ever so slightly, revealing a white rectangle, green writing, an orange circle in the center.

A Florida license plate.

Tendrils of worry climb up my spine as sweat trickles down it, because suddenly that hope I'd been holding on to flits from my fingers, and I can't move forward, backward, anywhere at all.

"My car," I whisper. "Elijah. That's *my* car."

TWENTY-ONE

A: You get my email?

W: Yeah. That place... Where is it?

A: It's not far from the house you told me he booked. I'll meet you there. You think you can make it?

W: Well...I don't know. I guess.

A: I'll make it worth your while. 😊

The closer I get, the surer I am. I'm not seeing things.

That's my little blue Mustang. The one I got for my birthday. It's brand new. And it's...destroyed. The front end is smashed in, the hood is tented, and it's submerged in brown bog water up to the windows. *Past* the windows, because as I get closer, I realize the windows are open and there's water inside the car too.

My first thought? *Mom and Dad are going to kill me.*

It's a stupid thing to think at a time like this, but I can't stop replaying how happy I'd been on my sixteenth birthday. I'd woken up, gone downstairs, and found the keys waiting for me on the center island in the kitchen with a note that said, *Love Mom and Dad.*

I was happy, but nervous. It was so beautiful, and I worried about getting into an accident. Like I said, I hadn't wanted a car for that reason. Still, I'd taken it right out and drove up and down the street by August's house, hoping he'd be home to see. He wasn't, but the sheer thrill of it being mine overshadowed my inability to share my sweet ride with him. Later on, I'd sent him a message with a picture of me leaning against it with the top down.

It had been pristine. And now...

Oh God. What happened?

I jump off the edge of the bridge and head into the weeds where the ground is muddy and sloppy underfoot. Elijah puts a hand on my shoulder, holding me back, but I shake him free.

"Careful, alligators," he whispers, but I'm already barreling ahead, my eyes on the car.

The mud becomes water, sloshing against my ankles, and it only grows deeper until it's up to my knees. I don't let that hold me back. Even if the car is destroyed, there are answers there. Answers I've been desperate for.

I will get to that car if it kills me.

Overhead, a raven caws. The car might have floated downstream, but it's resting against the trunk of a large dead tree the color of ash. The raven...the tree...the rotting smell...all of it should be a warning, but it's not. Nothing could keep me away.

By the time the water's up to my hipbones, I can barely push through it. It's not normal water. It's thick like mud, but oily and rancid and full of living things, dead things. I cut through it, disturbing the blanket of duckweed, scattering mosquitoes and flies like a puff of breath scatters dandelion seeds.

I come upon the back door first. I grab the handle, but of course, it won't open. I peer in and notice the flowered straps of my backpack in the murky water. Grabbing for it, I yank it out, triumphant.

"My cell phone's in here. Well, if it's not in the cup holder," I say to Elijah, feeling through the pocket. "I know it's probably waterlogged or dead, but maybe we can fix it, and if you ever get the generator…"

I rummage inside, feeling nothing but a slippery coat of slime over my makeup bag, pens, gum. I know it's empty. Of course, it's in the cup holder. I never drive anywhere without my phone right next to me.

"Cup holder," I say to Elijah, trying to get to the front seat.

But he's in the way. I expect him to move back and let me through, but he doesn't. He just stands there, looking down on me, another stony expression on his face.

I nudge him. "Move. Let me…"

I stop when he shakes his head. It's his posture that warns me. It's so sentinel stiff, I wouldn't be able to knock him over if I had an army behind me. I narrow my eyes, trying to read what he's telling me. As usual, I can't.

But I know something is wrong.

Something is very, very wrong.

"What?" I whisper.

In a flash, I see pity in his dark eyes. Or sorrow. My breath comes in a series of gasps.

He doesn't want me to see whatever is in the front seat.

And that means…

I close my eyes. Count to three in my head. Really, how many times have I told myself this? *If things get worse, I'm out of here.*

When I open my eyes, he's reached into the front seat and pulled out my cell phone, which is coated in a fine layer of grime. Though Elijah's expression is stone, I understand with complete clarity.

Things are about to get much, much worse.

Time to get out.

But there is no way out. We're on an island. And we can't escape.

There is only one way to escape, and it's inside Elijah's backpack.

Deciding I can't feel any worse than I do now, I take a deep breath. And with all my might, I shove him aside. Incredibly, he moves. Not a lot. Just a few inches.

At first, I think it's not enough. I see the windshield, the dashboard, my butterscotch cookie air freshener tied to the visor. I take a step closer. That's when I notice the reflection in the rearview mirror.

It's the intricate, white-washed bones of a hand, clasped over the strap of a shredded seat belt.

Bones.

A hand.

A skeleton, inside my car.

A dead person.

My...

Oh God.

My mouth opens. A silent scream. The bottom of the bog drops out from under me. I feel like I am in the center of a slowly spinning maelstrom, about to be sucked into its depths.

I back up. There's a silhouette in the driver's side. Another person. What I thought was part of the head rest is not. It's the outline of a head, covered in a few scraggly wisps of hair.

Not a head.

A skull.

Silent no more, I finally use my voice—how can I not?—and this time, it's louder than I've ever screamed in my life.

This time, Elijah lets me.

TWENTY-TWO

W: Okay, then. YES. I'll do it.

I don't remember going back to the house, the house I'd hoped I'd never see again. Somehow, I lose the Birks, probably in the cement-like mud of the marsh, and I wind up trudging home in my bare feet. Part of the time, I walk, struggling to put one foot in front of the other. Part of the time, Elijah drags me. Most of the time, he carries me over his shoulder, the one that doesn't have his weapon slung over it. My hair hangs to the ground, and the world is turned upside down.

The world is already upside down. It is over.

I know I weigh too much for him. He may be big, but he grunts and stumbles, and his T-shirt is soaked and sour with sweat. I tell him, over and over and over again, that he needs to let me go. He needs to leave me to die. Put me where the alligators are most likely to get at me. Or the crocodiles. I don't discriminate. I'd be their meal. I wouldn't even fight.

But he doesn't. He doesn't tell me to be quiet. He doesn't tell me anything. He lets me cry and scream and mourn. Maybe he wants the monsters to come for both of us.

Though it took an entire day to get to the broken bridge, it feels like hardly a blink and we're back at the house. He shoves open the gate in the rusty chain-link fence, climbs the stairs, opens the creaking screen door, and sets me back on the stained mattress in Suzy's room. The room is the same as the first day I woke up here, but one thing is different.

Now, I don't want to live.

He goes to leave. Before he can, I whisper, "Give me the gun."

He stops. He doesn't face me, but his shoulders sag. "No."

I try to sit up, but I can't find the energy. My eyes follow him in the near dark. How dare he? "No? You *told* me—"

I swipe for the bag on his back, but he reaches out, quick as a flash, and grabs my wrist. Elijah stares at me for at least a minute before he says, softer now, "No."

I don't know if I want to hear the answer to my next question, which is why I have trouble letting it out. "Why not?"

He reaches into the bag, takes out the silver box, and opens it. Elijah pulls out the gun, opens the magazine, and shows me the bullets inside. Two of them.

All I need is one.

I reach for it, but he snatches it away. He sits on the edge of the bed taking deep breaths, and I can tell he's uncomfortable, debating whether he should tell me something.

Finally, he says, "Suzy."

I wait for more, but now he must be regretting even saying her name, because he shakes his head.

"You killed her?"

His eyes, dark in shadow, flicker to mine, full of malice.

Elijah swallows, the gun laid across his hands, like he doesn't want to hold it, but he doesn't want me to have it either.

"My mother used to read the Bible to her before bed. She loved the stories of the cherubim, watching over us. 'For he shall give his angels charge over thee, To keep thee in all thy ways. They shall bear thee up in their hands, Lest thou dash thy foot against a stone,'" he recites. "Kids see things we don't see all the time. She used to look up at the sky for hours. I think she thought the clouds were angels. Watching out for us.

"She used to do that on her swing. Tilt her head back and look up at the sky. Or sometimes, she'd lie in the grass, and I'd have to tell her that her shirt was riding up and she needed to cover her belly. Hours and hours she'd spend, just looking."

He makes a sound like a laugh, but can it be? Does he laugh? I've never heard him do that before.

"She'd call out the things she saw there. Dogs. Unicorns. A cowboy riding a dinosaur. Mickey Mouse. A mermaid. All this stuff." He shoves the magazine back into the gun, and the click is the loudest sound I've ever heard. "Then, right before she went after Granny, she started seeing angels. Up there. Down here, she'd see the worst things. Bad things, telling her to do bad stuff.

That's all she saw. So she kept looking up at the sky. Wanting the angels to save her."

She started seeing things.

Like me.

"I've had visions, but never of angels," I whisper. "I think I'd like that."

"No. You wouldn't. She couldn't get them out of her head. She tried, but they were always there. Voices telling her to do bad things. She kept looking for the angels, waiting for them to save her. But the bad voices disguised themselves as angels, and she couldn't tell the difference. The voices got so bad that she told me she wanted to see the angels." He lets out a shaky breath. "That only they could keep her safe. She wanted me to take her to see them."

Despite the heat, my skin is cold. I'm shivering.

"I told her no, just like I told you. I wouldn't do it. She was my sister. But she made me promise her. She made me promise that if she ever did anything to hurt anyone, I'd do it." He shook his head. "I told her if I did that, I wouldn't be able to live with myself. So we made a pact. If she's gonna see the angels, she ain't goin' alone."

My voice isn't my own. It's hollow. "What happened?"

His voice matches mine, even quieter. He stares at his lap, and his shoulders sag. "Simple. I couldn't do it. She shot my parents while they slept. Then she went after Granny. After that, after I stopped her, she told me we had to do it. Right then.

"So I...shot her. From behind. I didn't want to see her. She didn't go right away. I shot her and her little body flew forward and she curled up in a ball, crying. So I shot her again. I watched her die and then I held the gun to my head and I...I..."

He shakes his head.

I know. He doesn't need to say more.

"She went alone," he says. "All alone. I know she's up there. And she's watching me. But she's not watching over me, like angels are supposed to do. No, she's looking down at me, wondering *why the fuck I'm still here.* Because I *promised.* She's laughing at me. And sometimes I think this is happening, that things keep getting worse and I am living this hell over and over again until I finally get the balls to do what I promised."

I roll over and stare at him. He's had that gun for so long. As much as I've wished for the end, contemplated sticking that gun against my temple and pulling the trigger, thought of it until I'm nearly mad...I know he's done that too, times a thousand. Times a million.

The pills may have broken me. But he's just as broken. Maybe worse.

"Will you?"

He shakes his head. "No. I can't. I've tried, but I can't kill myself. I can't leave the world like that. I have to make it up to her. Somehow. I wanted to fix it this time, but..." He lets out a bitter laugh. "I fouled that up. Again. Like I fouled up all the other times before."

He slowly retreats, probably to wallow in his own misery.

I roll back over in bed as darkness descends, and the mice swish and whisper in the corners, louder now that the cat is gone. I feel like they're multiplying under the bed. Soon there will be thousands of them. As the human race dies out, they will rise up and rule the world.

Maybe they will do a better job of it than we have.

The moonlight hits the glass over the pictures across from me, setting the room alight. I'd almost believe it's the light of hope if I didn't know better.

I peer at the picture beyond the glass, and what should pop into my head but the verse of a book my mother used to read to me when I was a child. *Goodnight Moon.* With the cow jumping over the moon, the three little bears, the bowl full of mush…and my own quiet lady, whispering hush.

My mother is dead now.

That lady who used to bounce me on my knee, singing songs, reading me books. She went over a bridge in the Everglades in the brand-new car she bought me, and somehow died. Maybe she was infected by the monsters.

It doesn't really matter. She's gone. She is in a marsh, slowly being consumed by the earth and whatever lives in those waters.

I look up at the ceiling. I should've been with them. Maybe they are laughing at me too. Maybe all of heaven and hell is laughing at us and the mess we've created.

I roll on my side and try to close my eyes, but I can't. A fat, gray spider climbs out from the gap between the planks on the floor. It's an endlessly wide gap. I'm not sure why I never noticed it before, but it has a little knothole in it.

In movies, that would be the secret compartment where the treasure was hidden.

But in this, the story of my life, it's probably home to something awful.

Nevertheless, I'm wide awake. I have no reason not to look. If it's Pandora's box or storage for a severed head, I'd probably just laugh at this point, shake my head, and say, *Just my luck.*

I reach down and hook a finger through the hole. For a second, I expect something to bite it off before the plank comes loose. But that doesn't happen. I lift it to the side.

I gaze at a cartoonish picture of a little rabbit chewing on a carrot.

I thought I was all cried out after my parents.

New tears spring to my eyes. I reach inside and find a whole stack of packets, bound together with a rotting rubber band that falls to pieces in my hands. That's okay. I spread out the little envelopes, marveling at each one.

Carrots. Peppers. Cucumbers. Pumpkins.

And yes, even tomatoes.

Seeds.

I pile them up and gather them to my chest. I'll tell Elijah. But right now, I'll enjoy them for myself, a little secret only the man in the moon and I know.

I look up at the sky. If the angels are laughing, maybe the moon is on my side.

If that's all I have, I'd better learn to be friends with the dark.

PART TWO

NINE MONTHS LATER

TWENTY-THREE

It's afternoon when I find it.

It's funny how something so small can set events in motion. Or tear things apart, depending on how you look at it.

I'm digging in the dirt to plant a new row of vegetables when my fingers scrape something hard. This thing, buried in the earth for who knows how long, is not pliable like a root, or dense like a rock. I clear the soft dirt around it until my fingers can pry it loose.

I pull it up and stare. It's bottle top from a Coca-Cola liter bottle. A little black nub I'd have tossed in the garbage without a thought once upon a time. I can even see the swirly script letters on top.

I'd say I miss Coke, but I really don't remember how it tastes.

I think I am seeing things, but I don't do that much anymore. Sure, sometimes I'll see Suzy or my father. But I've learned to blink them away, like Elijah has learned to ignore the sounds. They don't hurt me. They haven't gotten worse or better. I don't think I'm becoming Suzy. I don't think he is either. I think, just like E had hoped, we didn't get enough of the medicine in our systems, and we're going to be okay.

I drop the cap in the pocket of my strawberry dress and don't think much of it for the next few hours. I lose track of time in my garden. It's the only thing I've ever really created on my own, and I'm proud of it. I have carrots and cucumbers. Little turnips. Radishes. Peppers and tiny heads of lettuce. It's all growing at my ankles, nurtured by me.

It gives me purpose. It's life sustaining, life affirming. Crazy to think that once upon a time, I sang for thousands of strangers on the internet, but this? This little garden is probably the greatest thing I've ever done.

The sun is dipping behind the horizon by the time I finish, but I'm not nearly ready to be done. Problem is the days are shorter now. They bleed into one another like the colors on the horizon. Every day is the same, except the darkness comes sooner.

If you'd told me a year ago that I'd be a master of the garden, I'd have laughed at you. But these days, I am. I know just where to plant each seed so it gets the adequate amount of sun. I know how to shield the plants so they don't drown when the deluging rainstorms come. I know the peppers aren't happy in direct sunlight and the tomatoes do better when I pick them every single day. I haven't gone as far as naming the plants, but maybe I'll do that soon.

E walks by to check on my progress. He gives me a look.

Everything okay? I answer with one that says, *Yes, mind your own business, thanks very much.*

We don't talk much. We have our own silent language.

I give him a smile. He smiles back.

E has teeth. Oh, they're crooked, and I only see a bit of them when he smiles, but he's so stone-faced most of the time that the sliver of not-quite white can truly turn around my day. One minute, I'll be grumbling because I'm running low on pumpkin seeds and another plant is dead, and the next, he'll give me that smile, and I'll remember I used to hate all that pumpkin spice shit in autumn, so who cares?

E's building a fence around the place. There was an old shed behind the outhouse, with a caved-in roof and the decaying remains of old farming equipment. He's using the wood and some old, rusted chicken wire to go all the way around the house, adding ancient tin cans and metal things at intervals to alert us if something gets caught in it.

So far, nothing has.

I'm not sure how many days it's been, as I've lost count, but the dying world has left us alone. I've left it alone too. Or I try to. When thoughts of August used to come into my head, I'd savor them, replaying even the smallest detail again and again. Now, I force them out. I hardly think of what I've lost. I don't think of before.

Only now.

Now is all that matters.

I gather a pile of bounty into a basket—the reddest tomatoes, the longest cucumbers, the cutest little radishes—and carry them inside, laying them out on the counter as Elijah watches from the kitchen table. We eat a lot of vegetables, obviously. Sometimes E will shoot a seagull or some other bird with an arrow. That's all.

But not tonight. Tonight we'll sit together in silence and have crudités, minus the fancy sour cream dip. I set everything out on plates as I've done a hundred times before.

But I'm not tired of it. I've learned to be thankful.

Thankful I haven't seen the gun since we returned. We left it, at first, on the mantle in the silver box. Then, gradually, we decided to set it away. Accessible but not visible. It's in the pantry, on the very top shelf, behind an empty cannister that says TEA. I'm thankful it's put away and yet thankful that it's there. Just in case.

E never fixed the generator. After a few more weeks of trying, I told him not to. His mood was already bad, and tinkering with that broken old thing only made it worse. He showed me the part that was broken, a round knob that had corroded and cracked in two. He's been trying to find something to use in its place, but nothing has worked.

We've dealt. The days have been getting cooler anyway, and I don't mind sweating and heat as much as I once did.

He's much happier now. Well, as happy as someone like E can be. He smiles anyway. A bit.

Wait. The generator.

He turns to look at me, almost as if he can sense my thoughts, even from halfway across the yard. He comes over as I reach into my pocket and pull out the bottle cap. I press it into his palm.

I don't have to explain. He knows. He inspects it closely, then shrugs. *Maybe.*

He does an about-face and hurries toward the generator. Excitement bubbles in me, so I follow him. It'd be amazing if after all this time, I found the magic piece to fix that stupid hunk of machinery.

He pushes aside the sheet and crouches in front of the rusting monstrosity. Holding the cap between his thumb and forefinger, he tries to twist the bolt onto a protruding nodule. I'm not sure what it does, but it's crazy that so much depends on that. It reminds me of a poem I studied in school, about a red wheelbarrow.

So much depends
On a cola bottle cap
Found under the earth...
Beside the beautiful garden.

His heavy sigh draws me back. He has a wrench out and is trying to tighten on the bottle cap. He shakes his head when he lets go and the thing slips off.

Then he looks up at me and frowns. *Nope.*

My spirits do a little nosedive.

Oh well. I'm thankful anyway. Thankful for everything we *do* have.

We wash up at the bucket beside the house and go in for dinner. Even without electricity and running water, we have a good life.

It took me a while to be able to say that, but it's true.

It's especially true when he grabs my hand and pulls me onto his lap. He holds me there, looking into my eyes, running his fingers down my spine, his other hand tangled in my hair, his eyes on mine, still asking, always asking, *Are you okay?*

This is my favorite time of the day. Our work is done, and we can rest, be together.

We don't talk about the gun. Or the pact. Or the outside world.

In this world, there is just us.

And that is enough.

He pulls my face to his and kisses me softly.

He's always tentative, even now. I know I'm the first girl he's ever kissed. We took forever to get this far. For him to get the courage to take my hand. He is gentle, though his calluses scrape my skin. I don't mind them. In fact, I like them. It's usually me trying to push things further. Hell, it's the end of the world, so why not? Why should we die virgins? But he is the one who is nervous. He is a good kisser, but they're soft, sweet kisses that could be so much more.

I drag my hand behind his neck and try to pull him closer,

my body aching the way it used to when August and I used to chat. But this is more. So much more, because he's here, and my parents aren't downstairs. We can do anything we want...

He tenses. The moment dissolves in an instant.

I sigh against him. Foiled again. I catch his warm breath in my mouth when I inhale, and as I do, I hear a sound.

Not the metal cans in the fence. I can't place it. It has been so long since I've heard such a thing. It's a far-off puttering, like...a lawn mower? No. It's different.

I stare into his widening eyes. "What—"

I jump off his lap, scampering in bare feet for the door. He grabs for my hand but is not quick enough. I'm down the hall and pushing open the door, searching the darkness. No moon. There's only the outline of the distant trees against the velvet sky.

The sound draws my eyes upward.

It's cutting across the sky, red lights blinking on each wing. I haven't seen a plane in ages. It's a tiny prop plane, heading somewhere, who knows where, forging its way through the dark clouds. This is the first sign of human life I've seen in ages.

For a moment, my mouth opens, but I'm unable to say anything.

Then I look back at E, who's watching the sky silently. I expect that little sliver of a smile, that little sliver of *hope*, but instead, his stone face is back.

"A plane," I whisper.

He wraps an arm around my waist, squeezing me tighter. "A plane."

TWENTY-FOUR

We don't talk about the airplane. Not for days.

It's weird, but the days melt together, and we rarely talk to begin with. We communicate with gestures and looks. So the plane never comes up.

But I think about it. Do I ever.

I wonder who was in the plane. If they escaped someplace terrible. If they were going someplace better. Someplace with other people. Someplace where the world goes on and civilization is beginning anew.

Without us.

E, however, doesn't seem to care. It seems the airplane flew out of our line of vision and flew out of his mind too. Which is strange, considering. We're out here, in the middle of nowhere. I doubt we'd see a plane even if the world hadn't gone to pot. But when he saw one…nothing. No emotion whatsoever.

I should be happy. I'm alive, and things are good. E seems happy too. Well, happier than he was at least. I was only with him a few weeks when that sliver of smile appeared. I'd like to think that was my doing. I'd slipped in mud while tromping through the marsh, trying to catch a frog, thinking we could eat it, since I once heard it tastes like chicken, and damn do I miss chicken. I got covered in thick black marsh mud from head to toe. He actually laughed when he saw me, a sound that I still think of every time our situation starts to feel hopeless. His laugh was deep and nice, and I felt it low in my belly as much as in my ears. He called me a marsh puppy.

I love his laugh. I love a lot of things about him. I both love and hate how shy he is. He has never been with another girl. I know that for sure. I don't think he talked to any girls besides Suzy before me.

He put up a flowered bedsheet near the side of the house, by the barrel, so I'd have privacy to wash up. He pretends he's not watching me, but I know he is, or at least the outline of my body as the sun plays against the fabric. Every time I come out, skin scrubbed and clean, his cheeks are a few shades redder.

I know his parents were very strict. He obeyed them to the letter. His father was disconnected from society and kept them that way too. A fortress against the world.

It's a world he didn't want me in at first. But gradually, he opened up to me. He let me in. And now I am as much his family as they were.

Except he knows what he lost, so I think he treasures me even more.

I guess I treasure him too. I've lost a lot myself, though I don't like to think about that.

There is so much about him—about *all* this—to like.

I may not be religious, but I have a confession to make.

I have been thinking about the world outside.

I don't think he has.

Not at all.

Of course not. He has never been a part of it. He doesn't know what he is missing. One night, in the darkness, he confessed he's barely left this marshy island. I think what's beyond this property is too scary—scarier, even, than the monsters.

But I *do* know what I am missing. Whenever I think about it, it pulls tears from my eyes.

I try to avoid those thoughts. It's so hard, but I try. I also don't want to upset E. I know he likes me. I think maybe he has come to love me. I think I might love him too. And he has lost so much. I don't want him to think he could lose me too.

Tonight, E and I eat by the light of the moon. He doesn't like to make smoke, so we don't light fires, and except when he catches a seagull, we eat all our food raw. I don't mind raw carrots, turnips, cucumbers. I think radishes are the greatest food on Earth because they've got a little kick. I cut everything into different shapes, wedges and circles and sticks, to shake things up. Before, I used to say how healthy my diet was. Now, it's just food. Life-sustaining. I've lost so much weight that joking about a diet doesn't seem funny anymore.

His eyes get almost completely black as he sits across from me during dinner. It's like the moonlight refuses to touch them. As usual, we eat in silence with our fingers, grabbing little circles, squares, wedges and popping them into our mouths. He lets me have the last piece of pepper.

I wonder if there will be another airplane tonight. I've hoped for one every night.

So far, nothing. Not in seven—um, maybe eight days. Like I said, they all bleed together.

It probably *will* be nothing again tonight. I've come to expect it. Maybe the plane was a figment of my imagination. Without E to confirm it, did it exist at all? We create our own reality here. We are masters of this domain. Anything in the outside world is no longer our concern.

At least he thinks that.

Maybe I should too. Everyone I love is dead.

Except…

August is probably dead too. If he's lucky. Plus, I'm not sure I ever cared about him. Or he cared about me. Maybe it was all in my head.

Like everything.

When we are done, he whispers, "Do you want to go up?"

I nod. I love that. He hasn't asked me since before the plane.

He takes a lantern, one tiny candle, small enough to be a firefly, and we go to the window in my room. That's the way we always climb up because of the rotting tree, which even though the weather's getting cooler and more hospitable to life still has yet to sprout anything resembling leaves. He climbs up first, and then I step on the window ledge, one foot on the tree, and he pulls me up to the eave near the window on the second floor. The window to his parents' room, which has always stayed completely closed behind a shade.

From there, it's a quick climb to the top of the roof, where we sit, back to back at the apex, like we're on top of the world.

We are. On top of *our* world at least.

We can stay out here for hours. It's so peaceful with only the crickets' song and the call of an owl here or there. Nothing else.

Tonight, there are no clouds for the angels to hide. He says that when it's like this, Suzy and the other angels aren't gone—they're simply allowing us to see all this beauty. And it is beautiful. There are so many stars tonight.

No planes, though. Of course. I get the feeling we are so remote that this place never saw airplanes to begin with.

Once, when we were up here, I saw a falling star. It shot all the way across the sky, disappearing somewhere near the Atlantic. I said I'd have liked to catch it, but E didn't say anything. That—out there—is a different world to him. It might as well have fallen to Mars.

He never would have gone to Fort Lauderdale all those months ago, even if the bridge hadn't been out. I'm convinced he would've found some reason to turn around and come back here. He is fine to live out the rest of our days here. Just like this.

Maybe I should be too.

But here's another confession. That plane has gotten me to think, and not necessarily healthy thoughts. I don't like the way it's pulling at me.

Nevertheless, it *is* pulling at me.

Before, I'd been happy. Content.

But that plane opened a longing inside me. I wish I could stitch it closed, like a wound. I've tried that. It's not working. You can't fill a hole by pretending it doesn't exist.

A growing part of me can't be contained. It wants out—despite our failed attempt, the horror of what we saw. I'm afraid this desire is going to grow and grow until the madness comes back.

I haven't seen Suzy or my father in over a week. It's pushing my luck to think I might be cured, so I try not to think about that either.

"Hey," I whisper as we sit, braced against each other's backs, our legs hanging over the eave. I'm looking out toward the east, toward my fallen star. "Do you think it will always be like this?"

"I don't know."

"Do you think it will get better?"

After a moment, he lets out a long breath. "I've never gotten this far before. Usually, I…"

He trails off. He always does that when it comes to *us*. Stops talking, too embarrassed to say more. I get that this is uncharted territory for him, but I also think he must've tried and struck out with girls before. Badly.

It's kind of adorable how awkward he is. Adorable and maddening. Because if he thought he was missing something by being shut off from the outside world, maybe...

"Do you think we'll be doing this when we're old and gray?"

I feel his back tense. "Is that so bad?"

"No. But..." I swallow and ask what I'm really thinking: "What if...the world is better now?"

He's silent for a long time. "Not a chance."

"It could be. Maybe, somehow, they got it under control. Maybe that plane was taking people somewhere safe. I forgot there were other people alive in this world. It's nice, you know?"

He shrugs. "Things are bad."

"What—how do you—"

"It's too soon. They're not going to get better anytime soon." His back tenses against my shoulder blades, pushing me forward. "Maybe one day we'll try again. Not now. It's too soon."

I gnaw on my lip. Too soon. We should wait a few more months. He's probably right. I shrug. "I know I have nothing else out there. But I'm curious."

He looks over his shoulder at me, his stare drilling into me. "Is it so bad here?"

"No." I feel guilty for suggesting it. He told me that, all the way out here, his family got their news from a radio, but that died with the generator. "But you don't know. We don't have any idea what's happening out there. And—"

"Are you done?" he snaps, standing up, so that when I turn

toward him, I nearly lose my balance and slip backward down the other side of the roof. "You know what happened the last time. You want that again?"

Before I can answer, he does a little tightrope walk in his bare feet along the ridge where the two sides of the roof meet before sliding down to the eave. He slips out of sight and disappears beyond the rain gutter. A second later, I hear his feet hitting the ground. He doesn't come back.

Leaving me, for the very first time, to climb down by myself.

TWENTY-FIVE

E didn't come into my room last night.

For the past three months, we've had a routine. I go to my little toddler bed, roll over, face the window, and pretend to sleep. About a half hour later, he comes, squeezes in behind me, and holds me. Sometimes he'll put his lips on the shell of my ear or bury his face in my hair. He wraps his arm around me and holds my hand. Not too physical, really. Maybe a little. Once, I think he kissed my shoulder, if his lips grazing my shirt could be considered a kiss. He's too shy for much more than that.

Though the days bleed together, I remember how it started. It was the first day I saw him cry.

He's always mumbling. At first, I thought he was cursing God or whoever put us here, but that day, he'd been mumbling more than ever. And when I listened, really listened, I realized he was talking.

To her.

Suzy.

A lot of it was nonsensical. But then he'd say something like, *Bet you're glad you aren't here* or *You would've liked it.*

He'd been especially mumbly that day trying to fix the generator. At least that's where I thought he was. But when I went outside, I'd found him, crouched, head buried in his arms, bawling his eyes out and murmuring *This isn't working* and *I can't* and *How can I get this to work?* over and over and over again. He kept hitting his head with the heel of his hand.

That was when I knew he wasn't the emotionless statue I thought he was.

I suppose even the most unemotional person, when stuck on a never-ending hamster wheel of misery, would eventually want to get off.

I don't know what possessed him, but that night he crawled into bed with me. He was very stiff. He didn't touch me. I grabbed his hand and pulled it around me.

The first few nights, I doubt either of us slept. It's weird, sleeping next to another person. I was acutely aware of his every breath, his every movement, even the flutter of his pulse. Gradually, I got used to it. Gradually, my body craved the closeness, even during the hottest nights.

But last night, I slept alone, cold despite the sticky heat. It felt like a part of me was missing. For someone who has always been isolated from others, he sure knows how to hit a person where it hurts.

Strange how we can change so much, so quickly, when the situation calls for it.

When I wake—well, I never really slept—I roll over when I hear floorboards shifting in the kitchen. I get up and go down the hall. He is standing barefoot, facing away from me. He freezes. I know he can sense me, just like I know the weight of his body, the way he moves, the sounds his joints make when they crack and his teeth make when he's worried and grits them, which he always does.

I know him.

So I'm not entirely surprised when he turns and stalks past me, out the door, without looking at me.

That ruins my entire day.

Kind of funny, isn't it? Everything is different from my old life, and yet I still get mopey when a boy I like ignores me in the hall.

Like August. Who did that *constantly*, until that one day…

Ugh. I can't think of August. Not now.

E's outside, but my routine's the same. I get up and go to the side of the house and wash up before starting the day. I don't plan to change that because he's angry at me. I stalk out, focused on that sheet at the side of the house, only minimally aware that he's standing at the edge of the marsh, stretching and surveying the fence to make sure it's intact, which is part of *his* morning routine.

I go to the outhouse to do my business. No longer am I scared about the moaning figure beneath the seat. That was a hallucination. Still, I only use the outhouse in the daylight. There is nothing down there except excrement. The thing that scares me most is the stench. Not that I spend much time investigating. I try to spend as little time in there as possible.

After I finish using the outhouse, I slip behind the sheet and ladle water into a basin, which I use to wash my face and brush my teeth with a pink Barbie toothbrush that belonged to his sister. I was disgusted at first, brushing my teeth with something that belonged to a dead girl, but everything I use belongs to someone who's gone. I pull off the big T-shirt that belonged to his dead dad and slip into his dead mom's strawberry dress, which I washed and hung out to dry on the line last night. This is not the time to be picky. It's the time to be grateful I'm still here.

I pull the dress over my head and tromp through the weeds to where I left the other bucket. I'll pour the dirty water from my washing into it and use it to clean my clothes later. When I'm done, I'll use it to water the garden. Not a drop wasted.

I find the bucket under the rusted boat. That was the boat I'd hoped to escape in so long ago. Crouching in front of it, that idea seems so silly. The boat is more rust than anything, and there's a pretty big hole eaten into the side.

As I'm staring at the boat, I hear the porch creaking behind me. He's there, probably watching me again, but when I throw the sheet back, he's disappeared.

I'm sure there are plenty of vegetables to pick. I see them, ripe and fat on their vines. Tomorrow, they'll be mush.

But forget it. I don't need to eat today. The only way I can think of getting back at him is by not making him anything to eat. He can go pick his own vegetables.

Besides, my stomach hurts, mostly because of him.

I asked him a simple question last night. It's not bad to want things to get better. Doesn't he want that?

Or is he scared of losing this? Losing me?

A couple days ago, he got the idea to try to fix the generator again. Almost as if having lights and AC would make this place so attractive to me that I'd want to stay. I know it's a lost cause, but I'm not going to burst his bubble. I'm also not going to go near him, since working on the generator always puts him in a bad mood. Since he's already in one, it can only get worse.

I make myself busy inside.

There is actually plenty to do. The window panes are absolutely atrocious, so covered in mud and dust that you can barely see out them. But E told me not to touch them, because there's nothing we should want to see out there when we are inside. Almost as if he wants to cocoon us more than we already are.

He didn't say anything about the floors, though. They are so covered in dirt, the wood planks are barely visible. The white linoleum floor of the kitchen is practically black. Our footprints track through the house. And lucky me, I found a bucket, a mop, and a little container of Murphy's Oil Soap in the closet of my room among Suzy's dresses and T-strap patent leather shoes.

Defiantly, I go outside. E must not have been listening for me, because he whirls around when I dip the bucket in the rain barrel to fetch the water. His eyes darken, and he gestures with his hands. *What do you think you're doing?*

I shrug innocently.

He grabs my arm, but I shake him loose.

"Willow," he whispers, making my insides somersault. I can't take it when he says my name like that, because he very rarely does. "We don't have enough water for you to play around."

I press my lips together. It's nonsense. At least I think. It rains a lot, or at least it did during the rainy season. But now we're in a different season, and okay, yes, the barrel has never been this empty.

I guess it wouldn't be wise to take chances. We're clearly stuck here.

Glaring at him, I pour the water back and go inside.

Into the muddy, mucky, might-as-well-be-outdoors indoors.

Not that it matters. No one is going to visit us.

I'll find something else to do.

I shove the soap and the mop in the bucket and carry it to the closet. I shove it back where it came from, atop the messy pile of shoes. As I'm doing that, the handle of the broom falls over, knocking some of the clothes off their little hangers.

I found the key to this closet a couple months ago in a kitchen drawer. It's full of things that once belonged to his little sister, which is why I avoid it whenever possible. I've done a good job of ignoring most of the traces of Suzy in this room, but now I can't. I reach down to pick them up, frowning at how tiny they all are. How delicate and soft and pink. The Suzy in my head used to look so cute in these. I sniff them. They even smell faintly of baby powder, and it's the nicest thing I've smelled in a long time.

As I'm reaching down to pick another up, I notice a shelf on the side of the closet that I hadn't seen before.

I stoop and pull out a little pink box. It's slightly bigger than a music box, with a tightly fitted lid with a picture of a fairy sitting on a rock.

No…it's an angel sitting on a cloud, with stars in her hair. Her eyes are closed like she's looking down on the world, and she's sprinkling golden dust over it.

I smile, thinking of Suzy, looking for angels. Wondering if this is what she thought about that very last moment, before E…

I catch myself mid shudder. Even though I've seen him use that bow and arrow, it's hard to imagine the E I know doing something like that…shooting his little sister…

Pushing the thought away, I get down to business. It's easy to pry off the lid. Inside, I find a bunch of newspaper-wrapped bundles. I take one, carefully unrolling it, because something about the way it's packaged tells me that its contents are fragile. When I finally get to the end, a little angel figure rests in my hand. It's dainty and porcelain and wearing a flower wreath, its arms open at its sides, as if for a hug.

I set it down and take out the next one, unwinding the paper with as much care as the last. I find another cherub, coddling a tiny white lamb.

As I unwrap each one, I set them up on the dresser like tiny angel soldiers.

There are ten in all, and each one draws a smile to my face.

When I unwrap the last one, I see it's lost its head. It isn't there, among the paper. It must've broken off before.

I place it next to the others anyway. But my smile fades as I think of the little girl who these figures belonged to. A family's littlest angel trying to murder an old lady while she slept by wrapping the chains from a swing around her neck.

Suzy lost her head too.

I take the figure down and am about to wrap it up when I hear the door open and close. A second later, E peeks in and peers at me, kneeling in front of the closet.

What are you doing? He doesn't seem angry. Just curious.

But then he sees the angels and his whole face changes. No anger. Instead, he's stricken, the wind squeezed from his lungs. His eyes darken with a memory. He slumps back against the doorjamb.

Then he whispers, "I'll help you clean the floor if you want."

Kneeling on the floor, I'm practically knee-high in dust bunnies. I shake my head. It doesn't really bother me anymore. Not enough to die of thirst.

He stares at me for the longest time.

Actually, no. That's wrong. He stares at the figures between us. The little angel army. His eyes practically burn holes in them until a fly buzzes in his ear and it rouses him from his stupor. Slapping it away, he nods and heads outside again.

I have no doubt he was thinking of Suzy, of how these were her little dolls. Maybe the only dolls she had, because I haven't seen others, and these seem rather well-loved, their faces and features faded from handling. Maybe she cried for ages when that one angel broke. Maybe he used to play make-believe games with her.

Whatever it is, I don't like the look on his face. I don't want to bring him more pain.

So I carefully take them, one by one, and rewrap them in the scraps of newspaper.

As I'm doing so, something catches my eye on the newspaper itself, which is yellowing. It's an ad for Meltz's Furniture Store, a place that, according to the radio ads, has "the best selection in all of Florida with seventeen locations to serve you" and where my parents got most of the furniture in our house. There's a picture of a dark-colored La-Z-Boy, the kind with the lever on the side that sends the footrest to the moon.

My father had one like that. He used to work so many hours at the lab that on Sundays, his only day off, he'd sleep in that thing all day, snoring so that the walls of the house shook. JT used to sleep right next to him.

JT, my Akita. Now he was a good dog. I had him trained to do just about everything for me. He could bark "Jingle Bells" on command. Sort of.

I don't know what brings me back, but I find myself staring at the price, $897, and wondering if that's a good deal.

Then I laugh at myself because if the world is as dead as E thinks, I could probably have 897 La-Z-Boys for free if I desired.

Then I scan to the date.

January 26 of this year.

I stare at it for the longest time.

I don't know what day it is, but the days are getting shorter and cooler. I know fall is coming, or maybe it's already here.

I stare and stare until the letters bleed together, exactly the way E stared at those angels, and I remember something he said. *It started a year ago. With the pandemic.*

Unfolding the newspaper, I press it flat on the ground. It's the lifestyle section, so there are recipes. Articles about taking care of one's pets. A gardening piece. A crossword.

Funny to think that people were still gardening and baking and doing crosswords when the world was crumbling around them. But I suppose people needed something to keep their minds off it.

Fingers working frantically, I start unwrapping all the newspapers, looking for one page in particular. I flip through the paper, blackening my already dirty fingers, searching for it.

On the second to last clump of newsprint, I find it. Section A. The front page.

There is a gaping hole where an article has been carefully clipped out. Huh. I wonder what that article was about. Whatever it was, it was a big story that took up several columns in the very middle of the front page.

196 | CYN BALOG

I scan for other headlines. The president's nominee for a new head of the Department of Homeland Security. A shooting in a mall in Fresno. A new push for universal health care. A major car accident on Route 4. Disney World's newest ride in EPCOT.

There is one article about the Ventex shortages. Sure enough, people were hoarding it. But good news—several pharmaceutical companies were banding together to produce more.

Maybe someone clipped out an article about the second plague, the one E said was getting out of hand, turning people into monsters. For what reason, I can only guess.

But that doesn't sit right with me. A story that massive wouldn't be mentioned in *one* story but dozens of them. *All* of them. The crumbling of society would have tentacles, worming their way into every facet of life and every page of the newspaper.

Flipping to pages two and three, I read faster, getting more and more frantic. I check the date again and again, sure I am missing something. How can this be?

No mention about the second plague.

It's almost as if it never happened at all.

TWENTY-SIX

I don't tell E what I'm thinking.

Not the next day at least. Instead, I keep turning questions over and over in my head.

I thought I must've been seeing things, so I went back and scoured the pages of the newspaper again.

Then I figured the second plague must've happened later. That was possible. But I distinctly remember my father sitting at Christmas dinner, telling us that I didn't have to worry about getting sick like my classmates. I even asked E what year it was to be sure about my timeline. He probably thought I was insane.

He's been looking at me like that a lot lately. The thing is, I haven't seen Suzy in ages. Or dead grannies. Or anything weird. BST-14D might turn people into monsters, but maybe I didn't have enough of it. Maybe we both got it out of our systems in time.

It's been three days, and E stays in his bedroom at night. He works on the generator or up on the roof, repairing the lost shingles and the rusted gutters. I get the feeling that he never did any of that stuff before. Surely the generator would've been fixed by now if he had. Maybe his father handled all the repairs around the house. Or maybe he's dragging out the repairs because he doesn't want to be in my company.

I don't need more reasons to be suspicious of him. I don't want to be. I am sure there is a reasonable explanation; I'm simply not thinking of it. I can't ask him or it'd make him angrier.

So instead, I sit up at night and think. Why would a national crisis that brought an end to the world not be mentioned in Florida's largest newspaper?

I was in a car accident, obviously, and I hit my head. Maybe everything got muddled in my brain, and my memories aren't real.

Maybe the BST has melted my brain, and I'm so far gone that I don't even realize how crazy I am.

The thought scares the hell out of me. Maybe everything I consider to be true, to be real, is not. Maybe nothing is. Maybe my parents weren't dead in that car. Maybe there is no August or JT or *me*. Maybe I am a stranger, even to myself.

The sun comes up after I've driven myself mad with thoughts like those.

We have no vegetables in the house, so I go out to the garden and pick some. I grab the wood-slatted bucket from the countertop and head out, not pausing to wonder where E is. The sun's barely up, but he's usually up before me. He's around somewhere. If I beat him to the side of the house, we don't have to work there together.

I don't think I can be that close to him and not ask the question.

As much as I want to know… The truth is I'm scared to death of the answer.

When I'm done picking the veggies, I head inside. The room across from the nursery is making the same, familiar banging sound. Shadows play in the strip of light underneath the door. *Just the wind.*

I remember how silly I was in those early days, thinking it was zombies.

Now, it doesn't feel quite so funny. Because I still don't know for sure what is making that noise. I've taken everything E says as gospel…but why? He's keeping me alive, the only other person here, my lifeline…but he's still a stranger.

I'd tried to peer through the window from the outside, but it's over the generator and too high up to reach without a ladder. It's cracked open just a sliver, with a white shade pulled down tight, like most windows in the house, so the sound *could* be the wind.

But it also could be one of many, many *other* things. Things he doesn't want me to see.

Gathering my resolve, I reach for the knob and twist it, not entirely surprised when it doesn't budge. I shake it a little. That's no help.

Wandering back to the kitchen, still cradling the basket of veggies to my chest, I think about what he told me. *It doesn't work.*

It smells. I suppose that's a reason to keep the door locked. And the door upstairs?

If the rooms are locked, they have keys. He's opened them before, so he knows where those keys are.

They must be nearby.

My eyes drift toward his room.

There.

In the kitchen, I peer through the window over the sink. I can see him heading toward the far end of the property with a coil of chicken wire. Still making that fence.

That'll keep him busy and out of my hair for a while.

I slap the basket of veggies on the table, pop a tomato into my mouth, and head for his room.

All this time, and I've never crossed the threshold into his bedroom. It's not that I felt unwanted exactly, but he's always tensed when I appeared in the doorway. I figured it was because his religious parents told him not to have girls in his room, so I respected that.

He's never actually closed the door. It's always partly open, like an invitation. I've been curious about him, except snooping in a person's room seemed wrong.

But that seed of doubt has been planted, and I won't be able to sleep at night unless I nurture it, like the vegetables outside.

What I notice first when I hover in the entrance are the things I'd seen before. The unused drum set, the bookshelf lined with textbooks, the neatly made bed. The longer I stand there, the more I see. Brown blood still dots the sheets near the head-board. Despite having lost his faith, a worn old Bible sits on the bottom shelf of his bookcase. Even though this has been his bedroom, likely since he was a child, it has an impersonal feel to it, like it's been used but never really lived in. I used to keep jewelry and knickknacks and all sorts of mementos on my dresser, but the surface of his is clear. I used to put posters on my walls, but he has none on his.

I'd say he didn't want anyone to know the real him, but who is *anyone*? No one had the chance. *I'm* the only one from the outside who has been here.

Maybe he simply likes his space clean and uncluttered.

That seems to be the case when I open the top drawer of his dresser. The clothes are neatly folded into little squares. Boxer shorts and T-shirts. He has rolls and rolls of white tube socks that I've never seen him wear. They're so bleachy white I wonder if he wore them before.

I quickly close the drawer, feeling like a voyeur, but then I open the next one. It's more of the same—neat, nerdy-looking polo shirts and khaki pants he's never worn around me. It doesn't fit the person he is now, with the piercing and tattoo. All he wears is a rotation of two holey T-shirts and dirty jeans. But I guess he doesn't have anyone to impress; plus, we're saving water, and doing laundry without a washing machine isn't exactly a joyride.

Behind the door, I notice a closet with accordion doors. I never saw it before. I pull the knob and the first thing I see is a black suit. I pull it out and try to imagine E dressed in it, but I can't. Besides, it's clearly several sizes too small. Other than that, there are more clothes and several pairs of shoes I've also never seen him wear.

As much as I try to imagine an E before this, all I see is that awkward boy in the photo in the living room. It's a huge jump to the ragged E who's working on our fence, almost as if they're two different people. My mind can't compute.

I want to know him. Just as much as I wanted to know August. Probably more. August would freely offer details about himself. E? Not so much. It's definitely like pulling teeth.

Here I am, about to pry open his box of secrets.

I look up at the top shelf of the closet. There's a pile of shoe-boxes stacked neatly in a pyramid. I stand on my tiptoes and try to swipe down the top one, but I can't quite reach, and if I grab any of the lower boxes, I'll likely cause an avalanche on my head, which will bring E running.

So I close the door, just as I found it, and turn to the bed.

He has almost the exact same night table beside his bed that's next to the little bed in the nursery—honey-stained, with a clear glass–beaded pull. I bet they were part of a bedroom set once.

The back of my neck prickles. If he's hiding a key, it's there.

I sit on his mattress, then slide the drawer open.

The first thing I see is a small, folded piece of paper printed with the words *Istruzioni per l'uso*. I pull it out. It has a number of languages on it, none of which appear to be English. There are no diagrams or pictures, so I can only guess what it's for. I set it on top of the nightstand. There's a wire-bound notebook, a couple of pennies, a small pocket Bible, and a pencil.

Then I pull out a photograph. It's Elijah and his sister, but this one isn't posed. They're probably a bit older than in that other picture, and they're sitting together on that metal boat, holding fishing poles. Suzy's looking at the camera, mouth open in a laugh, but E's looking at her with amusement, pride, and love, like, *You really think you're so cute you can get away with anything, don't you?*

From the look on his face, the answer is yes. He'd have done anything for her.

I'm busy staring at the photograph, trying not to think of how horrible her last moments had been for the two of them, when there's a sweeping sound out in the hallway that I know well.

The screen door closing.

Then a creak and a shift of the floorboards.

I throw the drawer's contents back inside, close it, and rocket to standing as E appears in the doorway.

His eyes first hold a question. A second later, it's accusation. *What are you doing?*

That tells me all I need to know. He left the door open, but it wasn't an invitation.

I shrug lightly and run a hand over the night table. *Just thought it was getting dusty in here.*

I walk to the doorway, intending to sweep past him into the

living room, but he stays stiff, blocking my path. His eyes drill into me.

Eventually, he moves.

I go into the kitchen, and he follows. *Want something to eat?*

My attempt to change the subject fails. He places both hands on the counter, fingernails black with dirt. *What were you doing in my room?*

I smile, but I feel it cracking on my face. So fake. *I told you—*

None of that bullshit about dusting. What were you doing?

I swallow. I've hurt him. Betrayed his trust. All he's ever done was try to keep me alive. If he wanted me dead, he could've killed me a million times by now. There's probably a simple explanation for those newspapers. I just need to talk to him.

I clear my throat and point to my bedroom. When he doesn't say anything, I go and retrieve the newspapers. I lay them out on the counter, smoothing them with my hand.

At first, he shrugs. *So what?*

Where are the articles about the second plague? The end of the world? Why is—

He holds up a palm. His face is turning red underneath his tan. I think I've caught him in a lie when he mouths the word *Stop*. He's not looking at me. This has all been a lie.

So I press on. *No, there's something wrong here, and I need you to—*

"You're serious?" He says this aloud, his voice so jarring and cold that it makes me shiver. He locks his eyes on mine again, my certainty draining away. "You don't remember the cover-up?"

Cover-up? I shake my head. How can he ask me that? He knows I don't remember anything.

He grabs the paper and crumbles it in a ball. "Yeah. There was a cover-up. The media couldn't report on it until it was too late. Then everyone was calling it fake news, and nobody knew what was true and what wasn't. By the time people realized we were in trouble, we were in *trouble*."

Oh. That made sense. My father used to tell me to be careful on social media because there was so much misinformation. "They'll go through a lot to make you believe something that isn't even real."

Now I feel stupid. Not because I asked the question, because it's a good one, but because of the way he's looking at me.

You really don't trust me, do you? he mouths.

I do, I mouth back. *I was exploring. Sorry. If you don't want me in there, just tell—*

"I don't." He turns and strides toward his room, shutting the door behind him.

Leaving me to wonder, more than ever, what the hell he is hiding.

TWENTY-SEVEN

Two days later, I find out.

There's been a tenuous peace between us. I follow the rules, which means I don't go exploring, even though I desperately want to. I pretend everything is fine, which I'm good at.

But deep inside, I know something is wrong. I want to ignore that feeling. I want everything E is telling me to be the truth, because I've come to accept it.

I can't. It's eating at me. Curiosity killed the cat, and it will probably do the same to me.

Because whatever he is not telling me is too terrible to share, and I don't think I can survive any more terrible news.

That morning starts out like most mornings before that. I wake up, wrapped in his arms. Days ago, I thought he was there because he cared about me. Now I wonder if he's trying to keep me.

I disentangle myself from his arms and go outside to wash up. A little while later, he follows, lugging more chicken wire from the shed to fix the fence.

There was a hard rain last night, really hard, pounding and thrumming so relentlessly, I thought for sure it would never end. The wind slammed against the side of the house, making the windows rattle, supports moan under the strain. Lightning flashed in the sky nonstop, and the thunder was so loud, E wasn't the only one covering his ears.

Hurricane? Maybe. It's not like we have the Weather Channel to consult. I've lived through plenty of hurricanes, and I have to say, not having the weathermen warning you to be on alert and evacuate makes it somewhat less frightening. Or maybe I've been through so much that the weather is the least of my worries.

Anyway, the ground is mushy and waterlogged, squishing underfoot.

When I go to the garden, I sigh.

My proud little patch of earth is in virtual ruins. The stalks and sprouts are flattened against the ground, and ripe and unripe tomatoes and other vegetables are squashed and bruised in the mud. After everything I've put into it, and because it's one of the few things I care about now, tears fall from my eyes.

I retreat to the porch steps to mope. I've been saving seeds from the different vegetables, but I don't have much left from the original packages. I was hoping to stretch them for longer, to gather new seeds.

Then I get an idea. I go back to the garden. Most of the plants aren't destroyed; they're simply damaged. I saw some twine in the shed once. E usually keeps that door closed, but he opened it to get the chicken wire. I don't think it's off-limits. Maybe I can find some sticks and twine so I can prop up the plants and keep them upright so the vegetables can continue to grow. After all, they feed us both.

It's worth a shot. I push off the porch steps and tromp through the shin-high, still wet grass. The sun is already pretty hot. When I get to the shed, I peek inside, wondering if E will be upset with me.

But there's nothing to hide. An old lawn mower. A broken rake and rusted shovel. Gasoline cans. Burlap sacks and tarps and fishing nets and poles. A kid-size basketball hoop. An old coil of jump rope and some broken nubs of pastel sidewalk chalk that likely belonged to Suzy. A bunch of old plastic pretzel containers storing various odds and ends, like rusted nails and pennies.

The smell of fertilizer and gasoline in the stuffy, close space is dizzying. I scan for the ball of twine. Grabbing it from the shelves, I notice an old coffee can full of sticks. They might be too small, but then again, they could work perfectly. When I pull one out to look, I wind up knocking over the can. The sticks spill onto the ground, along with something that rolls in a circle, like a tiny wheel, before falling on its side at my feet.

I pick it up and stare at it for the longest time before I recognize what it is. I tilt my head to be sure, reading the words embossed on the side in white: BRIGGS & STRATTON, MILWAUKEE, WISCONSIN, USA.

Briggs & Stratton.

That's the brand of the generator. I know that because I've looked at that ugly hunk of junk long enough to burn each piece into my memory. This little black cap is *exactly* the size of the piece E said we were missing.

Sticks and twine forgotten, I nearly trip over my own feet running out of the shed. The grass around the property is taller than I am, but I head in E's general direction because he's flattened the duckweed on his walk. I follow it, half skipping with excitement, holding the part so tight it makes an indentation on my palm.

I burst out at the edge of the property. E turns, hands raised in fists, rigid and defensive.

Before he can relax, I grab his hand and press the piece into it. I grin.

He stares at it, unsmiling. His eyes flash up to meet mine. *Where did you get this?*

I answer, *The shed*, only cringing a little at his reaction. Before he can ask the inevitable question, I add, *I was looking for sticks and twine to hold up my plants. They're all flattened.*

No smile. And here I thought he'd be so happy.

Instead, he closes his fist around the piece and tromps back toward the house. I get it, he's pragmatic. No reason to celebrate until the generator works. But it sure is better than the Coca-Cola cap. I follow behind him, excitement growing, as he grabs a bucket and situates it in front of the old generator. Sitting on it, he takes the metal piece and affixes it carefully. Then he removes his wrench from his pocket and tightens the bolt, one, two, three times.

Nothing happens at first. Then he reaches to the side and flips a switch, and suddenly, the thing sputters a little. It's never done that before.

"Is it working?" I ask aloud since he's not looking at me. I step closer, but he nudges me away as the machine keeps sputtering. Maybe he thinks it's going to explode. It's making a *puh...puh... puh...*noise, like the little engine that could. Maybe it *will* explode.

Then it starts to crank, the motor inside running, not quietly but evenly at least. I hear that familiar humming I remember from the good ol' days, when we had some semblance of air-conditioning.

Oh yes. It's working.

Before he can do anything, I run inside, accidentally letting the screen door slam in my excitement. I try the light switch by the door. Dim light fills the space. *It works. It works. IT WORKS!*

I'm about to do a happy dance when the electricity goes off again. The humming dissipates. The only sound is the twittering of birds and the thrumming of bullfrogs.

Yeah, well, I guess it was too much to hope we could have AC. Light. Access to the two-way radio, the outside world.

I walk onto the porch as he's coming in. *Broke again?*

He shakes his head. *It works. But we shouldn't waste gas.*

He stalks inside, leaving me alone to wonder: *What exactly is there to save it for?*

TWENTY-EIGHT

I used to mutter under my breath when I didn't get my way.

Now that's our normal way of talking. Mutter, mutter, mutter, like everything in the world is wrong.

I mutter so much, so loudly, that it drowns all other sound in my head.

Why wouldn't he want to keep the generator going? Why does he want to live in absolute filth?

I know the answer. He's *used* to living like this. He doesn't adapt well to change, which is why me being in his life was almost the end of his world. He's gotten the situation back to where it makes sense to him. He doesn't want to upend that again.

But I don't care.

After the great discovery, he grabbed a handful of tomatoes from yesterday—probably the last ones we'll get for a while, since the rest are mush at the bottom of my garden—and, popping them into his mouth in a leisurely way, sidled out to the fence again. Like nothing happened.

It's almost enough to make me think he hid that generator piece on purpose.

No. I'm not going there. No sane person would want to live like this.

No *sane* person...

I sit on the steps, too depressed to even think about my garden when all I can do is picture AC blowing on my face, the glow of a light bulb, the goddamn *I copy* that we wrangle out of that radio...

It's almost too much to bear.

But maybe that's it. His world is so small. Controlled. He is the master of this domain. *We* are the masters because he let me in. He doesn't want to lose those comforts again. Maybe he thinks he will lose *me* if we have access to the radio. I'm sure he can't understand why I would want to give up this life. What could be better in a ruined world than being here with him in our very own kingdom?

He doesn't know, though.

He's scared. He doesn't realize how amazing it would be to find others. To be part of a larger group. Maybe we could rebuild the world, join—create?—a community...have a future. He thinks reliving the same day is a future, but I think we will never get back anything that we lost if we stay.

Looking over at the ruined garden, I *know* it. It's scary as hell that one storm means we might not have anything to eat for a week unless he can kill a bird or catch some fish.

We're balancing on a knife's edge, that close to dying.

I don't want that. I can't live like that.

In the silence of the morning, I drag in a breath of humid air, let it out, and rise to my feet. Then I march over to E. He's in the marsh, up to his knees in brown water, carefully unrolling the chicken wire around some posts that must've made a fence years ago.

I don't like the look of that water—there could be alligators among those reeds—so I stay on the bank, mud oozing between my toes like some nightmare. "We should try to use the radio," I say. It's a whisper but louder than anything for miles.

He has to hear me.

And yet he doesn't look up. He doesn't acknowledge my presence.

I try again. "E. We should use the radio."

Again, he says nothing.

Fine. I'll do it myself.

He whips around to face me, his hair falling in his eyes. "No."

It's almost like he's read my mind. I cross my arms and jut out my hip. "Why not?"

He goes back to his work, and at first, I think he's going to ignore me.

When I start to speak again, he says over me, "It isn't safe."

"Why? It is. We can—"

"If anyone's out there, they might try to come here. We could be overrun."

I stand there, feet sinking into the mud, the hem of my strawberry dress hanging into the dank water so that it'll likely smell like brine and dead things later. I'd never thought of that. Yes, it's a risk, but what makes him think anyone would consider this a refuge? We may be cut off from danger, but we're starving. Anyone who is stupid enough to overrun us would die with us. "Okay, but—but it might not be so bad. And if it is, we can escape."

He's silent.

"I know it's scary. I know it'll be different for you. But we'll be together. Always. I promise. I—you're everything to me."

He doesn't say a word, but the muscles in his jaw tense. For a moment, I think he may be softening.

I try to make my way over to him, to lay a hand on his arm and show him I care. That I won't leave him. But all I manage is an awkward shuffle. "Just think, if—"

"*No!*" he says with such finality, the earth beneath my feet shakes. That's his equivalent of yelling.

"Fine," I mutter, turning and stomping to the house.

He knows I like to make peace. All he has to do is say no, and I'll do as he says. But I know how he operates too. If I ignore him, if I stay away from him long enough and scowl when he comes near me, he'll give in.

I hope.

My hope lasts for most of the day. I spend that time in my room with the door shut tight so he knows not to bother me.

When I do come out, I ignore him. Pretend there's nothing but air where he stands.

I can tell it bothers him because he's usually so ninja-like, but when he's annoyed at me, he starts to make more noise than usual. His footsteps are louder, his breathing sharper, his movements less fluid.

I must fall asleep, because it's morning by the time he throws open the door to my room. I'm lying on my side in bed, staring up at half a moon that's pasted against a rapidly lightening sky.

He whispers five words.

"All right. Let's do it."

TWENTY-NINE

That morning routine, the one I've gotten so used to?

It's forgotten.

I don't bother to wash up or go to the outhouse. It can wait. The second he speaks those five magic words, I'm up like a jack-in-the-box, following him out to the main area of the house. His routine is disrupted too. It's almost as if he hasn't slept at all, up all night, mulling over my request.

That's him. It takes a while for anything different to settle in his brain and make sense. He smells like stale cigarettes. He must've wasted a few of his precious stash making the decision. Sure enough, there are new butts in the ashtrays.

Head down, like he's marching to his own funeral, he goes outside. A moment later, there's that caustic sputtering, as if the house is trying to cough up a bit of food that's gone down the wrong pipe. Then the walls start to vibrate, almost dangerously, before settling into that low, comforting hum.

He reappears, shoulders still slumped. His dark eyes don't

meet mine as he walks softly past me down the hall to the radio. He stands there for a few beats, staring at it.

Then he pulls out the chair tucked against the table, slides into it, and takes a deep breath.

He puts on the radio headset and twists the dial, listening. I hear nothing, but he must, because he keeps twisting the different dials. He told me this radio belonged to his father, and he had never been allowed to touch it, but even if he never laid a finger on the dials before, it looks like he knows what to do now. I'm sure after his parents died, he spent many hours listening to this radio for news from the outside world.

He presses the button on the base of the receiver and says, "Hey. Anyone got their ears on?" His voice is odd. He pauses. "Anyone there?" His expression doesn't change. He twists the dials and tries again. "Anyone there?"

I can't hear anything except a little residual static from the headset. All the while, his mouth is a straight line. I don't know what his expression would be if someone did answer. I don't know if he'd register surprise, because he's never been surprised, not once since I've met him. I get the feeling he wouldn't be happy, since anyone answering that radio would mean change, and change scares him.

After about ten minutes with my heart in my throat, my feet rooted to the braided rug, I start to wander around the living room.

He keeps going. "Anyone there? Anyone there?" After a half

hour of trying, he takes off the headset and twists the dial all the way to the right. I expect him to say, *See, I told you*, but he doesn't gloat. He simply says, "Nothing."

Nothing is such a depressing word. Is there no one out there at all? The world has faced crises before, maybe not an extinction-level event, but I always thought that our Earth was stronger than this. That it'd fight longer. I used to love television shows with end-of-the-world scenarios. There was always a group of people trying to eke out a new living in a changed world. Where are those people?

Maybe they've given up too.

"I'll try again later," he mutters.

He's giving up so soon. I want to try right now. Keep trying. Keep the hope alive at least.

"Can we leave it on? In case someone calls us?"

He shakes his head. He's right. If anyone is out there, they are probably as hopeless as we are. Wasting the precious fuel in the precious generator just so I can have a little hope? It's selfish.

"It might be too early," I admit. "Maybe we can try in an hour."

He stands. "Tonight. I'll try tonight."

Tonight. The hours of the day stretch, long and bloated, in front of me, an eternity of hopelessness.

Then he goes outside. A few seconds later, the walls stop humming. Silence settles around me, absolutely still, like the dead lying in their graves outside.

After that, E goes on with his usual routine. But I don't. I keep thinking of that radio, tucked in the corner. I keep thinking of random people across the world, sitting at their desks for their daily attempt at making contact and getting nothing but static in return. It's like searching for an outlet in the dark—you keep trying, hoping you'll hit the right spot in the wall.

The more times you try, the closer you get.

If you give up? You get nothing.

I try to keep busy, going to the garden and collecting food, but there's so little. Most of it is ruined, and the vines are entangled, shriveling in the sun. It only makes me more uneasy, more certain that we will not last here much longer.

I fill my stomach with carrots and radishes and a few bruised tomatoes, then pick the rest of the good vegetables for E. As I do, I keep looking at the generator.

It becomes a bit of an obsession. I can do nothing but stare and see all the possibility...

Before I know it, I have my hand on the switch. I watched E do it, so I know to crank the handle several times before flipping the switch.

I look over my shoulder.

E is gone, working somewhere in the marsh. I don't hear him, but I can see the tops of the tall grass swaying from his movements. I probably have time to start it up, make a call, and turn it off. Just once. Just for a few minutes.

As I concentrate on the handle, sweat trickles down my nose. I swipe it away and take a deep breath.

The handle is harder to pull than I thought, but when I wrench it toward me, it makes a zipping sound, like someone starting a lawn mower.

I stiffen. Am I really doing this? Yes. I have to. E doesn't understand. It's the middle of the day, and if I connect with someone, he will be so glad, he'll forget to be angry at me.

I hope.

Pulling again, I let out an uneasy breath. Another zip, louder this time. That sounds right. It's the noise the generator made with E.

Again, I pull. The sound gets louder. My fingers glide over the red switch. Do I push it now? Do I need to keep cranking? Why can I not remember how many times E cranked before he flipped the switch?

A fly buzzes near my hair and distracts me. Before I can reach the switch, a hand comes out of nowhere and grabs my wrist.

I gasp. E.

He demands with his eyes, *What do you think you're doing?*

"I'm…I want to check the radio."

He pushes against me, trying to get me to move aside so he can have at the generator. But I'm not giving up. He reaches for my other arm to pin me back, but I squirm away, scuffling with him, each of us groping for purchase in the small space.

"I told you—"

"I want to try again."

"*No*," he bites out, much louder than I thought I'd hear from him. It's almost a subhuman growl. Fear ripples through my body, and I'm not sure what happens, but while I'm leaning back against it, I must knock something, because the generator starts making a strange noise. It vibrates a little, the nails that attach it to its wooden pallet platform rattling. It's like a pressure cooker getting ready to blow.

He breaks his gaze from mine, and those black eyes fasten on the machinery.

Maybe it was not a good idea to try to start that thing on my own. I try to skirt away from it, except his hand is still clamped on my wrist.

I try to pry his fingers off. "Let me go," I choke out, finally slipping out of his grasp.

Suddenly a loud, crackling zap emits from the generator, and black smoke rises into the air.

E, hand still on the switch, stands there, his body trembling. At first, I think he is listening, that he might hear another one of *them* in the distance. Then I crane my neck to look at his face.

His eyes are rolling into the back of his head.

He's not scared. His hand is on the crank and his veins are bulging, wickedly blue, all the way up his arm. His mouth is slack and there is a thin line of drool dripping from his chin. His hair lifts and I can smell something burning.

His body isn't trembling.

It's convulsing with electric shock.

"Oh my God!" I don't know what to do. He's fixed to that machine, the machine I started, and he's being pumped with electric voltage that's going to kill him.

I'm going to kill him.

And I'll be here. Alone.

I scan the ground. The hoe from my garden. Grabbing it, I swing the wooden handle toward his hand, knocking it away from the generator.

He stands there for a moment, no longer convulsing, free of the current.

Then his knees buckle and give out. He slumps to the ground.

I stare at him. Actually, his chest. I watch it carefully, holding my breath, waiting.

But it's not moving. Not at all.

Oh God. He's not breathing.

THIRTY

I stand there, still as a statue.

The only thing that moves is my hair, rustling in the breeze, and a few insects, buzzing in the air.

The only sounds are my heart beating out the word *alone, alone, alone* in my ears, the birds chirping obliviously above, and a hum.

The hum of the generator I tried to turn on, because I'm stupidly selfish.

This is all your fault, Willow. E is dead. You are alone in this world and will be for the rest of your life because of this.

The first steps I take are at a slow creep, because I'm afraid. But then a voice says, *Hurry! You're wasting time. He might still be alive if you hurry!* I throw myself down beside him.

He's lying on his side, his body blackened and yet pale, his hair smoking. A sweet smell fills the air. I touch him, sure I'm going to be shocked, but I feel nothing. His skin is still warm. I angle his limp frame toward me and look at his face, eyes closed as if he's asleep. His chest isn't moving.

He's dead. And I am the one who killed him.

No. He can be revived. Right? He needs someone to start his heart.

I lie him flat on his back. Placing my hands over the center of his chest, I begin compressions.

I do not know how to do chest compressions. I know there is supposed to be a rhythm, but damned if I can remember what it is. "Staying Alive"? I think I saw that while bingeing episodes of *The Office*, and that's probably not where I should get my first aid advice. I did take a babysitting class that taught CPR when I was eleven, but that feels like ages ago.

My efforts are half-hearted, clumsy. I bend over him, pinch his nose, tilt his head back, and breathe into his mouth.

Nothing.

I do this, again and again and again. It's not good enough. I'm selfish and a failure.

After a while, I entwine my fingers with his. His hand, which was once warmer than mine, is now cold.

Maybe he's gone to his sister. Maybe now they are up there, laughing at me.

I tilt my head to the sky and let out a quiet sob.

This is the way the world ends, right? With a big whimper.

In the quiet, I hear something.

It takes me a moment to recognize what it is. Even though the generator is behaving very, very wrongly, it's actually still working. Humming, alive. There is electricity inside the house.

I can tell because I must've accidentally flipped a switch in the hallway, and the dull light is pouring onto the porch.

Electricity.

I nudge his body off mine and race into the house. Funny how easy things used to be, how I took for granted that I could call 911 and help would come. Now, there is no help to call. I am alone.

Destined to be that way forever if I don't figure out what to do.

I rush to the radio and switch it on. Slamming the headset over my ears, I twist the dials. Static. "Hello? Hello?" I keep shouting until I realize I have to press the button on the intercom. I jab at it. "Hello? Anyone."

Twist and try again. Twist and try again.

Nothing.

Oh God.

I let out a shuddery breath, and for the first time, I think about the gun. I think about pushing a chair to the pantry, stepping up, nudging aside the tea, and taking it in my hand.

E had been faced with the same choice. He hadn't been able to do it.

What makes me think I'm any different from him? I've been here so long, this place has become a part of me. I am more like him than I would admit.

Where I'm sitting, I'm facing the stairs. I don't know what I expect to find up there, but I break from the chair so fast that it topples. I run up them, taking them two at a time. They creak under my weight, something they never did under E's, and he's so much heavier than me. Maybe because I'm running, trying to get away from the gun in the kitchen or the idea of the gun, which is suddenly calling me loudly.

I try the door, jiggling the black iron handle.

Locked.

Of course.

It's one of those old doors, with a keyhole. I stoop down and peer through it. I see a sky-blue wall.

I look again.

Eyes.

There are eyes, wide, curious, unblinking, staring back at me.

I hitch out a breath and pull away.

There can't be someone here. That's ridiculous. There's no one else in this house. It's impossible. It's too small, and it's so quiet that I hear every little mouse step on the floorboards at night. I'd have known. *I'm going crazy again. From the stress.*

Willing my brain to behave, I inch closer to the door. It takes everything inside me to dip my head and press my cheek and eyelashes against the metal door plate. Inhaling sharply, I look again.

Gone.

Of course.

Just my imagination.

No, wait. I shift a little, and I see those wide eyes, trained on me.

It's a clown doll. No...a Harlequin. A giant one, in that black-and-white silk outfit, its long arms and legs sprawled over a wicker chair. It has the palest of porcelain skin. Through the black mask, its bead eyes are pinned on me.

I shudder. Was that his mother's? How weird. I've seen *Poltergeist*. I'd never be able to sleep at night with that thing staring at me.

As creepy as it is, it's a relief. Just a doll. Maybe I am not going insane.

But as I pull away, the hint of a shadow sweeps past the keyhole.

THIRTY-ONE

No. This isn't real. There is not someone living in this house with us. I've been here for months. Alone with him. Living and eating and sleeping. I would know if there was another person living in the house with us.

It's a hell of a time for my hallucinations to come back. But that's got to be what this is.

My voice pricks the air like static electricity. "Is someone there?" I whisper, my voice hoarse. "Hello?"

No answer.

"Please." I jiggle the door handle. "If there's someone in there, please open the door. There's been an accident and he—he's hurt. I think he might be dead. I need help."

Nothing.

"*Please.*" My voice cracks.

But there is only silence. I think about shaking the door harder, but I can't bring myself to do it. Maybe I don't want to know what is beyond that door. I'm scared to death. Because whatever it is, E was hiding it from me.

To protect me, of course.

There's no other option. Any other reason is too horrible to think about.

Tears slide down my cheeks. I wipe them away and go back down the stairs.

What I need is first aid. Is there a first aid kit anywhere? No, of course not. I've looked through every cabinet and drawer in the kitchen. By the time I get to the bottom of the staircase, I'm running. I go to the kitchen and start throwing open every drawer and cabinet anyway, spilling their contents—silverware, cooking utensils, oven mitts, pens and pencils and assorted junk. Not that a first aid kid will help.

It's been too long. He's dead.

"Shut up," I tell myself aloud. I'm not giving up. I repeat those words to myself again and again as I sift through kitchen tools. When I've made a mess in the kitchen, it occurs to me.

Where did my mother keep our first aid kit? Under the sink. In the bathroom.

I go to the door. Jiggle the handle. Nothing. What is that saying? Insanity is doing the same thing and expecting different results?

I shove against it. Bang on it. Throw my full weight against it.

Almost as if it heard me, that slow, rhythmic beating begins.

I stare at the door, backing away.

No.

This is insane.

I am insane.

"Hello?" I call out, my voice barely a breath. "Is someone in there?"

Nothing.

Again, insanity. *There is no one in this house with you, Low. And E will be dead if you don't get it together.*

Key. I need the key.

I do an about-face and race for his room. I know what he said about me being here, but he doesn't have that luxury now. I open drawers in his tall chest, pulling out clothes, looking for any damn bit of brass.

He'll be upset I went through his things, and if he does yell at me, I swear it'll be the sweetest sound I've ever heard. I'll thank God for it.

Because I can't be here alone.

I slip across his bed and go through the night table. Nothing new.

Then I slip to my knees and peer under the bed. My bed was a receptacle for all sorts of shit. I never cleaned under it. So not very long ago, I found a long-forgotten stuffed bunny named Boo that I thought I'd lost when I was four years old. It was covered in dust and looked as if it'd been chewed by JT.

E is extremely neat. My eyes narrow in on the only thing under the bed—a shoebox. Funny for a guy who never wears shoes.

I pull it close to me. It's some kind of Converse knockoff, a picture of the shoe on the side. I pull it open and there it is.

The key. It's brass, the handle rusted, with a tiny heart on the end. Too cute and magical for a house this awful.

Saying a little prayer of thanks—because something has actually gone right for me—I rush into the hallway and to the door. I turn the key in the lock, heart in my throat, thinking it'll be just my luck if it doesn't work. But it does. I hear the mechanism giving way, the lock disengaging, and then, for the first time, when I put my hand on the knob, it actually twists.

I start to push it open very gradually, not breathing at all. I'm finally going to see what is inside.

I catch the bubble-gum pink of old tile and a sliver of rusted mirror. No zombies, like I originally thought. Not a wild animal. Not Granny either. Rather, it's the ordinary things of an outdated bathroom.

I start to inspect the rest. Wide-open window, as Elijah promised. Toilet. Bathtub, not the clawfoot kind but the kind that's surrounded by walls. Sink with a rusted drain, similar to the one in the kitchen. Horrid flowered wallpaper, shimmering with gold. The same pervasive stench of mold that seems to settle over everything in this house.

In the reflection of the mirror, I notice a clear shower curtain, the unadorned *Psycho* kind. The type that serial killers use to wrap their victims on crime shows. A shower. I haven't seen one of those in forever. Sometimes I'd stand outside in the rain and think of how I used to sing in my shower at home under the rain spout, the water so hot that it turned my skin red, and the steam cast a dreamy haze over everything, like living in a cloud...

I'm jolted from the memory when something judders forward in the mirror, heading toward me at breakneck speed. Something big and black and...

Strong, because when it slams the door closed with a crash, it shoves me back with it so hard I stagger backward, nearly propelled to the toddler bed across the hall.

All I can do is stare. Shadows sway underneath the door.

This time, I know it is definitely not the wind.

And then the steady beat begins again, shaking the very walls around me. The sound is so loud I have to cup my ears.

THIRTY-TWO

It has been too long.

I know it has been.

E is gone. I'm sure of it.

Sounds are getting louder. Does that mean I'm getting sick?

Either I am hallucinating and am really getting sick, or someone else is here.

Whoever this someone else is, I don't want to see him as much as he doesn't want to see me.

I swallow an apple-sized lump in my throat as dread settles over me. There is so much I don't want to do alone. So much. Almost all of it.

Or…am I alone? I don't know anymore. What slammed the door on me? Will I hallucinate some friends so I won't even know I'm alone? Maybe E is a hallucination himself.

Gathering every bit of courage inside me, I walk to the window above the kitchen sink, overlooking the generator. Bracing myself, I peer out at the place where E fell. Eventually,

I will have to bury him. I will have to dig a grave and put him in there, like we tried to bury that man so long ago. But this time, I will be doing it alone.

I press my hands against the windowsill and my forehead against the screen, trying to see the space where he fell. But the screen is too dirty and the massive carcass of a generator is in the way. All I can see is the tall patch of grass where he fell. It's black, singed from the incident.

Maybe it's good that I can't see him. Maybe that's why I need to bury him, and fast—so I don't see his face, reminding me that I am the one who killed him.

I slide out of the kitchen, and I slink down into the chair by the radio. Time stretches out like an endlessly spiraling path, headed nowhere but downward.

The radio's still on. I put on the headset and listen. White noise. I used to have a machine like that, to calm my head at night so I could sleep.

Maybe I can take this to bed with me tonight. When I sleep. Alone.

How can I sleep in this house alone?

I peer at the bathroom door.

Do you really think you're alone?

I don't know. As I'm tapping my fingers on the table in frantic rhythm, getting sick of static, I look to the left, at the side of the radio nearest the wall, partly covered by some dusty blue damask curtains. There are two wires snaking from underneath the table through the hideous fabric. One is attached to the input in the radio, which makes sense.

The other…is not.

Had E noticed that?

Slipping my hand in the narrow opening, I grab ahold of the wire and feel for the opening with my fingertip. When I've found it, I plug the cord in place.

My fingertips prickle with electricity. My spine straightens. I take a deep breath, depress the button on the receiver, and say, "Hello."

Nothing.

Well, all that buildup. Of course there would be a big letdown.

I twist the dial, and suddenly, there is a high-pitched, whirring of changing frequencies.

And then I hear something E and I haven't heard in over half a year.

Another voice.

At first, I can't make out the words the man's saying. He's speaking slowly, in a monotone voice. "So went Satan forth from the presence of the Lord and smote Job with sore boils from the sole of his foot unto his crown. And he took him a potsherd to scrape himself withal; and he sat down among the ashes."

Someone is reading from the Bible. Is it a recording? A real person?

I depress the button again. "Hello?"

"Then said his wife unto him, 'Dost thou still retain thine

integrity? Curse God, and die.' But he said unto her, 'Thou speakest as one of the foolish women speaketh. What? shall we receive good at the hand of God, and shall we not receive evil?'"

I try again. "Hello? Please! Someone. I'm here alone and I need help."

"In all this did not Job sin with his lips."

It's like speaking into a void. No one can hear me. Maybe it isn't real.

I turn the dial to another frequency and start again. "Hello? Can anyone hear me? My name is Willow. Is anyone out there?"

Static.

And then, like a miracle, it happens.

There's a crackling, and a voice says, "I copy, Willow. This is Bob Simmons. What's your twenty?"

THIRTY-THREE

I simply stare at the receiver, unable to make a sound for a long time. A person. A real person. I am communicating with an actual human, who is communicating with me.

My mind goes blank.

What is a twenty? I'm afraid of messing this up.

Then I realize I'll mess up more if I don't say *something*. I press the button. "Bob. What is a twenty?"

"Where you at, darlin'?"

"I don't know." I really don't. There is nothing, no street sign, no named road, nothing that tells me where on Earth I am. "In the Everglades. I think."

"Well, nice to hear from you, Willow. What're you up to this fine day, over?"

He thinks this is a casual conversation. How can he think that? What is wrong with him? Doesn't he know what's going on out there? "My...f—" I stop because *friend* sounds wrong. That's not what E is. "Someone here is dying. Dead, I think. I need help. Please."

A pause. "Yeah, right. I don't have time for this, Willow, darlin'."

He thinks I'm joking? How could I joke about this? My funny bone broke a long time ago. "No! Please. I'm here alone with him, and he got electrocuted by our generator and I think he's dead. I'm all alone here, and I don't know what to do."

"How old are you? Over."

"Six—" I freeze. "No. Sorry. Seventeen."

"You don't got your parents there? Have you called for help? Over."

"No. I'm calling *you*. Can you help me?"

"All right. Where you at? Over."

"I told you. The Everglades."

"That ain't narrowin' it down much, darlin'. I'm in Naples so it ain't like that's around the corner."

Naples? People are alive and well in Naples! There is so much I want to ask him. The first being can he get here from there?

"You got anything else to go on? An address? A road? Over."

"No." I look around wildly, as if the address is going to be stuck to the wall. Does this place even have an address? It had a mailbox, so maybe at one time it got mail. "It's the Rowan place."

"The Rowan place? Huh?" A pause. "You got any landmarks?"

"We're surrounded by water. An island. That's all I know."

There's a long pause, and for a moment, I think I've lost him.

"All right, hon," he says. "You sure you ain't shittin' me?"

"No," I say, allowing a flicker of hope to spark inside me.

"Wait. There's a small bridge out there, um, and the nearest city is Fort Lauderdale. It's really far in the distance, though. Could be a hundred miles. Maybe more." I'm frantically trying to remember directions. "The bridge is north of me."

"Copy that," he says. "All right, Willow. Sit tight, over."

"Do you…" I whisper softly, then realize I'm not pressing the button. "Do you think you can send someone? Even with—"

A hand reaches across my line of vision, grabbing ahold of the wires attached to the radio's base. Before I can stop it, with one quick, desperate pull, the wires are yanked from the base, and the radio goes dead.

"*No!*" I shout, my hands flying out uselessly. But the deed is done, and the way the cords are frayed, I know it can't be undone. Not by me anyway.

But that is the least of my problems. The silence I've come to dread fills every corner of the room.

I look up, up, up, at the wall of a person standing quietly beside me. His smell is different, burning, *wrong*, but I know him by feeling, whether or not he makes a sound, which is why I'm more surprised I didn't notice him when he came inside.

Maybe because I really believed he was dead.

But he is not. E stares down at me with pure, unbridled disgust. His hair, his skin, is singed black.

His finger is at his lips, but they force out one word in a slow hiss: *HUSH.*

THIRTY-FOUR

I stand, staring at him. His hair is wilder, straighter. His eyes are bloodshot. "I thought you were dead! Are you okay?"

He doesn't answer, just keeps his finger pressed against his lips.

I pick up the frayed wire. Yeah, the radio's definitely unfixable. "What did you do that for? It wasn't broken! It just wasn't plugged in. Did you know that?"

I told you not to touch it, he mouths, which gives me a sinking feeling.

Yes. He did know. "But I thought you were dead! And I found someone. Someone who can save us."

He lets out a short laugh. *No one can save us.*

"But he said—"

E reaches out and snakes a hand behind my neck, gripping me so hard his fingertips dig into the base of my skull. He drags me close to him. "What did you tell him?"

All my breath leaves me, and the words die in my throat. I

can't even remember anymore. His black eyes suck every lucid thought from my head. "I...don't know."

When he lets me go, I fall back into the chair, almost knocking it over. It's only when he stalks away that I can breathe again.

What. The. Hell?

That's what I get for being concerned about him, for wanting him to be all right. For trying to save him. It almost makes me wonder why I even cared.

Because without him, Willow, you'd be alone. And you're as good as dead.

I think about Bob Simmons and my spirits lift, but only until I catch sight of the frayed electrical cord.

I'm fooling myself. Bob will never find us. Mr. Wants to Be a Hermit for the Rest of His Life broke the radio. Why did he do that?

Except now I know: There are people alive in Naples, and maybe other places too.

I start to head outside, which is where I think E went, but instead, I see him standing in the kitchen among the mess I made. He's not looking at that, though. His hands are braced on the peninsula, the muscles of his arms taut and tense. There is a scrape on his upper arm, bleeding a long, sinuous line to his hand. His chin is almost to his chest, but his pupils are fastened on me.

He stares at me, unmoving.

"I don't understand you," I whisper in a huff. "You really don't want to get out of here, do you?"

He doesn't say anything.

"You're scaring me," I tell him. I start toward my room. It's too stuffy in here. I need my own space.

As I go, I see the door to the bathroom, with the key still inside.

I got so wrapped up in the radio, I almost forgot. There was a person...or something...in there...

Somehow, it doesn't seem that scary with E by my side.

It is silent behind the door. I stop for a beat, thinking.

It only thumps when E isn't with me.

I get a crazy idea. What if the thumping was him? What if he climbed through the window and was trying to convince me that I'm...

It's more plausible than zombies.

And I have to know.

I put my hand on the doorknob. Twist. The latch disengages and I'm about to push when E bridges the distance and throws a hand over mine on the knob.

He pushes me away, turns the key in the lock, pulls it out, and shoves it into the pocket of his jeans.

"What...what was that?"

He nudges me back. Just a tap, really, like he doesn't want to touch me. *You don't want to know.*

Nice Girl me would've agreed. Would've taken whatever he said without question or challenge. But there's another me, some-one not so nice. I'm not sure if she was always there, waiting to come out, but she's getting impatient.

And *that* me is over this bullshit.

"Yes, I do," I growl. "Were you making those noises? Are you trying to make me think that I'm—that I was—"

You're seeing things again.

"No, I'm sure I'm not. I want to—"

Before I can say more, he crouches and grabs me by my middle, lifting me so my upper half falls forward over his shoulder. I'm dangling like a fish on a hook. I pound on his back as he walks, then start to squeal, but the second I do, he drops me on the floor, making the floorboards shake. It only occurs to me what he's doing when he's in the doorway, reaching for the doorknob.

I scramble up, but the last thing I see as the door closes are his spiteful black eyes. I hit the wood with such force that pain jolts up to my forearms.

A key turns in the lock.

Here I am again. In the cupboard under the stairs. Harry Potter trapped.

Something is wrong. Something is very, very wrong.

I listen with my ear pressed against the door. I can hear the light, barely there sweeping of E's movements. The slight creak of the opening and closing screen door. That's all familiar, but there is something new. A tension in his movements.

The walls stop humming. He's turned the goddamn generator off.

I back up and sit on the bed of rags. I'm right where I was before. Except one thing has changed.

That not-so-nice girl has woken up, and she's sick of the lies.

And if the truth kills her, it kills her. If this experience has taught her anything, it's that there are far worse things than death.

So she opens her mouth and as loud as her lungs will allow...

She starts to scream.

THIRTY-FIVE

I've been screaming for what feels like hours, until my throat is scratchy and sore.

I should know he can't hear me in here. And who knows? This time, he might leave me here for good. I'm completely at his mercy.

Maybe that not-so-nice girl needs to try another tactic.

I feel around, but there isn't much in this space. I go to the door. There's a thin strip of light underneath, the only indication that it's still daylight.

Reaching for the smaller inside knob, I twist. Of course it doesn't budge. It's locked from the outside.

I listen at the door but hear nothing. Couldn't he hear me screaming? Or was it a waste of time?

Maybe, if I bring my mouth right up to it, someone will.

Another, more terrifying thought occurs to me.

Maybe he *has* heard me all this time.

Maybe the monsters he is so afraid of are not the ones inside him or roaming the wide world. Maybe he's more afraid of *me*.

I shake that thought away. No. He's bigger than me, stronger. He's not afraid of me.

But Suzy…

It doesn't matter. I need to get out of here. That same dread that fell over me while I was tied to the bed is back…that helpless feeling that no one will come. That I might die here, waiting for someone to discover me.

But the not-so-nice girl is a girl of action. She refuses to wait to be rescued.

I run my finger along the metal plate, feeling for the keyhole. When I find it, I bring my eye up to it. It doesn't give any light. The key must still be in the hole on the other side. Jabbing my pinkie into the hole to push it out is a waste because even my littlest finger is too big.

Fanning out my hands, I try to find something long and thin on the floor, something that I can use to pop out the key. But it's like before; I am in here with nothing but rags and dust bunnies.

And the old stub of a candle that E once brought in here, many months ago. It's now a pile of hardened wax. Feeling around it, I notice something rigid sticking out of the smooth wax. I run my finger over it until it occurs to me what it is.

A wooden match.

That could work.

I use my fingernails to dig into the wax, trying to pry the match free. The stuff collects under my nails but I keep digging, loosening it. Then I wiggle it, first a little, then a lot, until it comes loose. *Ha*.

I scoot to the door on my backside, find the hole again, and stick in the match. Sure enough, it encounters the resistance of the key, then I can feel the key giving way, sliding out.

There's a hollow metallic thud of the key hitting the wood floor.

Still doubtful this will work, I press my cheek against the floor and try to find where it landed. With my luck, even though it landed with a heavy plunk, it probably bounced away from the door.

But no, I'm wrong. It's right there, actually...maybe a few inches from the opening.

Careful, I think. I bring my eye to the keyhole and look out. I expect to see something terrible, like the last time I looked in a keyhole. A grotesque Harlequin or E, staring back at me. But there is nothing. Only that old, overstuffed sofa, with the neatly folded afghan laid across the back. The sun is setting, silhouetted in the kitchen window, but the lights don't flicker.

He's not here. At least I don't think so.

When it gets dark, he'll come in.

I don't have a moment to lose.

Jamming my flattened hand into the space, I stretch my fingers out as far as they can go. My knuckles catch on the rough underside of the door, the skin scraping, but I can still shove them a little farther. A little more. A little more...

My middle finger grazes the metal.

I take a deep breath, trying again. I try to swipe my fingers to the side, hoping the momentum will draw it nearer. But it only pushes the key out of reach.

Dammit.

Now my knuckles are wet and raw. They're bleeding.

Gnawing on my lip, I decide to try my left hand. I don't have the dexterity I do with my right, but it's worth a shot. Doing the same thing, I inch my fingers under the door.

I must have thinner fingers on this hand, because this time, I can touch the key. My heart does a little dance in my chest as I stretch my middle finger, capturing the key underneath, and slide it, ever so gently, toward me.

It only budges an inch or so but that's far enough for me to catch the edge of the key with my pinkie and swipe it back under the door toward me.

I pick it up and run a finger over its contours, hardly able to believe my plan worked.

Then I stick it in the keyhole and turn it. The lock clicks to release. Wincing because I don't want to make noise, I turn the knob as slowly as I can. I gingerly pull open the door and peer outside.

The coast is clear.

Pulse pounding in my ears, I crawl out, then climb to my feet.

When I do, I hear something. A voice.

No, voices. Rising, falling. Back and forth.

It's the unmistakable sound of conversation. And here, I nearly forgot what that was like.

The sounds are coming from the front of the house. It's a place I've rarely been, because the front door is blocked from the outside by all those milk and vegetable crates, and the windows are clouded with dirt and rusted screens, so there is barely any view.

But I'm curious.

I creep forward, following the sound, then stop. There's a ringing, loud and vibrant, like a bell.

Laughter. A man is laughing.

What is going on? Is this whoever was locked in the bathroom? *Was* there someone else living here with us? Who are they? It feels like a party I was not invited to.

I push aside those hideous damask curtains by the fireplace, trying to peer outside. No go. The dirt is far too thick, streaking down the windows, as black as asphalt on a newly paved road. It's not so bad up higher, but I'm too short for that.

Looking around, I grab the chair from beside the table with the radio, set it into position, and climb onto it.

Better.

I peer out onto the front yard, with its dead grass and the mailbox full of bees.

And I see something incredible.

A police car.

My heart leaps. There *was* another way onto this island after all?

Saved.

That's the first word that comes to my mind. This police officer is going to take us somewhere safe. I called Bob, Bob somehow got in touch with the authorities, and now they are here to rescue us.

I did this. I saved us.

Now I'm laughing with relief too.

The man wears a gray uniform and brimmed sheriff's hat. He has a rather unfortunate pot belly, but he looks neat and tidy, like he's largely escaped the events of the past few months. Not like us, that's for sure. E's closer to the house, and he looks like a wreck in comparison, but as he chats with the sheriff, a smile breaks out on his face, and I know everything is going to be okay.

I dare to smile too.

I should go out there. See what they're talking about.

I'm about to jump off the chair when the officer turns and heads back to his car. I watch him sidle along it, open his door, and pull out his radio receiver. Standing behind the open door, he starts to talk into the receiver, maybe to tell them that he found us. We are alive.

I'm so busy watching him that I don't notice E, who must've gone back toward the house.

Seemingly out of nowhere, something black whizzes through the air and buries itself in the officer's chest.

His smile dissolves. Still clutching his radio, he staggers back a bit. Then he slumps forward through the open window of the police cruiser, gasping and trying to stoop for cover.

Before he can, another arrow sails through the air, this time hitting him straight between the eyes. It's the money shot, sending him sprawling, his head splitting open like a smashed melon.

I forget I'm on the chair as I scream and lose my balance.

The last thing I see before I fall is E bolting for the back door.

THIRTY-SIX

I scramble to my feet and run to the back door. It's my only escape.

After that, who knows where I'll go? I doubt I can make it to the police car. I'm trapped. But I'm more trapped in this house, with him.

His strides are longer, and even though I have less ground to cover, he flies up onto the porch as I push open the screen door.

I skirt away from him, pressing myself against the side of the house. "Get away from me!"

He tries to grab my wrists, but I yank them away.

I pummel his chest. "You killed him! You killed him! You killed that police officer!" I shout incomprehensibly because I'm crying hysterically.

He tries to put a hand on my mouth to shut me up, but I wrench away from him. "Shh," he repeats. "He'll be back."

Not that again. Liar. He's *dead*. I'd been so wrecked when I thought Elijah was dead. I thought that I'd die without him. How stupid was I?

He has the bow strapped to his back, but as I push him away, my hand gets caught in the string. There's an almost pretty musical *twang* before the thing snaps. E lets out a low curse, the only sign that he's the least bit perturbed by the way I'm carrying on. In a flash, he manages to squeeze my wrists, rendering me immobile.

At least he can't use that bow on *me*. By now, he knows he doesn't need to. He can wound me in far deeper ways.

"Listen to me," he says calmly. "Willow, just listen. I'm trying to protect you. Protect—"

"No. You're a liar! And a murderer! Don't tell me he was one of those monsters. He wasn't. He was normal, like anyone. I *saw* him."

"You're right. He was normal," he says. "But he wasn't good. He would've taken you. And I promise you, he'll be back."

I shake my head, refusing to listen, but the words seep in anyway, probably because there's a part of me that still wants him to be on my side. "Taken me?"

"Yeah. I heard it on the radio before. Rumors. That's why I didn't want you talking on it. When things went bad, there was no law. A group of police officers started taking advantage of everyone. They trade girls—girls like you—for the things they need to survive."

He's speaking evenly, but he's not looking at me. I've heard of that of course. In *The Walking Dead*, society devolved so that it was every man for himself. "They would've...traded me?"

He's quiet for a long time. "Or worse."

I shake my head, hardly believing this is happening. Not five minutes ago, I was thinking we were saved. Now there is no being saved. Not from the police anyway. Unless… "You said there was no way onto the island. How did he get the police car here?"

"That's what he was telling me. They fixed the bridge. Enough to get his car over it."

The bridge is fixed. That means we can get out.

Or at least I *can get out.* I'm not so sure who E is anymore.

"What are we going to do?" I ask, studying his face.

If he is a liar, he's a very good one. He lets go of my wrists. There are red marks where his hands have been.

He says, "If there was one, there will be more. We got to move the body."

I shake my head violently. "I'm not doing that."

"All right." E wipes his hands on the thighs of his jeans. "I will. But help me wheel the car into the back. We got to let the marsh swallow it."

I frown. "Why?"

"I told you why. There're gonna be more. If they see the car—"

"But don't you see? With the bridge fixed, we can finally get—"

I stop. He has a *Hell no, never in a million years* look. I get that he's afraid of what's out there, but he has to know that we can't survive here much longer. And with the car, we can escape.

A chill skitters down my spine. *That's the last thing he wants.*

"We have to move it off the road at least," he says, starting for the car. When I follow him, he stops and does an about-face. "Wait here while I drag the body into the back."

Good. Because I don't want to see that officer again. I already know what I'm going to see tonight when I close my eyes: that arrow cutting his head in half, his brain matter exploding out the back of his skull.

I watch E round the corner of the house and start to go inside, hugging myself.

Then something occurs to me.

I slip back outside and jump off the side of the porch, walking through the tall grass, down the long driveway.

E stands by the dead officer and the open door of the police cruiser. The two arrows are sticking straight up from the man's chest and head. E must not know I'm there, because he doesn't acknowledge me. He stops, puts a bare foot on the man's chest, and wrenches the arrow out. It lets go with a sickening pop, spattering chunks of bloody flesh in the air. E wipes the tip of the arrow on his jeans, leaving a grotesque red smear, then tosses it on the lawn.

He does the same with the other one, but I squeeze my eyes closed.

When he starts to drag the body toward me, I angle away from him. As he goes past me, he mumbles, "Not going anywhere with those tires."

Startled by his words, I open my eyes. The first thing I see is the man's head, leaking a long line of black blood on the dirt.

I turn toward the car and sneak over, thinking, *Great, does he have a flat? Does he have a spare?*

It doesn't take long to see that E is absolutely right. Two of the tires on the passenger's side are completely flat, but not from any small puncture or gravel on the rutted road.

No, there's a long gash in each one, as if someone slashed them deliberately.

Someone...

Don't be stupid, Willow. You are the only two people here. Unless...

I look at the house, almost expecting to see a face looking at me through one of the windows. But E has stopped and is watching me instead.

As our gazes meet, he continues on his way, dragging the dead man to the back of the house as if he hasn't a care in the world.

THIRTY-SEVEN

I watch the body bopping over the ruts, the man's big, bleeding belly jiggling.

Like a bowlful of raspberry jelly.

The thought makes me hunch over, gasping, wanting to vomit what little is left in my stomach. The police car is not an escape.

It's a liability.

That is, if the police really have turned lawless and are out to get us.

Which…I don't know.

Of course you do, Willow. Those tires didn't slit themselves.

Blood rushes to my head and sweat spills in my eyes as I try to think of what to do. Red ants climb on the dusty ground, oblivious to my skinny shadow looming over them. I could leave on that rusty old boat if I could drag it to the water, if I knew where I was going. Maybe it could take me wherever the current went. Anyplace would be better than here.

Or is it? How far would I get before it filled with water and left me as alligator bait?

The crackling of a radio jolts me.

A disembodied female voice says, "Bruce? You there?"

The cruiser's radio! How stupid was I not to even think of it?

E must've forgotten about it, or else he'd have pulled it from the dashboard, rending the receiver from the base, like he did the radio in the house.

I creep closer to it, all the while watching the side of the house for any sign of E. In the quiet, I can hear a shovel. He's digging. When I get there, I stop. I don't want to see the spot where that police officer died.

"Bruce?"

I snap my head toward the car. It's loud. Too loud. He's going to hear it and come running.

I wait for a beat. Two. Instead, I hear the shovel, plunging into the earth again.

Maybe he didn't hear.

I don't want to take the chance that he won't hear a third time, so I hurry to the passenger-side door. The handle is so hot from the sun, it scalds my fingertips when I lift it. It's locked.

I have to go around. To the other side.

I *really* don't want to do that.

The voice says, "Hey, Bruce?"

The woman has enough grit in her voice to make me think she's older. Grandmotherly. An older lady who wears sun visors and dangling costume jewelry earrings that match her shoes and purse.

Would a sweet, grandmotherly lady work for a bunch of rogue police officers that trade young girls for toilet paper?

Maybe. Possibly. Possibly not.

What choice do I have?

Bracing myself, I scramble around the back of the car, keeping my vision trained on the side of the house. The sun is high in the sky, reflecting off the chrome fixtures and the red and blue police lights. It occurs to me the car has just been washed. There's so much dust on this road, but nothing on the bumper, the windows...

Until I come around the taillight and catch sight of what was once the officer—Bruce—spattered on the cruiser. There's a large puddle of blood where Bruce fell too. The radio's curly cord is stretched, the receiver almost bathing in it.

I stare at the bloody puddle like it's lava. My vision bends, and I see it in double. My knees wobble. Taking a deep breath and gritting my teeth so hard my jaw cracks, I race for the door and dive inside, not before I realize that the seat is covered in droplets of blood and brain matter too. It's everywhere—on the front windshield, the mirror, the steering wheel, the seat. Everywhere.

Oh God.

I try to ignore it, but my hands are slick with sweat and the radio is sticky with the officer's blood. Together they make an impossible combination. I try to pick it up the receiver, but it doesn't want to stay in my hand. I wind up fishing it up by its cord. I hold it away from my mouth and depress the red button on the side. "Hello?"

The response is so loud it makes me jump in the seat. "That you, Bruce? Can't hear you. Speak up, honey."

I scramble to find a dial to lower the volume, but they all look the same. The cabin of the cruiser smells of body odor. But there's also a scent I haven't smelled in quite some time. It stirs up memories—Friday nights around the dinner table, me and Mom and Dad, JT at our feet under the table.

Pizza Fridays.

As I press the button, I notice it, sandwiched between the door and a black backpack. A white, grease-stained bag. On the front, a picture of a happy man in a chef's hat, twirling a round of dough over his head. *Nonno's Piz...*

Pizza.

He's eaten pizza. Maybe not today, but recently enough that the smell lingers.

Where, in this dead world, did he get pizza?

I reach over, unzip the backpack, and rummage through it. I find a sleeve of gum, some flares, an old balled-up navy-blue T-shirt, and a small, cloth-bound kit, wrapped in a tie. I'm not sure what it's for.

"Bruce?"

I stare out the blood-spattered windshield toward what will soon be Bruce's final resting spot.

Everything you know is wrong.

My hand shakes. I break from my trance and press the button. "This is not Bruce. Bruce is dead. He's been murdered. And I need help."

THIRTY-EIGHT

After I give the lady my message, I manage to find the switch to turn off the radio.

In a daze, I walk to the back of the house. E is still digging. He's about knee-deep in the grave, tossing dirt over his shoulder. He has another foot or so left to go if he makes the grave as deep as the last.

At first, E doesn't look up. Then he stops and swipes a hand over his forehead. *You okay?*

No. I'm not.

I nod anyway and point inside. *Tired. I'm going to lie down.*

He nods and goes back to his work.

I go inside. Contrary to what I told him, I do not go to bed.

Instead, I take a deep breath and open the bathroom door. I don't do it slow. I throw it open all the way.

Just a bathroom.

I don't understand. There's nothing about it that E should want to hide from me.

Except the door bangs against something and bounces back. Something won't let it open all the way. I peer in, and my breath catches.

The pedal kit for his drum set. What is it doing in here?

I look closer. The beater—the part that is supposed to strike the drum—is attached to a thin string.

My heart thuds as I follow the path of the string with my eyes, up the wall and into a small hole in the ceiling.

The truth that dawns on me is too terrible. I won't entertain it. I *can't*.

But sure enough, as I reach over and lift the string, the beater strikes the door, making that familiar sound I once thought was the living dead.

Trembling, I back out of the room and close the door, wishing I could unsee it. But I can't. And now I have only more questions, begging for answers.

This time, when I climb the stairs, I know which ones make noise and I avoid them, like traversing a minefield. Not that it matters. I can hear E, busy outside. Still pushing the earth around with the shovel.

That gives me the time I need.

Kneeling in front of the door, I peer through the keyhole again. As much as I try to avoid the Harlequin, it's the first thing I see. Then shadows pass over the far wall. Just a flicker.

"Hello," I whisper, not expecting a response. I don't get one.

Because I know what that is. I may have been in this

technology-free world for the better part of a year, but I haven't forgotten everything about the world before.

I haven't forgotten what the dull blue-white light from a television looks like.

I pull the little black kit from the folds of my strawberry dress, then unroll it and run a finger over the various tools. I have no idea what most of them are for. To me, they all look the same—about five inches long with various, differently shaped heads. I select the smallest one. Gripping it in my clammy fingers, I shove it into the keyhole and root around, trying to connect with something. I twist and push, push and twist.

Nothing happens.

Wiping the sweat from my brow, I try another thicker one. Too thick: It doesn't slide in.

The third one I take hold of makes me think of those bears. Maybe this one is just right.

I wiggle it up and down and back and forth. Just when I'm about to give up, I hear the click.

Reaching for the glass knob, I turn it. It opens. Holding my breath, I push in.

Part of me thought that this place was sacred to E because his parents died here, and they meant so much to him. Part of me wondered if he kept it as a shrine to them, leaving everything exactly the way they had, right down to their bloody sheets. I'd imagined that was why he didn't want me upstairs.

As I go in, my thoughts hold true. There is a full-size bed in the corner, neatly covered in a patchwork quilt. Two pillows are propped against the wooden headboard, a smaller needlepoint pillow in the center that says, HIS LOVE ENDURES FOREVER. A woman's pink robe hangs from the post on the footboard. There is a vanity in the corner with an oval mirror and an organizer filled with various creams and lipsticks and other cosmetics. Big, worn men's slippers are positioned at the side of the bed, ready to be scuffed into.

I scan to the Harlequin, its mischievous eyes watching me, trying to orient myself. Its expression is decidedly sly, like, *I know something you don't know.*

If it did, I wish it'd tell me. Because I'd seen that shadow from outside the room. A shadow I was convinced came from a television set. A *working* television set.

But there is no television in this room. It is as I'd always thought, a neatly kept monument to his parents.

Then my eyes catch on a small door.

It's partially open, the top slanted to allow for the eaves. It has hooks for clothes and is so covered by them that it's nearly hidden.

I cross to it and inch it open, not liking how much it creaks.

The first thing I see is the computer screen. It's definitely an older model, but it has wires and other hardware hooked up to it, a tech geek's dream. It has a screen saver of a figure eight, slowly turning and twisting. A working computer…here…when the generator isn't humming.

That's interesting.

No. That's…impossible. Isn't it?

I follow the cord, which rather than disappearing into an electrical outlet skirts up the wall and out the window. To where? A solar source? Wind?

Doesn't matter. What matters is that all this time, he had power. He played with that generator. We ate by candlelight. We couldn't use the radio. And why?

You know why, Willow.

I look to the side of the computer, to the pictures taped on the wall. So many pictures, news clippings, and printouts, all featuring one subject.

I stare, hardly able to breathe. My vision clouds. This must be a mirage. But no matter how hard I blink, I can't unsee this.

E might have kept the upstairs bedroom in memory of his parents.

But this tiny cedar closet?

It's devoted to *me*.

Photographs of me from my yearbook. A map of Pensacola with a red circle around my house. Pictures from my Instagram. My goddamn junior-year school schedule. And a notebook, scrawled with notes that wouldn't make sense to most people:

August Rule
JT dog akita Justin Timberlake
Mascot Tiger white maroon

BD April 12
3rd period history
BFF lavani Singh
August GF Jana Wilson

Oh, but it makes sense to me. Every word of it—and it goes on and on for pages. I feel dirtier and dirtier. I want to close my eyes, but I can't.

My gaze hitches on a sheet of paper with dog-eared edges, creased and dirt stained, tacked to the wall. From its prominent placement to the number of times things have been crossed out and rewritten in different ink colors, it's clearly important. It's a list of dates:

July 13 (?)—trials start Suzy
August 6—trials start ER, SR, DR
???—trials start VK, ST, BL, MS, NV, CS
September 1—SUZY
September 6—VK
9/13—MS, BL
9/18—ST
9/20—CS
9/24—NV
10/1—VL fired from Latrobe
??? (possibly Dec?)—WL
1/26—Miami

2/3—First cases Pensacola

2/7—lockdowns

2/19—NG called in

2/22—END

I stare, trying to make sense of what I'm reading. What is *Latrobe* doing there? Two words are written in red and outlined thickly: SUZY and END.

END.

I can't pretend to know what any of that means.

There is so much newsprint tacked to the wall. The closest one says:

PLANS SCRAPPED FOR HIGHLY ANTICIPATED NEW DRUG

Oct. 1—Latrobe Scientific announced today that they have scrapped plans to continue research on their highly publicized new drug BST-14D in order to concentrate their efforts and funding on a bunyavirus vaccine. Once touted as a miracle drug that would make humans immune to any virus, BST ran into several issues in development, most recently the departure of lead scientist Dr. Vincent Lafayette.

The biggest article on the wall, however, right beside the computer screen, features a photograph of my face. It's a professional picture my mom had taken at a studio, so I had a headshot for my big break. I'd tried to look deep and sultry and interesting.

Instead I looked mildly disturbed and embarrassed, like I'd shown up to an appointment at the wrong time.

I never thought the world would see that photo.

Judging by the size and shape of the cutout, most of Florida saw it. Because it was on the front page of that newspaper I'd dug out of Suzy's closet.

An article about me.

With the headline *Young YouTube Star Vanishes in Miami.*

Miami. Of course.

With that, the pieces fall into place, and everything comes back.

THIRTY-NINE

"*Don't be afraid,*" *my mother said, peering over her shoulder at me from the front passenger's seat.*

"*I'm not,*" *I said, nose buried in my phone.*

But really, I was. My father was acting strange. It wasn't just that he insisted we take my car when we left, but his hands trembled on the steering wheel. He was going ninety on the highway. He kept peering in the rearview mirror as if someone was following us.

My mother murmured, "Don't you think you ought to slow down, Vince?"

He grunted. I wondered if his mood had anything to do with the man neighbors had seen lurking in our yard. The man who'd thrown a rock through our window with KILLER on it.

I received a text: Can you meet me at the Econo Lodge on 1st at 10? Room 102.

I stared at it for, like, a thousand years. He'd come all the way to Miami to be with me. August wanted me...alone in a hotel room... with him.

I googled the place. It was a dump compared with the secluded mansion on the beach my father had rented, but it was only ten minutes down the road. I could do it. I could tell my parents I was going for a walk, drive down to the hotel, spend a few hours there, and come back. Easy.

My stomach lurched at the thought of being alone with him for the first time. I'd like to say it was all excited butterflies, but there was something sour there too. I thought I knew what August felt for me, but I'd never interacted with him that way in person. What Lavani said stuck in my mind: He's just playing you.

It didn't matter. If he was, I'd accept the consequences.

Because August was good for me. When I messaged with him, he gave me courage, believed in me. And I craved that time alone with him. Finally. It could change everything.

I looked up at my parents. They only wanted the best for me. I couldn't disobey them like this…could I?

Yeah, I could. What they didn't know wouldn't hurt them.

So that night, when we got to the house, I dressed in my nicest romper, and I told my parents I was going out for a walk on the beach and would be back soon.

They were so absorbed in my father's work issues, they didn't even notice I'd swiped the car keys from my father's jacket.

And I took off, feeling free. Butterflies not only in my stomach but everywhere.

I was going to be with August.

He'd acknowledge me, and I wouldn't be some random face he passed in the hallway or saw on a computer screen.

I wanted it so bad, I was shaking. Touching him. Kissing him… oh God, could I kiss him? Would he want to kiss me? I popped an extra piece of gum just in case.

When I pulled up in front of the hotel, though, the place seemed almost abandoned. I stepped out of the car.

Something tickled the back of my neck, told me this was wrong. But I wanted so badly for it to be right.

I hesitated near the front of my car, telling myself that I could still leave. It wasn't too late. I could go back to the house, to my parents, and no one would ever know about my broken heart.

The door to room 102 opened. When I saw the boy who filled the doorway, I wanted to cry.

I'd been fooling myself. Of course I had been. Like August Rule would ever want someone as ordinary as Willow Lafayette. Stupid, stupid, stupid.

Everything I had believed was a lie, and in my confusion, my hesitation, this boy—this stranger—lunged and grabbed me.

FORTY

I'd woken up here. In that demon nursery, tied to the bed.

E had done this.

E had done all this. Every last diabolical detail.

He'd kidnapped me, knocked me out, drove me all the way to this house in the middle of nowhere, kept me as his prisoner, and made me believe I was going insane. He'd gotten his grandmother to play along.

But it had started long before that. As I look at the computer and the pages and pages of notes on my life, I realize it started *way* before that.

Maybe from the first message August sent me, back at the beginning of the school year.

August. Was that even August? Or was it E? Was he lying to me, catfishing me, this entire time?

I lean over, wanting to retch. Protect me. What a joke. All he's ever done is punish me.

And why?

I think and I think, but no answer comes.

I snatch the article from the red pushpin adhering it to the wall and read it:

A PENSACOLA TEENAGER VANISHED FROM THE VACATION RENTAL SHE WAS STAYING AT WITH HER FAMILY

Jan 27—Willow Lafayette, 16, told her family she was going for a walk along the ocean shortly after nine in the evening.

Lafayette is the daughter of Dr. Vincent Lafayette, a scientist at Latrobe Scientific. In the past few weeks, the family has called the police several times to report suspicious incidents relating to an individual they believed was watching their Pensacola home.

Security footage shows the teen going to the garage around 9:45 p.m., getting into her car, and driving away.

"It's not like her to drive off like that," her mother, Dr. Beatrice Lafayette, said. "We're worried about her. We just want her back safely."

I stare at it. There's no mention of any crisis with the second plague. The whole thing must have been a lie. But what I can't stop looking at, what makes my insides turn to jelly, is those words spoken by a woman I thought died months ago. My mother gave a quote after I went missing. About me and my disappearance.

How? I saw them. In the car, half-submerged in the marsh. They were dead.

Or are they?

I can't be sure of anything anymore. The more I see in front of me, the more I doubt. I notice a string tied to the base of a lamp and run my finger over it. It's the same as the one I saw in the downstairs bathroom. I pull it, once, twice, and can hear it, beating on the door downstairs.

It would be enough to drive someone crazy.

Which is exactly what he wanted.

Only someone absolutely diabolical could plan something like this.

I clamp a hand over my mouth, because if I don't, I'm sure I'll scream. Tears blur my vision.

This isn't happening. Am I that stupid that I let Elijah, this man—no, this *monster*—fool me, not once but again and again and again? Somehow, he faked everything. How many lies did he tell me? Everything I thought was real, every detail of my life for the past year...is all a lie.

I squeeze my eyes closed, and this time, when I lean over, I retch. I have nothing in my stomach, so I heave bile onto the wooden floor.

Those bodies in my car...are they my parents? Are they strangers? People he killed to maintain the ruse, his diseased mind thinking they'd "come back"? Did he put them there? Stage them? Touch their dead bodies like it was nothing to convince me of his grand lie, because he was so far gone, because he's not even human himself?

The men he killed in front of me. They weren't zombies,

monsters, shadows of the people they once were. How did I believe that? Except he orchestrated everything to make me doubt what I knew. He drowned my car out by the bridge with two bodies to convince me my family was dead. He manipulated my environment to fit with his story. He murdered people to keep his lie going.

Elijah is the monster.

And somehow, I always knew it. I was too scared to trust my gut.

There's a sound outside, faint at first but growing louder by the moment. I look away from the sad, pathetic shrine of my life, listening.

Sure enough, I recognize gravel pinging against the side of a car.

A car. Another car is nearing the house.

Oh God. Another car is nearing the house. I see that arrow hitting the policeman between his eyes on loop. I close the door to the closet, then the bedroom. I rush down the stairs, trying not to make a sound. When I reach the front of the house, I climb onto the chair as a black-and-white car comes into view.

More police.

They're doomed.

The only saving grace is that I broke the string on his bow, and he's probably been too busy digging that grave to fix it.

A lanky man with a mustache steps out, spitting on the grass. He goes to the mailbox, opens it, looks in, closes it quick, waves his hands to ward off the wasps.

My stomach drops.

He's younger than the last one, but he's smaller than E. Likely weaker too. He's no hero. His partner looks, well, plump. Like he spent too many nights behind a desk instead of out on a beat. They're unprepared for what is about to happen. E could probably take them both down, even without his bow. E has the element of surprise. They have no idea what kind of trap they're running into.

My gut tangles. I need to get out there. Stop him.

I look down to navigate off the chair when an arm wraps around my knees.

I let out a yelp. It's E. He quickly and effortlessly lifts me, setting me right on the floor. He's not looking at me but out the window, and I'm glad for that. There's no way to hide the hatred on my face.

"Look. There's another one," he whispers to me. "Stay here and be quiet. Let me take care of it."

"What are you going to do?" I whisper. "You don't have your bow."

He looks around. His eyes land on the pantry, and it hits me. He bolts for it. He's tall enough that he can swipe the tea canister down without standing on the tips of his toes.

"Wait…no. You can't."

He stops. "What?"

My breath catches. Thinking quickly, I say, "Two bullets. One for you. One for me. Right? If you use it on them…the sound…"

He pauses. "Right." He looks down at the open canister and closes the lid. Then he opens a drawer and takes out one of the big butcher's knives. "Stay here."

He disappears outside, letting the door slam. Of course. Because that whole being quiet thing? It's bullshit. A rule he made up to keep me in line.

I could scream right now if I wanted to.

And dammit, I want to.

I want to scream so loud the whole world will hear me.

Instead, I listen to his voice speaking plaintively with the officers on the side of the house. He sounds accommodating. Helpful. Polite.

What bullshit.

Quietly, because for some reason that's my life now, all I am capable of anymore, I open the door and let it bump closed with barely a sound. I pad around the side of the house to where Elijah is standing, reasoning with the officer, the blade tucked securely behind his back, pointing between his shoulder blades.

I walk three steps, lift the gun, and cock it, just like he showed me.

The click isn't loud, but it's loud enough that he hears. Or maybe he doesn't. Maybe he sees the police officers' expressions shift first.

Either way, I don't move. Not a single muscle. The officers draw their guns in alarm, almost in unison, and point them at me.

"Drop it!" one of them says.

They think I'm pointing at them. I'm not.

Oh hell no.

Elijah slowly turns, his dark, fathomless eyes as emotionless as the day I met him.

"Low," he mutters. "Don't."

Low. He called me Low. Only one other person ever called me that.

"Drop the gun," the skinny officer barks.

No, thank you.

I take a deep breath and say in a loud, clear voice I don't recognize, "I am Willow Lafayette of Pensacola, Florida, and I am being held here by this man against my will."

Elijah shakes his head. He drops the knife. And then he almost smiles, no teeth, but a definite upturn of the lips. There's a peculiar look on his face that can only be described as relief. He whispers, "See you later."

My fingers are greasy on the trigger. At first, I think I might not be able to pull it, but then I squeeze a little, and it gives. I can. I will.

Two bullets, I think. *One for you.*

The other for you too.

I pull the trigger. Once. Twice.

The resulting roar is so loud that it practically bursts my eardrums.

I absolutely love it.

FORTY-ONE

The ride in the police car is frightening.

I haven't been in a car, moving this fast, in a lifetime. The landscape blurs by the window at breakneck speed. I feel helpless but in an entirely different way. Like I've been standing still for an eternity, and now I'm a falling star, hurdling toward Earth with no way to stop before the inevitable explosion.

The police officer in the front of the vehicle is nice to me. Exceedingly so, like I'm a time bomb he's expecting to go off. A *miraculous* time bomb, actually.

That's what he'd said. He tried speaking low when he got me into the car, when he called for backup. He'd said, his voice cracking, "You're never going to believe who I found. Remember that girl?" Turns out people were looking for me, even in the face of all that chaos. His voice cracked and he beamed as he said, "Yeah, that's her. Willow Lafayette. She's right here next to me. I know, right? Yeah, she's all right. It's a miracle."

I'm a miracle.

I spent so long being little more than nothing. I don't know what to do with this information. Me. A miracle.

Also...*am* I all right? I suppose I have all the requisite limbs, and I'm not bleeding. But I don't know. *I'll have to get back to you on that one.*

Now, he keeps saying things like, "Can I get you anything? Want me to crack a window? You okay over there?" Like that's exactly what I am. A perfect miracle. He's afraid that if he blinks the wrong way, I'll disappear. His eyes constantly shift to the rear-view mirror. Every time I catch him looking, he focuses on the road.

The road.

The road that is leading me away from that place. From this nightmare.

I think the road has been here all along.

Where we'd gone right, toward the broken bridge...the police car made a U-turn in the drive and went *left*. Left, in what E called the wrong direction. He was wrong. Or lying. Or both.

If I hadn't given up, if I'd had the courage to explore, maybe I would've discovered that months ago.

Turns out this wasn't an island.

We weren't cut off from the world. Oh, the house was remote, yes. Out in the absolute middle of nowhere, which was what the state police officer, whose name is Farrow, said. "But not too far out. Ain't many places in the US of A these days where you can't get a phone signal, where you don't see any sign of life at all. This is about as rural and remote as you can get, but it ain't a dead zone. You can still get internet out here!" He's been chattering on, saying things like that, observations about the world, but I've been mostly silent. We've been driving for an hour, and I have yet to see anything but trees and more trees.

The world has survived, and as I feared, it has gone on without me.

A little ways later, we pass a stand on the side of the road. It's nothing, really. A ramshackle wooden platform with one of those old, aluminum-webbed lawn chairs beside it and a flimsy umbrella decorated with ducks. *Fresh tomatoes. Five for a dollar.* No sign of life, but it's a little seed, deep in my brain.

Your whole existence is a lie.

Your whole miraculous existence is HIS creation.

A few miles later, there's more to see. An old house with a broken-down pickup in the drive on blocks. Windows with screens so old, rust is bleeding down the siding like wounds. Overgrown grass. The place could be abandoned, could be home to another victim of the end of the world.

Until I see the large old woman in the flowered housecoat waddling in the drive. She has socks pulled up to her fleshy knees and sandals. Even though she's wearing a visor, her gray ponytail threaded through the hole in the back, she shields her eyes with her hand to look at us, then continues lumbering toward the mailbox.

The first thing I think: *She's one of them. Quick, where's the bow?*

The second thing I think: *E isn't with me anymore. I have to take care of myself.*

The third thing I think is that I'm going to have to relearn everything.

I close my eyes. Then I whisper, my throat dry as the desert floor, "When did they win?"

"What?" Farrow turns down the radio. "Did you say something?"

I try, louder now. "When did they win. Fighting the… second plague?"

"The *second* plague?" He laughs. "You mean the second wave of the screw?"

"No. I mean, the stuff that happened after the screw?"

He licks his lips, like he's trying to think of a delicate way to explain a touchy topic.

"They *did* win, didn't they?"

He glances back at me, and I see it clearly, because I know that look well. There's worry in his eyes.

Maybe I'm not the miracle he thought.

FORTY-TWO

The closer we get to the Florida State Police precinct, the more my worst fears come to life.

We drive into Fort Myers, a place I've never been before. I only know that's where we are because of the sign. I watch through the window like I used to view a movie. Detached, some small, broken part of my mind understanding the scenes playing out before me aren't real.

They can't be. They're all wrong. I look around, thinking how much it looks like the Florida I remember. Too much traffic. A homeless man begging for change at an intersection. A bunch of kids my age hanging out on a picnic table eating pizza. A harried mom wheeling her cart of groceries to her car.

It's all make-believe. It can't be happening. I'm certain if the officer powered down my window, it'd be like a curtain going up, revealing the real world.

The broken world I've envisioned for the better part of a year.

Smoke. Death. Broken buildings. Wreckage. The remains

of a once-great civilization. *Look on my Works, ye Mighty, and despair!*

"Fort Lauderdale burned," I murmur.

"What's that?" Farrow's voice is all too cheery. I can't remember ever hearing a voice like that.

"Fort Lauderdale. The city burned down?"

"No. Fort Lauderdale's right as rain. Pretty far from where you were. Doubt you could've seen it from there."

Oh. *Lie. What other lies are waiting for me?* I press my nose against the window.

"It must be great to get back, huh?"

"I have never been here before," I whisper.

He drums his fingers on the steering wheel. "Right. Yeah. Well, we'll get you home. We just need to bring you in, ask you some questions, have a doctor look you over, make sure you're all right. Right?"

I cross my arms over my body. "I'm all right."

If it saves me from a doctor pinching and poking me, I'm all right. I'll *make* myself all right.

"Even so…"

"What happened? With the second plague?"

He looks in the mirror at me again. "With what?"

Right. The second plague was a lie. Zombies were a lie. It's only now that I realize how ridiculous it sounds. How stupid it makes me. "The cure?"

He lifts a shoulder. "You mean the pill? Ventex. That's what we all take. It was a little dicey for a while because of the short-ages, but we managed to get the virus under control six months ago. There are pockets that emerge here and there, but we know what to look out for, keep taking our Ventex, wearing masks in group settings. It's no problem."

I rub my eyes. "So there was no cure?"

"I…" He laughs good-naturedly. "Far as I know, nothing's come through yet. I hear they're working on a vaccine, though. Those things take time."

We pull into the parking lot beside a one-story brick building that says Florida Department of Law Enforcement. There is a group of people waiting outside. Law enforcement. Reporters. People standing around holding signs. The only one I can make out has my name on it. WE LOVE YOU, WILLOW!

"Dang," Farrow says. "We'll go around back."

"Why are they here?" I watch as he leaves them all in his dust.

"For you."

He goes past a fence and pulls into another lot behind the building. This time, he pulls right up to the curb, cuts the engine, steps out, and opens the door for me.

"In you go." Before I can stand, he hands me a disposable mask. "Don't forget this."

It's been a long time since I wore a mask, but now I'm thank-ful for it. I slip it on, glad it covers my face.

It's only two steps to the back door. Inside, there are at least a dozen officers. They applaud for me. I think they're smiling broadly under their masks. A large white-haired man, ignoring all protocol, shakes my hand and tells me he's the captain of something. The unit? The squad? I'm not paying attention. I stare at the ground.

I never thought I would crave the solitude of that awful nursery room.

After a few seconds, I feel dizzy.

"Whoa," Farrow says as I slump against him. He and the white-haired man frantically urge everyone to back up, giving me space. They take me to a small room with a table and chairs, one of those bare interrogation rooms in the movies where the police question a suspect until he cracks like an egg. They don't have to question me; I'm already cracking.

I slump into a chair as Farrow says he's going to get me something to eat. I nod, though I'm far from hungry. I don't even know what hunger is anymore. When the door closes, sealing the crowds out, I whisper, "Why are they doing that?"

I venture a glance through the veil of my greasy hair, and the white-haired man smiles at me. "Doing what?"

"Clapping."

"That's for you, because we are all so happy to have you back," he says, reaching out a hand to me, like he expects me to take it. I don't. "We thought we'd never see you again."

———

Farrow brings me food. A can of Coke, a bag of potato chips, a sleeve of Twizzlers, and a package of Devil Dogs…he must've ransacked the vending machine. Funny, I never thought I'd see any of these foods again. I vaguely remember how they taste, but it's the memory of that taste that makes my stomach churn. He lines them all up on the table across from me, but I don't dare touch any of them. I'm craving tomatoes.

They ask me questions about how I am feeling and what I went through. I answer as best I can, numbly, because that's what I am. Numb. Just as they can't believe what happened to me in the Everglades, I can't believe any of what is happening around me. I want to pinch myself and wake up, wake up and find myself back in that old house, where things, as terrible as they were, made sense.

After about an hour, someone buzzes the captain and tells him that the ambulance is waiting outside to take me to the hospital. I shake my head and tell them that I'm fine. I don't want to go I don't want cheering crowds or people looking at me, dissecting me like a frog stretched and pinned in some classroom lab. I want to go home.

"We still need to get you checked out," the captain says. The shiny brass plate on his chest says Lincoln.

I'm too tired to fight.

I start to stand, but before I can, the door swings open. *What now?* I think, expecting more applause or more questions, neither of which I can handle right now.

Instead, I see two familiar faces.

Doctors Beatrice and Vince Lafayette.

My parents.

Contrary to what I remember of them, lying dead in the car in the swamp, decomposing in the heat… They are here, and they are very much alive.

They rush to me and surround me, hugging me and weeping. "Oh, my darling," my mother says. "We thought we lost you."

Yes, I think. *You have.*

"We love you so much," my father says.

"I love you too," I say and start to weep too.

PART THREE

ONE MONTH LATER

FORTY-THREE

My life is a study in absolute opposites.

I lie in my bed, watching the reflection of the waves from the gulf rippling on my ceiling, trying to choose.

Should I?

Should I not?

It is a question that has plagued me for the past three days. Three days of packing my school books, reading over my schedule, and making sure that I have everything I need. Christmas and New Years have come and gone, and now it is time for the show.

Yes, school—real, in-person school—started in the fall after the screw was successfully eliminated. Now I get to be a part of that.

And it's weird, because I'm actually excited. I've been going to therapy with a young, cool psychologist named Kristen Slick. She's nice. She's helped me work through my issues. She's been preparing me for today.

I think I'm ready. Every day is a little easier, and even though I know everyone will be looking at me and my performance will be the test of whether I'm *normal*, I think I'm going to be okay.

I shower and change into the new jeans and tank top my mother bought me. She wanted to take me on a shopping spree, but I was scared about people recognizing me, so we did all my shopping online. At first, I'd lost so much weight that nothing fit, but I'm much healthier now. My mother's delicious holiday cookies really helped with that.

I curl my hair and apply makeup, then hoist my backpack onto my shoulder. *Ready.*

Downstairs, my mother and father are waiting for me. My father used to go into Latrobe early, so I'd never see him in the morning, but he works from his lab in the basement a lot now. The smell of bacon and coffee wafts toward me, so I follow it to the breakfast bar and sit down.

"Good morning, honey," my mother says, setting a plate of bacon and my father's famous pancakes before me. "Hungry?"

The television in the corner of the kitchen used to spout the morning news, but now my parents keep it off. To protect me, of course. I don't have a phone anymore either. I don't think I'm on the news every day anymore. Reporters still camp out on our front lawn among the palm trees, but there are fewer of them.

The last time I watched television with my parents was when I was on *Good Morning America*. It was an exclusive, viewed by over forty million people. I'd gone to New York for the taping.

They'd done a good job with it. On the ticker while they inter-viewed me, it said, *FROM TRAGEDY TO TRIUMPH.* In the segment, they'd talked about how I was getting better. Back to my old self. How I was prevailing.

At one point, the interviewer asked, "Have you had any con-tact with your kidnapper, Elijah Rowan?"

The camera switched to me, and I, very calmly, with a nonchalant little shake of the head, said, "No. Thank God!" And smiled.

The studio audience had erupted in applause for me.

I try to keep that in mind as I pick up a forkful of my break-fast. As I do, I can feel my parents' eyes silently regarding me before trading anxious glances.

I pause with the fork inches from my lips. Elijah said that my father was crumbling his medication into my food. Making me test his medication.

Ridiculous. These are my dad's pancakes. There's no secret ingre-dient in here but applesauce.

I trust my parents more than I do Elijah. Yes, according to the dribs and drabs I've heard, cases of the virus are practically nonexistent now. Latrobe and other pharmaceutical companies have been working on a vaccine so we can stop taking the Ventex, but it's far from approval.

And no, they haven't caused a zombie apocalypse. Those things I was seeing? Slick tells me they were the result of the stress I was under after being abducted. Perfectly normal, not to mention that my kidnapper's gaslighting hadn't helped matters. And she must be right, because the hallucinations went away. Oh, I still wake up trembling, expecting to be back in that bedroom with the walls closing in on me, but baby steps. I'm getting better.

Finally my father asks the question that is on everyone's mind this morning: "Are you going to be okay, kiddo?"

I smile. "Sure I will. Just hope I don't have a lot of homework."

They both grin in response.

When I stand up, my parents practically tackle-hug me. JT hovers nearby, wanting to be a part of the family huddle.

We hug a lot these days.

I tell them everything's going to be great, then rush upstairs and brush my teeth.

Don't get me wrong. I'm nervous. There's a gnawing in my stomach that won't go away. But like I told that interviewer on *Good Morning America*, "If I've survived that, I can survive anything. That's what we do as human beings. We don't curl up and die. We press on."

I'd gotten a standing ovation for that one too.

As I brush my teeth in front of the mirror and make sure I don't have dried toothpaste on my lips—not that it matters; we all still must wear masks at school—I get the feeling I'm going to receive more applause today. Like I said, my life is opposites. People either try to treat me normal, which means paying special attention to ignore me, or go all out, making simple events into a three-ring circus. Considering the principal of Pensacola High,

Mrs. Foster, had a mural painted in my memory in the art wing, started a Do Something Nice for Willow Day last month, and had the entire student body sing "You've Got a Friend in Me" from *Toy Story* in a video when I finally came home, I'm getting three-ring circus vibes. Knowing my popularity before, though, I'm also thinking there will be a lot of purposeful ignoring too.

But that's okay. I'm ready.

As I'm packing my lunch into my bag, my mother calls to me, "Don't forget your mask! Did you set up your laptop? I think you should bring it. They're doing more things online these days."

"Oh. Okay." It's funny. I've been without technology for so long that I barely think of it anymore. There was a time when my fingers got itchy if I didn't check my phone once every two minutes. Now, I don't miss it. Not at all.

I rush into my room to grab my laptop. It's a tiny Mac, perfectly portable, a Christmas gift from my parents, since we agreed I didn't need a phone. Not after what started all this. We never actually talked about that, because my parents figured I'd learned the *No talking to people on the internet, even if you think you know them* lesson. My parents got the computer for me solely because they knew I'd need it to do schoolwork. I've been good with it, because even though it's hooked to the internet so I could check into my classroom and make up work to stay with my class, I haven't strayed off my school account.

It is a tool for schoolwork. Nothing more.

I open the lid to make sure it's properly charged and notice a message has popped up in the Pensacola High School messaging app. That's not abnormal. I've gotten about twenty messages from Mrs. Foster and my teachers trying to make me feel welcome and a few from students asking how I am.

I stare at the message:

August Rule: hi

It's replayed in my head a million times when my father calls to me to hurry up or I'll miss the bus. August Rule is messaging me.

August Rule is messaging me.

That's what started all this. Or did it?

I rush downstairs, trying to refocus, the question filtering through my mind: *Should I? Shouldn't I?*

My father drops me at the bus stop on the corner. I'm the only one there. I already told him I don't want a ride to school, and I'm not driving myself. Ever again. I never wanted a car to begin with, and now I really don't want one.

As we're waiting for the bus to arrive, my father says, "I'm so proud of you."

"I know." He's said it at least a hundred times.

"You going to be okay?"

"Yep." He should know, because I've said that at least a hundred times too.

"Good." He pats my shoulder. He's so nervous for me that

he's shaking. I have to admit, it's cute. But unnecessary. I'm going to be fine.

"Are you?"

He nods, looks out the window to where the bus should be, then scrunches his face as if he's trying to stop himself from sneezing. His voice cracks. "I just don't want to let you go again."

"Oh." I want to cry, but I have on new mascara, so I shake my head. "You have to let me go sometime, right?"

He nods and opens his mouth to say more, but thankfully the bus comes. I told myself that I would never, ever say a casual goodbye to my parents again, so I don't. I hug my dad tight. "I love you."

He smiles. "Love you too, Willow girl."

He would do anything for me. Anything.

Pulling my mask up over my nose, I push out of the car with my backpack and hurry to the bus. I can't see her mouth because of the mask, but the driver's eyes seem to smile down at me like she wants to say something but isn't sure what. "Hi," I say.

"Hello."

I climb the steps and stand at the front of the narrow aisle. The few kids on the bus are in the purposefully ignoring camp. So we're going to play that game? Fine with me. I'm great at ignoring what's wrong and pretending everything's fine.

I slide into the first available seat and look out the window at my dad. I watch him waving at me until the bus turns a corner, out of sight. We drive along the coast, the gulf shimmering brightly and blindingly in the distance. I slip on a pair of sunglasses.

Then I slump down, open my backpack, and pull out the letter.

It's from the Charlotte Correctional Center. I run my finger over the scrawled writing in the top corner and take a deep breath.

My parents have been corralling the mail, keeping it from me, but they missed this one. I don't know how many he has sent. I don't think he's allowed to contact me, so he must sneak them out. But I found this two days ago. And I've been going back and forth. *Should I? Shouldn't I?*

I look up at the clear blue Florida sky and wonder how much Elijah has been able to do that from his prison cell. He always loved looking at the sky. Looking for those angels.

I have seen none. Not a single one. And I don't think I want to.

See you later. The nerve of him. Is this what he meant?

"No, you won't," I whisper under my breath. I rip the envelope in half, shove it in my backpack, and watch the endless sky where the gulf water meets it. *The end of the world.*

Just one of the many lies he told me.

FORTY-FOUR

School is as I expect.

Maybe worse.

There are crowds of students waiting outside before the first bell. It's just like before. The difference is that there are a couple of news trucks. Channel Six and Channel Eight and some cable news show I've never heard of. All the same trucks that used to park outside my house are now filming my bus arriving at the school.

Mrs. Foster is also at the curb, wringing her hands in a motherly way. There are two security guards too. They usually monitor the only entrance and lunch area to break up fights. What are they there for…me? I guess.

When my bus sails past the principal and stops a few bus lengths ahead of her, she rushes after it in her Crocs and boards as the door opens. She looks at me and a too-sweet-to-be-believed smile appears in her eyes above her *Make a Difference Today!* mask. She talks to me like I'm in preschool. "Oh, Willow. Come along with me."

Yep, they're my entourage. When she leads me down the steps of the bus, she guides me away from the fray with the two security guards flanking us. I don't look up, but everyone's shouting. I think they're saying my name. It's so disconcerting that I'm relieved to be surrounded by the drab gray lockers and the white cinder-block walls of my school. Mrs. Foster ushers me into the administration offices and closes the door behind me, effectively sealing me off from the cheers.

"Wow," I say.

She nods. "I knew it would be that way. At first. It'll die down by tomorrow. Come on."

She leads me to a room next to her office. There's a little desk there with a laptop. I notice the laptop has my name written in Sharpie on a piece of masking tape. "What about—"

"I think we should ease you into classes, don't you?"

I shrug.

"Great. You can attend your morning classes online. And then after lunch, I'll take you to history. All right?"

"Okay." I reach into my bag. "I have my own computer, though."

"Perfect." She picks up the old computer. "You have all your books? You've been studying?"

I nod. It's amazing how my lack of technology has focused me. I've read almost all my English, world history, and chemistry books.

"Great. And you have your spring schedule?"

I pull it from between two notebooks.

"Perfect. I'll leave you to it. Give a holler if you need me."

I realize my first class is gym. "Oh, what should I—" but when I look up, the door is already closed. I'm not sure if they expect me to do jumping jacks at my desk. I decide against that. I have my gym bag with my gym clothes, but any excuse to get out of that nightmare is one I'm going to exploit. Instead, when the bell rings, I spend the next forty minutes arranging my desk, getting ready for my next class, which is calc.

Then I walk around the room. There is a display on the wall that says, WE REMEMBER...

It has ten or twelve faces of students. Some I recognize. Some I don't. I read the fine print underneath the header that says, ALWAYS IN OUR HEARTS!

Did they die?

Was it from the virus? I guess.

I don't want to think of that, so I scuttle back to my desk.

My calc book has stayed closed. I started it, but I was immediately lost. I don't know if I'll ever get the hang of it, since I didn't finish trig last year. Maybe I should be in remedial math. I go online and try to read the assignments, so I can at least pretend I know something for my first official class of my senior year, but it might as well be Chinese. Maybe I should tell the teacher so she'll go easy on me.

I open a chat box to message her when another message pops up.

August Rule: hi

I stare at it for a long time. I've made the decision to delete it and pretend it doesn't exist when a new message comes through:

August Rule: why won't you talk to me?

I snap the lid closed.

But it's still there, taunting me. I open the lid and drag the chat box to my trash can. Then I empty it so I won't be tempted to respond. It's gone forever.

Of course, it's not. He's still there.

After a bit of struggling, I retrieve the app and figure out how to block his name. Better.

Calc sucks. As expected, I'm lost, and not only because I'm not in the same room as the teacher. The rest of my classes aren't much better. The teachers keep trying to talk to me on the computer screen; meanwhile, I can hear the other kids whispering in the background. They all want to see me. The freak.

Adults want me to get back to ordinary life. This is not ordinary. Not at all.

As I'm eating the turkey sandwich my mom packed me for lunch and tucking the Oreos away for later (Did she really think I'd want to go through the afternoon with a chocolate smile?), the door opens, and Mrs. Foster is there, smiling at me. She says,

"How are things going? I brought a friend to help you through the rest of the day."

She steps aside, and there is Lavani. I think.

Lavani Singh has been my friend since first grade. Since I've known her, she's never worn her dark hair any other way but pulled back from her face. Sometimes in a ponytail, sometimes in a dance bun. She's a dancer, and she makes sure everyone knows by wearing oversized sweatshirts that say STRAIGHT OUTTA DANCE CLASS and YOU GOTTA POINTE. I used to dance with her until about second grade, when I discovered I had all the grace of an army tank. Anyway, her hair would always give me a headache from looking at it. It looked *tight*.

But now her hair is down around her shoulders and kind of wavy. It relaxes her face, giving her a softer, prettier expression, even with the mask. She looks older, like without me, her life has come together.

She waves. "Hey!"

It's not like we haven't talked. We have. I still don't have a phone, but she called my parents, who got us in touch. We—well, *she*—spoke for hours that first call, like old times. Lavani filled me in on all the gossip. She has a boyfriend now, Evan Marshall, who is a senior and on the swim team. He's pretty cute. Hard for me to believe, considering the two of us used to moan in junior high that we'd never get boys to notice us.

I roll the remainder of my sandwich in the Saran Wrap. "So you're taking me to class?"

She nods. "I told you, didn't I? I'm in all your afternoon classes."

"Really?" She never told me that. Or maybe she did. That's exciting. Everything people tell me is like a whirlwind. There's so much new information to absorb, I miss large chunks of it completely. I'm still in awe of her hair. I know it's the same Lavani, but she looks nothing like the friend who used to hang from the U-bar on the swing set at our elementary school, her knees scabby and the tip of her ponytail touching the dirt. "I like your hair."

She fluffs it. "Oh. Yeah. I had to take it out of the bun because I was losing so much of it. Evan likes it better down anyway."

"I do too," I say, but then I don't know if that's mean. I have lost any social game I used to have. Not that I ever had much. Talking to people, anyone, even my friend, is hard. "I mean, you look great, no matter what."

She grabs my bag. "Come on. I'll take you to history."

I stand and my eyes catch on the *We Remember* poster. "Hey." I point to it. "What happ—"

"What do you think? It's that virus. I hope someone figures out that vaccine soon. It's so scary, like a bad dream. Whenever I think about what hap—" She stops. Her face goes red. "I'm sorry."

She has no reason to be sorry, but I know what she's thinking. The person to freak out most over it was Elijah Rowan. Apparently that's why he kidnapped me. Some long, insane story that started with his sister dying and eventually led to him targeting my dad as a revenge scheme, because he was a scientist and supposed to fix things. Supposedly *he* was our stalker. I've kept away from the news, but from the little bits and pieces I hear, some of what he believes is utterly *insane*.

And I fell for it. Stupid me.

"Don't worry. It's fine!" I say, extra cheery to show her how fine it is. And it is. Except I'd rather not think of Elijah Rowan again.

It's weird to walk in senior hall. I've never spent time here before, but people are moving through their schedules like automatons. The only thing that's unexpected, I think, is me. As I pass, people gape. Some wave. Some lower their masks and smile. Some even say, "Hey, welcome back!" but the overarching vibe is astonishment. *There is the girl who was kidnapped.*

The bits and pieces I heard from the news also said I was lured away, catfished by someone pretending to be a student at Pensacola. It said I was kept in a remote location by that unstable young man. It never spoke of the lies he used to keep me there or how I was convinced it was the end of the world, that Elijah and I almost…that he and I were as close as two people thrown together like that could be. I've never spoken about that either. Not to the concerned interviewer. Not to the police or my attorneys. Not to my parents. Not to Lavani. And not to Kristen Slick.

Lavani's talking about how she's senior editor of the yearbook, and there's going to be an entire spread dedicated to me, but I'm not sure on the specifics because all the eyes on me seem to stick to my skin, weighing me down. My backpack feels heavy.

Breathe in. Breathe out. Just like Slick told you. You can do this.

Room 538, my history classroom, comes into view. Finally. The hallway, with its cool blue lockers, seems to be closing in on me.

I'm about to duck inside when I see him.

August Rule.

The real August Rule, leaning against a locker, one foot propped up against it, talking to a bunch of girls.

He's grown out his hair. It's shaved around his ears and really long on top, a messy, flat, ill-shaped slice of hair falling into his face. There's no discernible style to it, or maybe *not* having a style is the style? Maybe he works hard with gel to achieve that disaster? Whatever, it works for him. He's hotter than ever. And I get the feeling that if he came into school with a dead animal on his head, people would warm to it.

The day I got back home, I learned I had never spoken with the real August. Of course, I knew I hadn't in real life, except that one terrible gym class freshman year when he ordered me to tend goal, but the person I *thought* was August chatting with me online had always been Elijah. Elijah turned out to be quite the tech geek—he took an advanced computer science curriculum in high school, I heard.

He'd ordered a copy of Pensacola High's yearbook, pulled my online information, found out as much as he could about me in our chats...a move I fell for, hook, line, and sinker.

I'm not sure if Elijah knew I was absolutely in love with August Rule when he decided to impersonate him. But all he had to do was flip through the yearbook. August is one of those people who every girl has to love. Varsity sports from his freshman year, National Honor Society, class president, grin to kill for... All the quiet girls drooled over him, hoping he'd look their way.

Girls like me.

August never interacted with me during Zoom classes, never called or FaceTimed me, even though we communicated every night via instant messenger. I assumed it was because of his girlfriend, Jana. Now I know why. I was being a fool.

In the second the crowd between us clears, he sweeps a wayward lock of hair from his forehead, and his eyes settle on me.

On me.

And he smiles. Or at least his eyes do.

"They broke up."

I realize Lavani is talking to me. "Huh?" I'm frozen in place in the hall.

"August. And Jana."

My jaw drops. He's still staring. This feels meaningful. Like the beginning of something.

Lavani tugs on the sleeve of my shirt and laughs. "Come on, girl. You're holding up traffic."

I tear my eyes away from him and follow her inside. "Lavani. Did you see that? I think August was staring at me."

"Duh. Everyone is." She points to a chair in the back. "Laughler said you can sit there. But don't freak out."

"Laughler?"

"World History teacher."

I slide into my seat and grab my pencil and a notebook. "Right. Why would I freak—"

All the air whooshes out of my lungs as I look up. He has a self-assured, cocky sway to his walk, which I never tire of watching. Rebel that he is, his mask is down slightly beneath his perfect nose. I think of all I thought he typed to me, warmth I thought came from his mind, and my face heats as he stops at the desk in front of me.

"Hey," he says.

Oh my God. He spoke to me.

I look down at the surface of my desk. Someone has carved there *Suck this,* with a crudely drawn penis. I can't focus when August is so close to me. Sweat trickles down my rib cage. My heart beats double time, a rat-a-tat-tat, before I will my mouth to open and whisper a "hey" that's mostly swallowed up by my mask's fabric.

He slides into the seat so all I can see is his mess of wild, dirty-blond hair, hair I've longed to run my fingers through for ages.

I can't wait to text Lavani an excited, *Can you believe he talked to me?* and mark this day in my diary at home. But then it gets better.

He turns, drops his mask, and cocks a grin. "You're Willow."

He knows my name? *Well, of course. Everyone in the nation does.*

I nod.

"I'm August."

Duh.

He reaches a hand out to me, I guess to shake.

I stare at it for too long—it seems people still don't shake, don't *touch* nowadays. But August must be used to people risking life and limb to make physical contact with him.

I take his hand. When I touch his skin, which is warm and perfect like the rest of him, an electric current, only a thousand times more intense, courses through my body. Just my imagination, I'm sure—but I quiver.

"Jolly Rancher? You look like a cherry girl."

He's pushing a wrapped hard candy across my desk. I take it. I *am* a cherry girl. I am an *anything August Rule wants to give me* girl too, pathetically. I remember how he and I discussed our love for caramel M&Ms. He doesn't remember that, though.

Because it wasn't him.

"So…why didn't you tell everyone you could sing?"

I stare at him. I am not sure I can actually speak in his presence. I never have before. I'd spent days, weeks, and months psyching myself up to say hello in the hallway. Never did. Now…

I swallow.

"I…I did…"

No, you didn't, loser. You told the OTHER August that.

"I read that you have a YouTube channel. You're good."

Was that an...*an August compliment?* Was he on my YouTube page?

The bell rings, leaving me gaping and red cheeked behind my mask.

August turns to face the front and rakes both hand through his luxurious locks. Every time he does, I smell soap, and I'm in heaven. Mrs. Laughler comes in and waves at me, then all the welcome festivities begin. She fawns over me as most students face straight ahead. Something tells me they were all warned not to stare.

When Laughler tells us to get out our books so we can discuss some war in the Holy Roman Empire I've never heard of, August turns back and smirks at me. "You going to watch the special tonight?"

Again, I stare, because I can't answer, even if I wanted to.

What special?

FORTY-FIVE

It doesn't take long to get the answer to my question.

I have dinner to suffer through first. A question extravaganza, full of nervous glances and cautious questions from my parents, trying to glean as much as they can about how my reentry went. They still walk on eggshells around me. Always will, I guess.

My mother made Parmesan-crusted chicken for dinner, my favorite, probably because she thought it'd be a terrible day. It wasn't. Not terrible, not life-changing, except for one thing.

August.

While my parents do the tennis match, taking turns lobbing delicate questions at me, I answer with "fine," "okay," and "great," mostly because I'm replaying every single word August said in my head. Real words, spoken words, from the real August. They feel truer, more important now. *You're Willow. So…why didn't you tell everyone you could sing? You're good. Jolly Rancher? You look like a cherry girl. You going to watch the special tonight?*

Especially that last part.

After dinner, I retreat upstairs to do my first-day-back homework. I tell my parents I've got it under control, no problem. It's all easy stuff, but I need to get it done.

They believe me. They believe everything I say these days, because they know the alternative is too heartbreaking to bear.

My parents don't want me on the internet, so they've limited my access. Fine by me. I've had enough of the internet for a lifetime.

But a teenager simply can't avoid it. It's pervasive. As much as we want to disentangle ourselves from the internet, it's sticky. Now I know why people used to call it the web.

Case in point: A lot of my assignments are online. The research I have to do? Online. Textbooks? Online. Communication with teachers? Online. Information about upcoming events? You guessed it.

My parents let me have access to three things: my email, the school portal, and CNN. Other websites temporarily, by discretion. They have some special alarm on their phones that alerts them whenever I try to do anything else.

I guess they thought that once I appeared on *Good Morning America*, the days of me being national news were over.

But that was only my story. And as they say, there's more than one side.

As it turns out, CNN has exclusive rights to the other perspective. According to the promo, they're "going behind bars for an inside look at the man who kidnapped all-American teen Willow Lafayette."

That night, after I finish my calc, I sit on the edge of my chair, staring at the promo video until its etched in my head. Elijah in an orange jumpsuit, hands cuffed together, head down, walking down a bare hallway. Sitting in a courtroom, wearing a tie, no emotion whatsoever. The only emotion comes when the camera shows a picture of Elijah with his family, the same picture that was hanging in his living room, the one in which he's smiling that childish, toothy grin. As the dramatic music fades, the words *Teenage Idol Abduction* appear, along with *Tonight at eleven.*

I stare at the screen, then play it again.

And again.

And again.

Teenage Idol Abduction. It's almost laughable. Like I'm some singing star. I have a bunch of followers on YouTube. I'm far from a teenage idol.

Unless I was to *him.*

I pause the video when he's sitting in the courtroom, looking up at the judge, putting on his best angel face. They must be feeding him well in jail because his cheeks have filled out. Clean-shaven, eighteen-year-old psychopath Elijah Rowan could almost pass as younger than me. A messed-up, scared little kid who didn't know what he was doing.

I bring my face close to the screen and touch his face.

I hear footsteps in the hall outside and slam my laptop closed with a force that I'm surprised doesn't shatter the thing.

The special report plays at eleven o'clock tonight.

Good thing my parents usually go to bed at ten.

FORTY-SIX

At ten to eleven, I'm already glued to the screen.

At eleven, when the show starts, I'm practically shaking.

And when Elijah's face appears for the first time, I can't breathe.

I won't lie and say I don't care about him and it's all behind me. Maybe that's what I said to the world on *Good Morning America*, but come on. That's what they wanted to hear. I gave them what they wanted.

Or it's what my parents needed. What *I* needed.

Now, huddled in my bed under a blanket, heart beating the way a race car's motor revs at the starting line, I need to hear from Elijah. I can't take my eyes off the screen. A dramatic and foreboding voice begins, "She was a talented, all-American girl with a bright future. He was a troubled young man with nothing to lose. You've heard her miraculous story of triumph. Tonight, hear from him, the Teenage Idol Kidnapper, in his own words…"

As the reporter speaks, there are a few school pictures and

home videos of me, mostly provided by my mom with my blessing, so they paint me in the most flattering light. Most of the video is of him, though: orange jumpsuit Elijah, plodding down a ramp with shackles on his wrists and legs. Baby-faced courtroom Elijah, pleading for mercy.

But the last picture is one that I've never seen before. It must have been taken shortly after his arrest, because he has a bandage on his face and he's thinner, hairier, disheveled—the way I remember him. The camera freezes on that picture so I get a good, long look at him.

I think of the way the tomato seeds used to stick in my teeth. The sound of the mice, scurrying around the baseboards at night. The smell of the place, stagnant water and humid air.

My stomach roils, and I want to be sick.

I don't dare. Leaning over to grab a trash can to vomit would pull my gaze from the screen. I don't dare look away, not for a second.

The announcer says, "In this hour, we'll take you into the mind of one of the decade's most notorious young criminals, with behind-the-scenes details about the kidnapping, including never-before-seen footage and an exclusive interview with the kidnapper himself."

I watch, awestruck, as the reporter sits in an ordinary room with two plastic chairs. It looks like it might be a classroom, with a bookshelf in the background and an American flag. A dark-haired boy ambles to the chair facing the camera and sits. It's the baby-faced, chubby version of Elijah. He's wearing a button-down shirt and tie, oh so grown-up and professional, like he's interviewing for his first real job. He says something to the reporter, but the announcer is speaking over the exchange, "Our reporter was able to get inside the Charlotte Correctional Center and sit down with Elijah Rowan just days after his sentencing."

Whatever Elijah is saying, he's nervous. I've never seen him nervous before. Good.

The reporter, a man I've seen on CNN for years, sits across from the monster who destroyed my life. They might as well be sharing a meal, it's so normal, so informal, two men sharing a chat.

"Elijah Rowan was a normal teenager. He came from a family that went to church every Sunday. He got good grades in school, graduated two years early with honors, and took computer science classes at the local community college during the summer. People in his congregation and at school called him shy but always willing to lend a hand."

The camera cuts to a girl with acne-spotted cheeks and dangling earrings. She's sitting in front of an altar at some church. I can see the cross behind her. She says, in a voice that if it were a color, would be bubblegum pink, "Yeah, he was nice! We collected food for locals one Thanksgiving, and he drove us around to give out the turkeys! He didn't talk much, but he seemed cool!"

"Things were looking bright for this young man. But something went terribly wrong. He began acting erratically. Shut away in his home for months during the lockdown, he became fascinated with the pandemic."

My sophomore-year photo from the yearbook, awful as it is with my weird low ponytail that simultaneously makes me look like George Washington and emphasizes my too-big forehead, lands in the shot. "This pretty teenager's father was a senior scientist working on drug research at Latrobe Scientific in Pensacola."

The reporter says, in a serious voice, "Take us back to the first day you saw Willow Lafayette."

"I can't. Time…it ain't the same for me as it is for you. For everyone."

"What do you mean?"

"I've come here to tell the truth, and I will. But you won't believe it. No one will."

Elijah has said more to this reporter than he said to me in a single day at that hellhole. I have to wonder, does he like the attention? Is he one of those people who won't speak unless he has a camera on him?

No. His neck is red. The shirt's collar is too tight on him. Maybe it was his father's. His hands in his lap keep moving, clenching into fists, then unclenching.

"We're listening," the interviewer probes, giving the aura of concern.

"Listenin' and believin' are two different things," Elijah says, and I imagine he practiced this in front of a mirror, like I used to practice all my oral reports so presenting in class wouldn't scare me to death. It's almost as if he knows it's a matter of life and death.

He said the same thing to me. *You won't believe me. Maybe I'll tell you someday.*

"I first heard of Willow Lafayette probably about five years ago."

I blink. That would've made me...eleven? Twelve?

"When she was a child?"

"No. You don't understand." He seems to backtrack in his mind, like he's trying to figure out how to best explain the solution to a difficult math problem. He takes a deep breath, and he starts to speak. "I knew about her for years because of some testin' her father was doin'. But it was about a year ago that I decided I had to find her."

"A year ago? Didn't you just say five years ago?" The interviewer seems exasperated.

"Yeah. That's because, like I said, time...is weird, you know?"

The interviewer harrumphs like he doesn't know.

"I might look eighteen. My birth certificate might say I'm eighteen. But I ain't. I've been this way for five years."

The reporter narrows his eyes skeptically. "I'm not sure I follow you. What happened a year ago?"

Elijah swallows, his Adam's apple bobbing. "It was right after Suzy." He looks away. Near tears. "It always starts right after her, so I can't bring her back. It's like...that chapter's done. Ripped from the book."

Suzy. Before I can summon a visual of that girl in the pigtails from the portrait on the wall, the camera cuts to footage of his little sister. There are photos of her. Dozens, all of them with her toothless smile. Videos of her hula-hooping on the front lawn, rushing to make a giant bubble with one of those big bubble wands, dancing in front of a bedecked Christmas tree in a living room that looks everything and nothing like the living room I remember from that house. The only indication it's the same place is that awful afghan on the ugly couch.

An announcer speaks over the montage. "Suzy Rowan was a carefree seven-year-old girl. But something changed. Suzy started acting strange. She began to hit herself in the head and talk to people who weren't there…"

I listen, hardly able to believe this. So…everything Elijah told me…was true? No mention of the second plague, but…is it possible the reporter didn't know she was part of the trial Elijah mentioned? That it's been covered up that well?

The reporter goes on, talking about how Suzy's parents did everything they could to save her. But by then, it was too late. "And then, one warm summer night, the unthinkable happened, and by the end of the night, Suzy and her parents were dead."

The camera cuts to Elijah, who says, "Suzy was in pain. She couldn't take it anymore. She kept seeing things that weren't there, and she was so scared. Scared about what she might do to other people. She wanted to die. And then she told me what she'd done."

"What had she done?"

"She killed them. She killed my parents. And then she tried to kill my grandmother."

"What did you do?"

Tears fill his eyes. He opens his mouth, but nothing comes out. He looks away.

The video cuts to the reporter in the studio. "Elijah claims that he shot his sister because she'd shot their parents and was choking their grandmother, who has since died of the bunyavirus. But the evidence that young Suzy committed these heinous acts is inconclusive. Prosecutors say that whatever the outcome was, it left seventeen-year-old Elijah alone, angry, and disturbed."

For the next half hour, the reporter details the plot Elijah hatched. How he stalked me on my YouTube channel. How he managed to track down a copy of an old Pensacola High yearbook so that he could get to know intimate details about my school and peers. How he'd hacked into the school's records to find my schedule and the schedule of August Rule, who he'd chosen not really at random but because somehow he knew that August was the kind of guy I'd be crushing on. How he'd even driven to my house and stood outside, watching me. Left me flowers. Sent my father death threats, escalating in seriousness until my father had no choice but to move us to a vacation rental in one of Miami's gated communities.

But that wasn't all.

It was bad enough that he contacted me, pretending to be

August. That might have been his original intent: to taunt me, troll me, see how far he could carry on the catfishing. But when I told him how my family was going to Miami, he realized he could take it a step further. Meet me in real life. Engage in a twisted fantasy of keeping the object of his obsession. So he arranged to meet me in Miami. Kidnap and take me to his place, gaslighting me into believing I was insane, so I'd never try to escape. Kill anyone who managed to come too close. He'd even put the bodies of two strangers—innocent people who'd wandered onto his property—in the Mustang and sunk it in the marsh, staging the scene so I'd believe the world was ending because of a second plague and we were the only ones left in it.

The more the reporter goes on, the sicker I feel. The sicker I realize Elijah is.

The camera scans to him. He's not crying. He looks rather resigned, shaking his head. "That's not...you don't get it. You'll never get it."

I shake my head too. I can't believe it. Because if I was a revenge fantasy to him, there were a lot of worse things he could've done to me. He could've killed me. Tortured me. He didn't.

The reporter shifts in his seat. "Then tell us. You have all of America wanting to know the truth."

Without a beat: "They won't believe the truth."

"You're never going to have another chance to tell it."

Elijah draws in a breath, closes his eyes, and then says, "I've done this five times. The first time, I thought I was insane. The second time, I realized I could change things. I focused on her father. But that didn't work. So I—"

The reporter looks almost angry in his confusion. "I'm sorry, but I'm lost again. Five other times? What do you mean? You've kidnapped five other people?"

"No. I've lived this period of time, from September 1 over a year ago, when Suzy dies, on…five times. There's something in an experimental drug I took that makes it happen." He leans forward, hands out. "It's like this. Every time I die, I wake up. Right after I pull the trigger and my sister is dead. Usually, it doesn't go on this long. Usually I die sooner. I tried to reason with Dr. Lafayette. He won't be reasoned with. So then I tried to kill him. But that didn't work either. So I decided to focus on his daughter. Willow. And this time, because of what I did, I stopped it. At least for now. But I don't know. If he's still workin' on this drug, and I think he is, then…"

The reporter looks uncomfortable, bordering on disgusted. "I'm sorry, you've lost me."

"I'm in a time loop."

The words linger in the air long after he's said them. It's like it's waiting for the *dun-dun-DUHHHH…fade scene.*

The reporter pinches the bridge of his nose. "Explain that to me."

"I can't go back far enough to prevent Suzy's death, but I can prevent the rest. I think that's why I'm here. To stop it. I just haven't been able to yet."

"Stop what?"

"The end of the world."

The voice-over adds, "This young man who kidnapped Willow Lafayette is troubled. He clearly believes every word he's saying."

The camera goes back to the reporter. "During your sentencing last week, the judge said you had no remorse."

Elijah looks startled. "Why should I?"

"You admit to killing seven people to avoid being caught. Four were police officers."

He nods. "It's unfortunate. But it had to be done to save the world. Anyway, they'll come back."

The reporter winces. "So you're saying you'd kidnap Willow again if given the chance?"

Elijah nods. "Absolutely. Yes. I will. I *have to*. Until I get it right."

"Even now that you're facing your entire life behind bars?"

"I won't be behind bars forever. Maybe I've stopped it, and if so, then I'll be happy to be right here for the rest of my life. But if I haven't, and I'm not naïve enough to think I did, in a few days or a month, the monsters will take over the world and everything'll go to shit. I'll die. And then I'll wake up again, the gun in my hand and Suzy's body at my feet." He's not looking at the reporter anymore. He's looking directly into the camera. At me. My heart's thundering as he says, "And it will start all over again."

"And then what will you do?"

"I'll change the plan. It took me four times to even figure out who started all this. Who was patient zero. This time, I screwed up."

"How did you *screw up*?" The reporter's toying with him, humoring him so that he can prove to the world how psychotic Elijah truly is.

Elijah continues. It's almost like he doesn't care. And why should he? If he's right, in a few days, everything will have gone to shit. "I should've killed her when I met her in Miami. But after Suzy…after talkin' to Willow for so many months online…I couldn't kill her."

"After what you did to those other people? Sounds like you fell in love with her."

"Yeah." He's quiet for a moment. "Next time, I won't. I can't. I'll do something different. Change something slightly, and then it'll reflow the whole course of events. I'll be able to get out of this nightmare. Alive or dead. I don't care. I'm just…tired. So tired."

His eyes are glassy. Whatever crazy yarn he's spinning, he's clearly tired, and it's clear he believes every last word he's saying.

But I'm stuck on something else. He…fell in love with me?

I'm as agog as the reporter. "I take it that if you had a chance to talk to Willow Lafayette, you wouldn't apologize. What would you say to her?"

"I'd tell her not to eat anything her father puts in front of her. He means well, but he's sick. And if she can…do what I couldn't."

The reporter looks at him quizzically. "You're saying…patient zero, the person who triggered the end of the world, is…"

"Willow Lafayette."

"And how does she 'end the world'?"

"With a medication her father gives her without her knowing. She was already taking it when I kidnapped her. She's a time bomb waiting to go off, patient zero of the coming apocalypse, the second plague, which will make the screw look like child's play." Elijah shrugs, then his eyes lock on the camera, and I swear, he can see me. He looks entirely serious. "You've been warned."

I let out a yelp, slam my laptop closed, and burrow under the covers as far as I can go. But it isn't far enough. I can't get away from the memory of what he said.

Something tells me I never will.

Elijah believes that I am the start of the second plague. He was keeping me away from the world to save it.

A time bomb waiting to go off.

FORTY-SEVEN

The next day, when I come down the steps in the morning, I look at my father. He's so normal, handsome, balding a bit on top. He has a brilliant mind. Yes, Latrobe fired him, but he's kept busy in his basement lab. A man like that, whose entire life is scientific research, can't simply give it up.

Sick. The word tears through my mind. Now that most of my memories have returned, it seems almost obvious. That look in his eyes when he lost his job. Frantic…wild…

You can't just play with people's lives like that, Vince.

Yes. He can.

"Pancakes?" he asks.

I shake my head. I don't know if I can ever eat them again. I've been eating them ever since I got back, and now…

"You sure?" He comes over and feels my forehead. "Everything all right?"

I nod. "Dad…" I start, not knowing where I'm going.

"Yes, Willow?"

There's no easy way to ask the question I need to ask. Because no matter how I put it, I'll be accusing him. Besides, things have changed. The screw is all but gone. There's no reason for him to experiment anymore. So I simply say, "Have a good day," hitch my backpack over my shoulder, and tell him I'm ready for school.

School. It's another step on the road to normalcy.

As normal as one can be after being called a ticking time bomb on national television.

People still stare at me. Some avoid me. Some treat me like I need to be swaddled in Bubble Wrap. But it's less awkward than yesterday. Even after the story on CNN, sitting in class and walking the halls are less uncomfortable. I think that maybe Slick is right. Maybe, in another few weeks or months, they'll forget about the story altogether.

Maybe I will too. Maybe one day, Elijah's face won't be the first thing I see when I wake and the last thing I see before I go to sleep at night.

One can hope.

That afternoon, I slide into my seat behind August's chair. I expect he'll be bored of me now. I'll savor the occasional whiff of that pleasant, piney hair gel every time he puts his hands through his thick hair.

That would be enough.

But as he struts down the aisle toward me, mask lowered past his chin, a smirk on his face, I discover he's not done with me.

He slides into his seat and says, "Hey, Time Bomb. Some story on CNN."

He's going to go there? No one else has. Even Lavani didn't mention it. Of course, my parents haven't said a word. It's like everyone has been living under express instructions to not discuss the CNN program with me. *Keep quiet, and she'll never know it's out there.*

Everyone except August.

"That guy was *nuts*." He spins a finger near his temple. "He really believes you're going to start the end of the world. That's *insane*." He laughs. "But kind of hot."

I nod, my cheeks flushing. Did he just call me hot?

"Did you have any idea that guy was a total freak?"

I look around. As usual, people are turning to look, to listen, partly because they always do when August is concerned. But I also think they want to know what I have to say. They must've all seen the special.

I was the victim. And yet I know enough about the internet to know that not everyone was on my side. Hell, when a local kid died in a car crash last winter, half of the comments on the article I read said, "RIP" while the other half said, "Idiot. Probably speeding." I know armchair quarterbacks are saying I'm a stupid loser for falling prey to an internet predator.

I don't know if August Rule is one of them.

But then he shrugs and says, "It was cool. How you got out. Glad you made it back, Lafayette."

Thanks. I think it, maybe half mouth it. I definitely don't say it, because no sound escapes my stunned mouth. *He knows my full name.*

My heart swells in my chest. For the entire period, I don't hear a single thing the teacher says. I start counting down the forty-two minutes until the lecture is over so that maybe, just maybe, he'll talk to me again.

When the bell rings, he simply glides out the door like I don't exist, leaving me to wallow in misery. How pathetic was I that a single sentence from the "kid every girl in school would be crushing on" made my day?

I look over at Lavani, who, oblivious to my freak-out, winks at me and tells me she'll see me later. I gather my books and head out the door for my locker.

As I walk down the hall, I feel a presence next to me. It's him.

August.

He waited for me.

He says, "So…why haven't you responded to any of my messages?"

I gape. He can't be talking to me, can he? It's always hard to tell with these darn masks. I venture a look at him. He's walking closer to me. He waves at a couple people but then looks back at me, expectant.

Holy…he *is* talking to me. *He's the one who has been messaging me? For real?*

I take a deep breath. "I'm not allowed," I whisper, my voice mostly drowned by the sounds of kids talking over one another and slamming locker doors.

"You're not?"

He keeps pace with me, which is a shame, because I forgot where I'm going. I know my locker is around here somewhere, but damned if I remember which one it is. And the combination? Forget about it. I'll go to my next class and say I forgot my book. They'll let me slide.

"Oh shit," he says, making the connection. He sweeps that flat part of his hair from his eyes. "I forgot. I get it. Makes sense. I watched the whole special last night. Shit. Sorry."

We're at my next class. I stop at the door, wondering if I should go in. As scared as I am of talking to August and as much as I want to flee, I'm a moth looking straight into the flame.

He stops too, looking up and down the hall. He waves at a few people, who do a double take. They're probably thinking, *What the hell is he doing with her?*

I'm wondering that as well. He must want something from me. Why message me? Walk with me? "Did you…need something?"

"Yeah." He flashes that dimple, reaches out, and touches my arm. "Hey. So why don't we go out. Just you and me? Are you allowed to do that?"

I stare. This isn't happening.

I don't know. Am I? I don't think so. I never asked. A few months ago, I thought I'd be dead. I never in my wildest dreams thought I would be here, in front of August, the *real* August Rule, being asked out. This has to be a dream. I am still on that bed, my sweat seeping into the mattress, listening to the mice scurry along the baseboard as the world outside whimpers to an end. I must be. Because this is too good.

Too normal.

Too impossible.

"Why?" I finally squeak out.

He laughs. "Because I want to get to know you. More than what was on the TV. You sound really cool, Willow. Like someone I want to be friends with." He drops the mask and grins that cocky grin I dreamed about a million times. I always imagined it just for me, but I never quite knew how it would feel.

I can't breathe.

I can't think.

Everything inside me is exploding with excitement. I'm sure it must be visible from the outside. I know my face is bright red, and I think it's probably obvious that I'm trembling too.

"Wherewouldwego?" It comes out like that, one quick word.

He shrugs. "Movies? You like movies? I'll let you pick what you want to see. Maybe the diner after?"

I nod. It's a date. A real date. He's seriously asking me out. I need Lavani. I need some sort of crutch to lean on. Because I'm totally about to lose it. My knees wobble.

"Friday night? Seven?"

"Uh…yeah."

"Cool." He gives me thumbs-up as the bell rings. "Shit. Gotta go. See you."

And then he's off. He doesn't look back, and the moment he disappears, I have a hard time believing it even happened.

FORTY-EIGHT

This is my life now.

I am that girl on *Good Morning America* with the bright smile and the new haircut. I am the definition of normal and well-adjusted. I have a best friend. I have a boyfriend. I have a dog named JT. I have a family that loves me. I have dreams for a bright future, with college, career, family. Despite the curve balls thrown at me, I have prevailed. I live a very privileged life.

I am Willow Lafayette, the triumphant.

The girl who survived. Who can survive anything.

That is what the world wants, and that is what they are getting.

My mother is watching me from the doorway as I apply my makeup: a little blush, mascara, and lip gloss. She's been there for five minutes, but I guess she doesn't want to disturb me. I know from the sound of her breathing and joints cracking as she fidgets that she is nervous for me.

I think she'll be nervous for me for the rest of my life, worrying that when I leave her sight, I might never come back.

Understandable.

She stands there until the phone rings. But then she's back a moment later, holding it out to me. "It's Lavani," she mouths.

Lavani knows. She doesn't text me anymore. She does things the old-fashioned way—calling me on my parents' landline.

She's probably calling to wish me good luck. I spent all last night freaking out with her about the date, about what to wear, what to say, what to do. Mostly, I kept repeating how I couldn't believe that he'd asked me out.

I take the phone and close the door, effectively shutting out my mom. "Hey."

"Hey." From the tone of that one word, I know she's not going to tell me anything good.

"What's wrong?"

"I don't know how to tell you this," she says.

"Just tell me."

A pause. "All right. I was talking to Tia."

Tia is the new, improved me. I couldn't expect Lavani to crawl into a hole and seal herself off from the outside world after I disappeared. We weren't that kind of close. Sure, she missed me, mourned me when she thought I'd died, held a special place in her heart for me. But she found other friends. Maybe they don't have the same wild backstory, but they're still somehow more interesting. Probably a lot more stable. Tia, I know, is Lavani's new BFF. They're in dance together and in the

French Club together and in several classes together too. When Lavani's not walking on eggshells around me, she's having real fun hanging out with Tia.

"And?"

"She said she heard from Lance. Her boyfriend. Who heard from Jim, who's on the lacrosse team with August. You know, they're pretty good friends, and—"

"And what?" I don't have time for this. August will be here any minute.

"And they were joking. He said that the only reason he wants to go out with you is to *be close to the drama*. You know."

No, I don't know. "What?"

"He wants to sleep with the Teenage Idol girl. Like a notch on his belt, I guess."

I don't say anything. Somehow that did cross my mind. Because he's not the August I know, the one who likes caramel M&Ms and walking barefoot. The fake August, E, is more August to me than anyone.

That's really effed up. But I always hoped...

Even when I had no hope, I wanted the dream August to be in love with me. To care about me. In my mind, I thought he did. I thought he'd swoop in, superhero style, and save me.

He never did. Not then and not now either.

"Willow? You there?"

"Hmm."

"Well? What are you going to do?"

I stare at my face in the mirror. I am the girl who can survive anything.

Even the real August Rule.

"I have to go." I end the call and throw the phone on my dresser.

I go to my notebook and pull out the envelope I'd ripped in two. If it's the last communication I'll get from E, the August who is not August, then I want to know what it says.

E cared about me. He wanted to kill me, but he didn't. He loved me. He said that on national television. Maybe he's crazy, but I trust him more than any other man I know.

I pull out the pieces of lined notebook paper and unfold them. Before I put them together, I already know what it says. It's what he said on television.

DO EVERYONE A FAVOR AND KILL YOURSELF NOW.

But he knows I can't do that. Just like he couldn't do it to me. He had the chance to end this all those months ago, and he couldn't.

So it's up to me. A study in contradictions. *Should I? Shouldn't I?*

The doorbell rings, making the decision for me.

It's time.

This is my first date ever, and I imagined it like prom on all those made-for-TV movies: The girl comes down the stairs dressed in her best, and the guy stands at the foot of the stairs, mouth open in awe. Except it doesn't happen like that. My dad's standing at the door, as wary as ever since this is his first interaction with a guy who has as many hormones as he once had. He's rooted there, legs set apart, holding his copy of *A Brief History of Time* like a loaded shotgun, finger wedged inside to save his place.

I have barely been able to look at my dad since I watched the CNN special. Since I heard Elijah's words: *With a medication her father gives her without her knowing.* I'd thought those pancakes tasted different, and it wasn't only the applesauce. I've faked a stomachache all week so I wouldn't be forced to eat them.

Still, it's inside me. I know it. I can feel it in my veins. Maybe not what killed the others but something. I bet he improved it. I bet he's thinking that this is the drug that will save us all.

And maybe it will. Maybe Elijah bought us time, and now my father's BST is finally a miracle.

I rush between my father and August. "Dad, I told you, this is August. We're going now," I say quickly and rush out to the front steps. When the door slams behind me, it hurts my ears.

"Wait," my dad calls, opening the door.

I turn.

"Remember: curfew at eleven." He looks at August, his eyes full of doubt. "Have her home before eleven, you understand, young man?"

August isn't intimidated. He's slouching and smirking in a way I know my dad's not happy with. And he's not wearing a mask. My father's probably wondering what's going on with August's weird hair too. "Understood."

Even his voice leaks subtle sarcasm. It's a wonder my father doesn't swoop outside and pelt him with his Stephen Hawking.

"I hope you have a mask!"

"Bye, Dad!" I mumble with a wave, holding up my mask as I rush toward the driveway where August's Jeep waits. I'm not sure if he will open the door for me, so I don't wait. I climb in myself.

When we're alone in the car, he looks at me. "You in a rush?"

I shake my head. Then I look at my house, with my father framed in the screen door, staring at us. "Just drive."

He throws the car into gear and does as I say. It's quiet on the way to the movie theater, but I don't care. I like the quiet. There's a strange buzzing in the car, and I realize I haven't heard anything like it since I was in Elijah's house. Then I notice a fly bumping against the window, wanting to get out.

When August does talk, he asks if I like the music he's playing on his iPhone. His voice is loud. Grating. The August I messaged with didn't like hip-hop. I don't like it either.

I furtively move a thumb to the window and crush the fly under it. It stills.

I don't think August notices because he's talking about why he likes this particular song. He's completely oblivious to everything but his own words and his own awesomeness. He keeps peering at his face in the rearview mirror.

Even though the fly is dead, the buzzing continues.

When we come to the corner, right before the movie theater, there's a panhandler lingering at the entrance to a supermarket.

He turns around, but it isn't a man like I first thought. It's a girl. A little girl.

It's Suzy.

My mouth opens. It starts to tell August that we need to go home. But he pulls into a parking spot and says, "We're here."

Again, his voice. Ouch. Everything. It's all so loud.

My limbs go cold, numb, as I follow him into the movie theater. He asks me what I want to see, but I tell him I don't care, and he picks some movie with a lot of shooting and car chases. He pays for the tickets, but we bypass the refreshment stand. He doesn't even ask me if I want anything. No caramel M&Ms to share. Not even Jolly Ranchers. We sit down in the very back row of the almost-empty theater.

Almost immediately, his hand is on my knee. I'm stiff. Not from the hand. Everything in my vision is going dim.

I saw Suzy.

I think I'm going crazy. No. I don't think. This time, there's no doubt.

She's a time bomb.

Except I *do* know. I know exactly how this ends.

The lights dim. The movie starts. I try to enjoy it, but it's so loud, eardrum-bursting, making me see stars.

Someone gets up from the front of the theater and heads down the aisle. I'm barely paying attention because I expect them to walk past me, but the second they get close enough, I notice the long, dark pigtails. Suzy.

She lunges at me, screaming. *You did this. You did this!*

I start to scream, batting her off me, but for a child, she's strong. A wall of bricks. I scream. August does nothing to help.

"Whoa! What's going on?" he asks, looking at me with utter horror as this little girl wraps her hands around my neck. Suddenly I'm flailing, choking, sputtering. I can't breathe.

I'm dying. And he's looking at me, disgusted. Like *what the fuck is wrong with her?*

Right when I think I'm about to take my last breath, she leans into my ear and whispers, *Get them before they get you.*

And so I do. I turn to August, who's looking at me like he made the biggest mistake of his life by asking me out.

And something comes over me.

Not regret.

Hunger.

Dipping my mask, I lean in, open my mouth wide, dig my teeth into his neck, and tear off a bite.

FORTY-NINE

When I wake, I'm in my bed, bright sunshine flooding in, painting the waves of the gulf on my ceiling.

I still taste blood. August's blood. Metallic and salty and pungent on my tongue.

Already, I know something is strange.

Something buzzes next to me. It takes me a moment to realize it's my phone.

The phone that I last saw somewhere in the middle of the Everglades, when it was old and broken. Now it looks brand new.

There's a text from Lavani. Can I hitch a ride to school?

I almost laugh. Maybe she doesn't know what happened to my car, but she must know I have no interest in driving ever again. I'm certainly not driving to school.

I sit up and look around. My room looks different.

I *feel* different. I can't explain it. I'm not sure I want to.

Lying on my bed, JT wags his tail, hopeful for a pet. I run my hands over his soft fur. He looks at me, confused, like only he can sense what is wrong.

Just then, there is a notification on my computer.

Climbing out of bed, I stumble over to it and read a message:

August Rule: You there?

I stare at it for a long time before I type: Maybe...who is this?

August. From history?

This isn't happening. But it is. It's right there on my screen.

What are you up to?

I type: I'm...not sure. What are you doing?

The response comes in almost immediately: Truth? I was thinking about you.

I know this. I've been here before.

And I'll be damned if I'm doing this again.

My fingers hover over the keys. Elijah?

A long pause.

Then: Who's Elijah?

It's him. It's got to be him. Please. We have to talk.

But the message is marked undeliverable. I try again and again but I get the same error message: USER NOT RECOGNIZED.

It's him. He is out there, in a house in the middle of nowhere, the victim of unspeakable tragedy. And it's because of my father and a drug he developed. One that might be inside me with the potential to destroy the entire world.

But there's a second chance. *We* have a second chance. Together.

This time, I'm not going to let it go.

This time, we're going to stop the end of the world before it's too late.

ACKNOWLEDGMENTS

I wrote much of this book prior to the pandemic, and what happened during that first terrible COVID year made me wonder if it was worth finishing. Many encouraged me to stick with it, and this book would not exist without them.

Deepest appreciation to Mandy Hubbard, my agent, who read the first twisted draft and said, "I have no idea what this is, but I love it" (or something like that), and my editor, Annette Pollert-Morgan, who agreed with her. Thank you both for your efforts—I can't tell you how much I have loved working with you these past few years!

Thank you to the entire team at Sourcebooks for doing everything possible to make me look good (no easy feat). I am awed by your talent.

Jennifer Murgia, thanks for listening to my incessant whining about how my ramblings are never going to make sense…day after day after day. Also, thank you for not laughing when I told you I had an idea for a horror novel based on *Goodnight Moon*. I owe you a trip to Palau.

Sara, thank you for the long walks and discussion. Not only did you talk me out of all my plot holes, you also helped curb my cellulite and kept me from going insane!

Gabrielle, thank you for your title idea. I'm sorry *Hush: A Silent Murder* didn't work. I'll let you pick the title for the next book, okay?

To my readers, thank you for sticking with me, even though I write some pretty odd stuff. Your notes keep me going! Stay weird—I'll be there with you.

And lastly, thank you to Brian. I still don't think I'll get an agent, but even so, you somehow like and believe in me.

ABOUT THE AUTHOR

Cyn Balog is the author of many young adult novels, including *Alone*, which received a starred review from *VOYA Magazine*. She lives outside Allentown, Pennsylvania, with her husband and daughters. Visit her online at cynbalog.com.

SOME SECRETS ARE WORTH WILLING TO PROTECT.
DON'T MISS CYN BALOG'S *UNNATURAL DEEDS*...

CHAPTER 1

Duchess—Police are investigating an apparent homicide after a body was found in a wooded area early Tuesday morning. Authorities have not yet released the name of the victim or the person(s) they are questioning in connection with the investigation.

—*Central Maine Express Times*

Is this thing on?

Ha-ha, I'm a laugh a minute.

Anyway, Andrew. It's me. Vic. I wanted to say I'm sorry. Sorry for... Well, where do I begin? I—

Cough, cough, cough.

Sorry. I'm losing my voice. Something bitter is stuck in my throat, and the air is so cold it's hard to breathe. This place reeks of decaying leaves, of the musty, damp rot of dead things returning to the earth.

There's something soft and wet under my head. I hope it's not brain matter. I can't raise my arms to check because of the way I'm twisted here. I think my leg is broken. Or maybe my back? Damned if I can twitch a muscle without pain screaming its way up my spine.

Somehow I managed to pry my phone out of my jacket pocket and prop it on my chest, but you know how spotty service is around Duchess. All charged up with zero bars—not that I'd be calling anyone but you. I wish I could see the background photo of you and me. It'd keep me company. You know the one. It's the picture of us at the Renaissance Faire when we were fourteen. We're both grinning like mad and you have your arm around me, claiming me as your own. It's probably the only time you were ever comfortable with yourself. With us. I miss that.

Anyway, you know how glass half-empty I am, Andrew. I wanted to record a note for you on my phone. You know, in case I don't get out of here.

Of course I'll get out of here. I wouldn't be lucky enough to die here. But maybe this'll be easier than telling you in person.

Cough, cough.

Where should I start?

It's so quiet. You must have left me, Andrew. But you'll come back. You always come back. You were scared, maybe, when you saw what you'd done. And now I'm all alone here.

I don't really know where "here" is. I think it's a drainage ditch on the side of Route 11. The last thing I remember is

rushing down the road near the Kissing Woods, feeling powerful. Immortal. Like everything I wanted could be mine. For an
instant, I felt like *he* could be mine.

But that's not possible now.

I know what people have said behind my back in hushed
whispers. They call me delusional. But I'm not. I know what is
real and what isn't.

No, wait. The last thing I remember is you with that fierce
look in your eyes. You sure surprised me. Who knew that my
boyfriend, quiet, unassuming Andrew Quinn, had *that* in him?

I thought I knew you inside and out, but...I was wrong.

I guess I should explain. After all, I have no other pressing
engagements. And you're overdue an explanation, aren't you? The
tall pines can be my witnesses. They can pass judgment as they
see fit.

I'm not sure when it all began, but Lady M said it best. Hell
is goddamn murky.

Whoops. Blasphemy. Yet another sin to add to my act-of-
contrition list.

Looking back, you knew when I started to change, didn't
you, Andrew? You know everything about me. It was that very
first day of school, the day my life began and the day it began
to unravel.

So here are the gory details. It won't be enough, but I'll
try. You can't know it all until you've smelled that intoxicating
cinnamon-and-cloves scent, read those texts that elevated even

the blandest words to poetry, and seen those heart-stoppingly blue eyes.

His eyes. Even now, I can see them with perfect clarity. I've seen them in my dreams, in the sky when the sun hits the clouds just right, and in my morning breakfast cereal. It all goes back to him. Every single thought always winds *right back to him. Always. Always. Always.*

It's no use. I want him out of my head. I wish I could scrape him out of my memory. I don't want to live with him etched in the deepest part of me. I don't want to die thinking of him.

But I know I will.

CHAPTER 2

Abigail Zell of 12 Spruce Street called at 8:33 a.m. to report her daughter's disappearance. The girl, Victoria Zell, 16, a student at St. Ann's Catholic School in Bangor, was not in her bed when her mother went to wake her for school. Officer advised Mrs. Zell that missing persons report can be filed after a 24-hour waiting period.

—Duchess Police Department phone log

Do you remember that night, Andrew? Right before I started junior year? We were crouched in our hiding place, between the rosebushes at the white picket fence separating our yards, you on your side, me on mine. Just like bookends. The grass stopped growing where I used to plant my backside, but it was thick on your side, probably the result of your mom's green thumb. It was already chilly, the crickets chirruping their summer good-bye.

When I was young, I used to count fireflies while we talked. That night, there were no fireflies.

"Vic," you whispered through the fence.

I giggled, lovesick. I adore your voice. It's so low and musical, even when you're not singing. If a voice made a whole person, I would be utterly, desperately in love with you. Most of the time, it's painful to watch you struggle to get the words out. Not because it bothers me, but because I know how much it bothers *you*. You've never liked yourself much, but I think you hate your wayward tongue most of all. How can something that behaves so angelically while singing music betray you so terribly the rest of the time?

You rarely stutter with me. When we were alone and darkness cloaked us, your voice was perfect. *Life* was perfect then. Stupidly, I didn't realize it.

"Y-you have fun at school tomorrow, OK?"

"Fun?"

You paused. "OK. Don't run screaming from school tomorrow. Better?"

"Much." I pushed a piece of foil-wrapped Juicy Fruit between the slats. A second later, I could hear you chewing the gum. "I wish you would be there."

I felt you push against the fence. You liked to fold the silver paper into squares and wedge them between the slats. "Save your wishes," you muttered.

It's true that wishing was useless. As if your mother would

suddenly decide not to homeschool you so you could enroll at St. Ann's. As if you'd be able to enter a classroom without crumpling into a panicky mess.

"You out there still?" Your stepfather's voice boomed from the darkness.

I peered between the slats at the lit tip of his cigarette, cutting through the darkness near your back porch. Since he worked so much of the time, all I ever saw of your stepdad was that tiny orange fireball. You jumped to attention and the fence rattled. "Y-y-y-yes, sir," you said.

I poked my head up and your stepdad muttered something about me. Nothing nice, I'm sure. Your stepdad has never been the sweetest of men, which makes him the opposite of your mom. You told me the story about a thousand times, about how they married when you were seven, mostly because your dad died unexpectedly and left you two in major debt… A "marriage of convenience" you'd said, but it never seemed very convenient for you. Your mother is prim and proper and likes the finer things in life, and your stepfather, well, doesn't. Somehow though, they fit together. There's only one piece in that puzzle that never seemed to fit. You.

I told you good night, then turned to go inside. My parents had the kitchen blinds parted in a vee, squinting into the dark yard in their attempt to spy on us. "Good night, Vic," you called to me. Most people call me Victoria. People are always formal with me. They think I am oh-so-serious and uptight because I don't know them well enough to say, "Hey, let's not be formal. Vic's fine." And, well, I can't help it. "Relax" is a mantra I repeat over and over in my head. And do I ever? Nope.

Victoria is a serious name, an old name. Everything about me screams old, from the way I dress to my often-hunched posture. Even my hands look old, veined and thin and fragile.

I guess we're just two peas in a pod, Andrew: You and your premature balding, and me and my old-lady habits. You and your agoraphobia, and me and my crippling anxiety. We belong together. And yet something in me wanted more. I am sorry to say that I wanted what I knew couldn't be. What *shouldn't* be.

And because of that, I blindly let him lead me.